The
Shining Men

A novel by
Nicky Heymans

malcolm down
PUBLISHING

Endorsements

The Shining Men is a fitting and fantastic finale to Nicky Heyman's trilogy about Joshua, Moses' successor. As Joshua finally gets to lead his people across the Jordan to occupy the promised land, he not only has to lay waste to Jericho but embrace the challenge of adopting the prostitute Rahab as one of his own people. Through every trial and ordeal, Nicky brilliantly portrays Joshua bearing his leadership burdens until the day when he receives the final reward for his faithfulness. As you travel with him on this last instalment of his heroic journey, you will be inspired and moved in equal measure by his dedication. And when you turn the final pages, your heart will be stirred to be strong and very courageous, just as he was those many centuries ago.

Dr Mark Stibbe
Award-winning novelist, ghostwriter, and CEO of BookLab

The Shining Men is a page-turning read, and an exciting and moving conclusion to the Joshua trilogy. Here, the author brings to life the story many of us are familiar with – Joshua leading the Israelites into their inheritance, the promised land. She expertly weaves character and plot together, through the adventure of Jericho and beyond, and in so doing, immerses the reader in the experiences of people who lived and breathed, had emotions and lost love, after the time of the exodus.

Joshua, his love for God, his relationship with Yahweh, his trials and adventures of leading the Israelites as a man alone and yet supported by friends and adopted family, finishes in an amazing and emotive conclusion as he passes from this life to the next.

I greatly enjoyed the trilogy, and the journey's end is tremendously touching. Authentic, honest, emotive – storytelling at its best.

Sheila Jacobs
Author of Nun's Drift

First published 2024 by Malcolm Down Publishing Ltd.
www.malcolmdown.co.uk

29 28 27 26 25 24   7 6 5 4 3 2 1

British Library Cataloguing in Publication Data
A catalogue record for this book is available from the British Library.

ISBN 978-1-917455-09-1

Cover design by Esther Kotecha
Art direction by Sarah Grace

Printed in the UK

Dedication

This book is dedicated to my beautiful daughter and now fellow writer, Talitha, who has been a loyal 'sounding board' for me from the very beginning of my writing journey.

Thank you, sweet pea, for being so willing to discuss my latest ideas or writing conundrums. I'm so thankful for your honest feedback, and for your steadfast encouragement and belief in me. You are a treasure and I love you to bits.

Acknowledgements

Once again, enormous thanks and my heartfelt gratitude go to my writing coach and mentor, Mark Stibbe. It's difficult to express just how much I appreciate your input, but hopefully you know how much your patient guidance and insightful advice have meant to me.

There were a few sticky moments during the writing of this book where I lost my way a bit. The scripture, 'Faithful are the wounds of a friend' (Proverbs 27:6) comes to mind! I'm so thankful that you care enough, and have the courage enough to rebuke and admonish me, as well as encourage me. Your input not only changed the whole direction this book was going in, but also radically altered the essence of the story. Thank you for pulling me back on track. Thank you for your continued commitment to moulding me and shaping me into the author that you seem to believe I can be.

Mark, you're a legend! Thank you from the bottom of my heart.

Note from the Author

Writing *The Shining Men* felt quite different from writing the first two books in this Wilderness trilogy. Being the first book I had ever written, *Into the Wilderness* was a fresh new adventure and every experience was a 'first', which made it challenging, as well as exhilarating. The second book in this trilogy, *Then There Were Giants*, was liberating, due to the fact that at least three-quarters of the book was totally fictional, so my imagination was let loose to run wild!

When it came to writing this, the third book in this trilogy about the life of Joshua ben Nun, I couldn't shake off the realisation that this book was not only the final book in the series, but that it was also the conclusion of Joshua's life and story. I have 'lived' with Joshua for three years during the writing of this trilogy, so I found the thought of saying goodbye to him really difficult.

The appearance of the 'shining men' is a theme that runs throughout this third novel, hence the title. Although Joshua did encounter these heavenly messengers in the first two books, in this third book they are far more predominant, and Joshua encounters not only these shining men themselves, but their glorious leader, 'The Man'. That encounter is based on the biblical account outlined at the end of Joshua chapter 5 and, although it is only three verses, it must have been a life-changing encounter for Joshua, and deserves to be highlighted. I hope I have done it justice.

In 'The Shining Men', I have endeavoured to bring to life some iconic events such as the fall of the city of Jericho, the story of the infamous prostitute, Rahab, and the conquering of the land of Canaan by the Israelites. However, this book also covers a period of time which the Bible says very little about – the last twenty-five years or so of Joshua's life.

I thoroughly enjoyed writing this book, but I must be honest: the chapters I enjoyed writing the most were the closing ones. There is a wonderful scripture at the end of Joshua chapter 21 which says, 'So the LORD gave to Israel all the land of which He had sworn to give to their fathers, and they took possession of it and dwelt in it. The LORD gave them rest all around . . .' (Joshua 21:43-44). They were finally able to settle in the land of their ancestors, Canaan, and could now rest. Wonderful! Simple!

Or was it?

I spent a lot of time thinking about what it must have been like for a warrior leader like Joshua, whose entire life had been spent fighting battles, both physical as well as internal, to suddenly be told, 'You can stop now and rest.'

Joshua had never rested. His whole life had been about war and conquest. Rest was a foreign concept to him. So, what might that have looked like? How do you go about changing the way that you have lived for eighty or so years? Our modern lives can be like that. Work, work, work, strive, push, be productive, prove yourself, make money, keep going . . . on and on, like hamsters on an ever-spinning wheel. But, over the years, I have come to realise something quite wonderful.

There is beauty in rest.

There is wonder in peace.

There is joy to be found in noticing the smaller things in life, if we will just take the time to allow ourselves to do that.

I love to believe that Joshua rediscovered the wonder of peace and rest in the latter years of his life. Surrounded by loved ones, settled in his own home instead of constantly moving around in a tent . . . what an amazing way to end a life that was well lived (and well fought). I must confess to crying as I wrote the last couple of chapters in this book, especially the one where Joshua dies, not out of sadness or grief, but because of the beauty of his passing.

I hope you enjoy reading about the epic battles and challenges that Joshua faces, the heart-wrenching conflicts that beset him, and his amazing encounters with Yahweh's shining men. However, my heartfelt desire is that when you finish reading this book, you will be left with an overwhelming sense of the beauty and kindness of God. I pray that He would reach out through the pages of this book and touch your heart, revealing Himself to you in a unique way, and that you would be perpetually changed, drawn closer to this immensely beautiful Being that we are so privileged to call 'Father'.

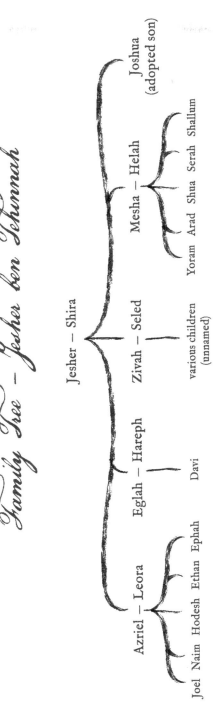

Family Tree — Jesher ben Tehinnah

Jesher — Shira

Azriel — Leora

Joel Naim Hodesh Ethan Ephah

Eglah — Hareph

Davi

Zivah — Seled

various children
(unnamed)

Mesha — Helah

Yoram Arad Shua Serah Shallum

Joshua
(adopted son)

Main Characters

Alya (f) – wife to Joel, matriarch of Joshua's family, mother of Sadie, Joash, and several other children

Attai (m) – grandson of a former elder, Abidan, from the tribe of Benjamin, husband to Mara, father of Eshton and Leah, Joshua's manservant

Azriel (m) – firstborn son of Jesha and Shira, married to Leora, father of Joel, Naim, Hodesh, Ethan and Ephah

Beerah (m) – trusted Israelite spy

Caleb (m) – warrior from the tribe of Judah, Joshua's second-in-command in the army, son of Jephunneh, husband to Johanna, father of Iru, Elah, Naam and Achsa

Eleazar (m) – high priest from the tribe of Levi, son of Aaron, husband to Bathshua, father of Phinehas and other children, grandfather to many grandchildren

Helah (f) – wife to Mesha, mother of Yoram, Arad, Shua, Serah and Shallum, grandmother of many grandchildren

Iru (m) – firstborn son of Caleb and Johanna, husband to Serah

Joel (m) – firstborn son of Azriel and Leora, patriarch of Joshua's family, husband to Alya, father of Sadie, Joash, and several other children

Joshua (m) – warrior leader of the nation of Israel, previously manservant to the prophet Moses, son of Nun, adopted son of Jesher and Shira, 'pet' name Yoshi

Mesha (m) – fourth born and youngest son of Jesher and Shira, married to Helah, father of Yoram, Arad, Shua, Serah and Shallum, close friend of Joshua

Moses (m) – prophet and previous leader of the nation of Israel, husband to Zipporah, father to Gershon and Eliezer, brother of Aaron and Miriam

Rahab (f) – Canaanite harlot living in Jericho

Salmah (m) – trusted Israelite spy, from the tribe of Judah

Samina (f) – wife of Yoram, mother of Miriam, Shaul, Malluch, Jarib, Adiel, and three more children, grandmother of many grandchildren

Serah (f) – daughter of Mesha and Helah, wife to Iru

Shallum (m) – youngest son of Mesha and Helah, brother to Yoram

Shining Men – Yahweh's heavenly messengers

Yoram (m) – first born son of Mesha and Helah, husband to Samina, father of Miriam, Shaul, Malluch, Jarib, Adiel, and three more unnamed children, 'pet' name Yori

Contents

1. Holding its Breath — 15
2. Debriefing — 17
3. The Crossing — 23
4. Shimmering Pillars — 27
5. The Other Side — 33
6. Gone — 41
7. The Beast — 45
8. Dissipated — 49
9. Foolishness — 55
10. The Man — 63
11. Conquest — 67
12. Just March — 71
13. Taking Jericho — 75
14. A Prostitute's Abode — 79
15. The Harlot — 85
16. The Smell of Death — 93
17. Rising Smoke — 99
18. The Attack on Ai — 105
19. Accursed — 109
20. Achan's Plunder — 113
21. Grieving Yoram — 119
22. Victory — 125
23. Covenant — 129
24. To Be an Israelite — 133
25. Becoming a Harlot — 141
26. Purification — 145
27. Persecution — 149

28. A Woman in Israel   153

29. Deception   159

30. Transformation   163

31. Blood Money   167

32. Cry for Help   173

33. Stand Still   177

34. Five Kings   183

35. Friendship with a Harlot   187

36. Taking the Land   195

37. A Wife for Joshua   201

38. A Husband for Rahab   207

39. Frozen   213

40. The Ravings of a Madman   217

41. Absconding   221

42. The Distance Between Us   225

43. Timnath Heres   231

44. Return   237

45. Inheritance   241

46. Farewell   247

47. A Little Touch of Paradise   253

48. Home   257

49. Me and My House   261

50. Cloud   267

1

Holding its Breath

The land itself seemed to be holding its breath; waiting, watching, yearning . . . compelling us to come and taste of its delights. I shivered, pulled my cloak tighter around me to ward off the early morning chill, and stared at the dim outline of the menacing city that loomed in the distance, dominating the skyline.

Jericho.

It was called the City of Palms, or so we had been told, but the beauty of that title was well unsuited to the gloomy mausoleum that glared back at me from across the plains.

The bright twittering of a desert sparrow broke my sombre musings, signalling that it was time; the dawn was breaking and a new day was upon us. I stood and watched the veil of darkness relinquish its hold, giving way to a broadening cloak of light as sunrise drenched the land with a golden glow. The dawning of the day was laced with birdsong. I could hear the rushing of the Jordan River's waters and see it glinting and dancing in the light of the sun's rising. A scuffling to my left revealed a lizard crawling through some dry leaves. It made its way to a nearby rock, where it lay like a statue, blinking a lazy welcome to the new day. The summer air was sweet, pulsating with the promise of what was to come. This day was new and unspoilt, exquisite perfection, tranquillity.

But I could not delight in it, for peace was far from me.

My mind wrestled with thoughts of war and battles and Jericho and – my shoulders sagged – harlots.

'Yahweh, forgive me,' I mumbled, 'but I do not understand why You have chosen to lead us on this path. You know of the desolation these women brought upon us in recent times. Many were seduced, led astray to follow other gods and worship idols. Thousands of

Your people died of a plague because of this great evil, and yet you would have us save the life of this pagan harlot and her family, and bring them here to live among us?'

The faces of the Canaanite women who had paraded themselves before us in times past flashed in my consciousness. Wild and wanton, heavily adorned with jewellery and piercings, their clothes revealing and their faces masked with heavy paints. The thought of meeting one of them, much less offering them sanctuary among us, sickened me.

Why did our spies make such a promise to this woman? Were they beguiled by her? Entrapped by her charms and seductive ways? Surely not? Salmah and Beerah were honourable men, brave warriors and men of wisdom. They had undertaken many missions on our behalf with great success, which was why they had been chosen to spy out the land of Jericho in the first place. I could not countenance these men being led astray by one woman's persuasive charms.

'Why, then?' I muttered to myself, staring at the ground, scuffing the dirt beneath my sandals. 'What hold does this woman have over them?'

Her name sent shivers down my spine.

Rahab.

2

Debriefing

They stood at the entrance to my tent, dishevelled and apprehensive. Attai must have told them of the urgency of my request, as it looked like they had come straight away, without pausing to wash or eat. I felt a pang of guilt at having disturbed them so early, but it was too late now.

'Commander, Salmah and Beerah are here,' Attai said.

'*Shalom*, Commander. You asked to see us?' they said, standing to attention.

'Mmm. Please, come, sit.' I motioned to a wooden bench that lined one side of my tent. They perched on it and Salmah, who was somewhat younger than Beerah, smoothed his hair, trying in vain to control the bird-like crest that stuck up on one side of his head.

'Attai, please ask Alya and Samina to bring some food and drink when they are able. We will break fast here, together, *nu?*[1] Salmah and Beerah smiled in agreement, looking somewhat pleased at the mention of food, but curious as to the reason for this unexpected early morning meal with their commander.

'Yes, Commander,' Attai responded, turning to leave. He had not been with me for long but, considering my initial reluctance to have a manservant at all, we had settled into a harmonious rhythm sooner than expected. I realised that what my advisors had told me about Attai was true; he was a trustworthy man, prudent in speech and well respected. Although I was reluctant to admit it, his assistance had made a significant difference to me, and I didn't find his company unpleasant.

'Thank you, Attai. I will have no need of you until later.' Giving me one of his characteristic smiles, followed by a cursory bow, he

---

1. *Nu* is a Hebrew expression.

went on his way. Salmah and Beerah sat straight-backed on the bench, looking apprehensive.

'Be at ease, please. This is not a day of trouble. I merely wanted to talk more about your time in Jericho.' Both men brightened and relaxed. 'Tell me again how you met the uh . . . harlot.'

'Rahab,' Salmah prompted.

'Yes. Rahab. Did she approach you or did you seek her out?'

Beerah spoke up. 'She approached us as we entered the city gates, asking if we were seeking lodgings for the night. The day was far gone and we were in need of somewhere to rest, so it seemed right to us.'

'And did you know that she was . . . what kind of woman she was when you agreed to lodge with her?' A familiar flush of heat rose up my neck and into my face. I was a time-weathered warrior, now leader of an entire nation, and yet still I flushed like a child when talk turned to harlots? It was foolishness! I fixed a look of astute indifference on my face and leant back in my chair.

'Not at first, Commander.' Beerah shuffled in his seat and sat up straight. 'Her manner of dress was immodest compared to how our women clothe themselves, but all Canaanite women seemed to adorn themselves in that way, so we thought nothing of it.'

'Hmm. And then?'

The spies went on to explain that Rahab had taken them to her home, a short walk from the city gates, and showed them their room for the night. She had just set about preparing some food for them when they heard a loud pounding on her door.

I leant forward in my chair. 'Yes?'

'It was the king's guards. They had been told that Rahab was harbouring two Israelite men, and the king had ordered them captured and brought before him.' Beerah and Salmah glanced at each other, then Beerah continued.

'In truth, Commander, our fear was great. We were trapped. There was no way of escape.'

'So?'

Salmah took over again. 'Rahab didn't hesitate. She motioned to us to be quiet while she spoke to the captain of the guard through the locked door. Commander, I saw fear in her eyes, but heard no fear in her words; they were sure and her voice did not tremble. She told him to wait while she . . . uh . . . clothed herself – although she was fully clothed already,' he hastened to reassure me, 'then she took us to her rooftop. She is a spinner of flax, and there were flax stalks drying on her roof. She scooped them out of the pallet, told us to get in, and covered us with the stalks, cautioning us not to move or say a word.'

'And you trusted her?'

Beerah's expression was without guile. 'What choice did we have? If she wanted to betray us all she had to do was open her door and let the guards in, but she didn't. We heard them pounding on the door and shouting while she was on the roof with us, but she remained calm.'

Salmah took up where Beerah left off. 'We couldn't see what took place when she let them in, but we heard the commotion.' He shook his head in disbelief. 'They plundered her home, overturned furniture and emptied containers in their search for us, but they found nothing.'

'Commander,' Beerah interrupted. 'Rahab even thought to take our bundles from our room and hide them with us under the flax. She has a quick mind and a prudent heart.'

'Hmm.' A prudent heart? A prostitute? No. I don't think so. 'The guards, did they search the rooftop?'

'They did,' Beerah responded. Looking down, he said, 'Commander, I cannot deny it, my heart beat so fast, I marvelled they could not hear it.'

I said nothing in response to Beerah's confession. I had been a spy myself; I knew well the terror that can seize a man's heart when he fears he has been found out.

'We readied ourselves to fight, should we be discovered, but Rahab drew their attention away from us and onto the view from the walls. She told the captain that she had ... uh ... entertained two travellers, but didn't know where they were from, and said they left just before the city gates closed.' Beerah tried unsuccessfully to hide his admiration for Rahab. 'She was most convincing.'

'Without a doubt,' Salmah agreed. 'She acted swiftly. Her life could have been forfeit, but she didn't hesitate. Our lives were in her hands. Were it not for her, we would now be lodging in the king's dungeons, or worse.' He looked down, hesitating before making eye contact with me again. 'She showed great courage and, in truth, wisdom in her deeds. She chose to put her own life at risk, to save us.'

'Why?' I demanded. 'Why would she do such a thing, take such a risk, to save two strangers – enemies of her people?'

Beerah's eyebrows lifted. 'We asked ourselves the same question. When the soldiers left, Rahab told us to stay hidden for a while longer in case they returned, but when night had fully fallen, we came out of hiding and were able to talk with her. We asked her why she had hidden us and not handed us over to the king's guards.'

Beerah paused, staring into thin air.

'And . . . ?'

He locked eyes with me. 'She said she believed that our God was the true God. She had heard the stories about the Red Sea and of our leaving Egypt. She even knew about the cloud and fire . . .'

'. . . and about the defeat of the giant, Og, at your hand,' Salmah interrupted.

'Commander,' Beerah continued. 'I sensed no love of Jericho or their gods in her, and we saw no idols in her home. I know this may sound like foolishness, but I sensed in Rahab what I believe could be a – a holy fear of the God of Israel, even faith in her heart towards our God, if that is possible?'

My contempt for that theory must have shown on my face, because a guarded expression came over Beerah's face; he looked away. At that moment the tent flap swung open, and the mouthwatering aroma of freshly baked bread cakes filled the tent. Alya and Samina brought in a platter loaded with manna cakes, figs and dates, and a jug of water. We greeted them, washed our hands in the dish of water, and dried them on the cloth they offered.

Moving to sit cross-legged on the mat, I said to Salmah and Beerah, 'Please take, eat. There is plenty, yes?' Their eyes lit up when they saw the food laid out before them.

'So,' I asked, pausing to stuff a piece of manna cake into my mouth, 'how long did you stay there for?'

Neither of them answered, both intent on filling their mouths with food but, after a long pause, Beerah swallowed and replied. 'Rahab said it would not be wise to leave straight away. The palace guards had raised the alarm and the city was alerted to our presence. She also told us we could no longer leave by the city gates. While we talked, she wove together strong cords made of flax, to let us down through her window, on the outside of the city walls.'

Salmah took a swig of water and continued the report. 'We stayed in her home until the third watch of the night and then made our escape, but that time was not wasted. Rahab's house is well situated. We saw all the land reaching to the Jordan River and beyond from her window on the outer wall, but the windows on her inner wall also provided a broad view of the city. She showed us the king's palace, the halls of meeting, treasuries, and the temple. She told us about Jericho's defences, where the watchmen and city guards are posted, and the timings of their watches. There is not much about the city she did *not* reveal to us.'

I grunted. 'True. We now have a detailed map of the city. You have done well, but there is one more question I must ask you.' Both of them stopped eating. 'Why did you make such a vow, a pledge of such importance, to a woman like Rahab – a harlot who you did not know and should not have trusted?'

Neither of them said anything.

They looked at each other, then Beerah spoke up. 'Commander, I understand why you question our decision. In truth, I questioned myself. It is not something I would ever have seen myself doing, but . . . it seemed right to us at the time.' Looking down at his clasped hands, he rubbed one thumb with the other. 'Yes, Rahab is a harlot. She is a Canaanite, a pagan, and a woman, but . . .' he searched for the right words, 'if Yahweh chose to use this woman to save us, and if she was courageous enough to choose that path, then who were we to spit in the face of such mercy?' He looked up again, almost daring me to contradict him. 'We did not ask what caused her to walk the path of a harlot, but my heart tells me it was not out of choice. There is goodness in her, I know it.'

Salmah took over. 'Commander, we have given Rahab our word. We made a vow to preserve her life and that of her family, in return for our lives. I beg you,' he said, leaning forward, 'do not make liars of us.'

I paused to look in the faces of these faithful men who were so intent on honouring their vow to this pagan harlot who they spoke so highly of. Part of me was frustrated because they hadn't told me any details of fresh significance. The greater part of me, however, was unable to deny the growing seed of curiosity which they had planted in me about this woman.

Looking them both in the eyes, I said, 'It will be as you have said. We will fulfil our vow to save this woman and her family, your lives for theirs, but only if we see the scarlet cord hanging from her window when we attack. That was the agreement, yes?'

The relief on their faces was so comical, I struggled not to laugh. I stood to my feet, indicating that our meeting was over. 'Come! There is much to do if we are to be ready to cross the Jordan River tomorrow. We will see Yahweh's hand move on our behalf once more, *nu*?' I said with a smile, hoping I sounded more confident than I felt.

I knew Yahweh *could* stop the waters of the Jordan from flowing, just as he had forty years ago at the Red Sea – but *would* He? He had done it for Moses, but Moses was gone and the burden of leading our people now rested on my shoulders.

Would Yahweh do the same for me?

That night I lay on my bed roll trying to banish all thoughts of city walls, harlots and fast-flowing rivers from my thoughts. I wrestled throughout the watches of the night, tossing and turning, knowing that I would not sleep much, if at all.

I was right.

I didn't.

3

The Crossing

All eyes were fixed on me, waiting for the signal.

'Joshua,' Eleazar's calm voice interrupted my brooding. 'It is time.'

I squinted at the silvery reflections of the early morning sun glinting on the surging waters before us. The Jordan River overflowed its banks weeks ago and now, this pounding mass of water was the only thing that stood between us and our promised land of Canaan.

The four men who stood before me had been specifically chosen for this task due to their stature and physical strength. Although he was high priest, Eleazar had lived many years and was no longer sturdy enough to bear Israel's greatest treasure. His son Phinehas had taken his place. Phinehas and the other favoured priests were aware of the great honour that had been bestowed on them. They were also well aware of the fact that this honour came with significant risk. The Jordan was deep at the best of times, but even more so when it was in flood, as it was now. The pull of its current was strong enough to sweep away large carts loaded with baggage, let alone mere men.

Their faces were set like flint, but the trembling of their hands and the rapid rise and fall of their chests betrayed the fear that beset them.

I made eye contact with each of them in turn, then gave Phinehas a nod. The four men bent down and gripped the golden poles. At his word, they hoisted their precious cargo, taking care to keep the Ark of the Covenant level, until the poles were high enough to be placed on their shoulders.

I turned to face the multitudes standing behind us. Raising my arms, I shouted, 'Rise up, O Lord! Let Your enemies be scattered, And let those who hate You flee before You.'[2]

---

2. Numbers 10:35.

My voice didn't tremble as I declared those words, but my heart wavered in trepidation. Why had Yahweh chosen to have this precious Ark of the Covenant, the tangible embodiment of His presence, carried straight into the pathway of this mighty flowing river?

The four priests walked towards the river, heads held high.

What if they slipped?

How would they bear the weight of the ark for hour after gruelling hour, while hundreds of thousands of our people crossed over into Canaan?

My heart pounded like the blows of a hammer, but it was too late to halt the procession; the priests had reached the water's edge. I held my breath. Phinehas and his partner glanced across at each other and, without even a moment's hesitation, stepped into the rushing waters, as Yahweh had commanded.

A collective gasp arose from the masses gathered behind me. All eyes were fixed on the four men as they waded into the river. My eyes narrowed, jaw clenched. The water swirled around their feet, soaking their sandals and the bottom of their robes. They found their footing and took another step.

Then it happened.

It started with a gurgling sound, like the gushing of water as it flows into an empty container. The ripples of water around the priest's sodden feet continued tumbling downriver, towards the Salt Sea, but the water that flowed in their place was much diminished. With each step that they took, the flow of water dwindled until only a trickle flowed down, snaking its way past their sopping feet. I held my hand up to my eyes and stared upriver, trying to see what has caused the stoppage, but the twists and turns of the riverbanks prevented me from seeing very far.

A flash of light drew my attention back to the four men who shouldered the Ark of the Covenant. What? There were no longer four men surrounding that priceless golden treasure; many men now formed a glowing hedge of protection around Yahweh's ark. A surge of exhilaration shot through me; I shivered as I realised who the newcomers were.

The shining men!

These, the strongest and mightiest of our priests, were completed dwarfed by the magnificent celestial beings who now stood around them, clothed in full battle armour and weaponry, glowing with a ferocious purity. Their presence seemed to give Phinehas and his fellow priests a boost of energy; step by step they walked on without faltering and, as they neared the middle point of the riverbed, Phinehas held up his hand. The four priests stopped, squared their shoulders, widened their stance, and prepared themselves for the back-breaking vigil which they knew was to come. The shining men positioned themselves around the ark and stretched out their arms, taking on the burden of the ark's weight with apparent ease.

They were mesmerising.

This was the fourth time I had encountered these glorious beings and yet, each time it happened, I discovered more about them. I was drawn to the fact that although they were sturdy and their muscles clearly defined, their strength did not seem to come from their physical form alone; it appeared to flow from deep within them. A glorious power cascaded out of them, like shafts of light rippling outwards. Their very beings seemed to be made of light, but a light unlike any I had seen before. It was brighter than the midday sun, yet I could look upon it without being blinded. The light that emanated from them was warm and white and yet, from time to time, strands of colour shimmered through the brightness. The light itself seemed to take on substance and form, causing them to exude a nobility, a surge of goodness that was without shadow.

Just as it had in the past whenever the shining men were near, doubt and fear lifted off me. My fast-beating heart no longer reacted in fear, but in excitement; their presence banished the disbelief that had scourged me.

'Joshua?' I turned to see Eleazar peering at me. 'What is it?'

'They . . . they are here,' I stuttered.

'Who?' Eleazar asked, looking across to where the priests stood with the ark.

'The shining men.'

'They're here? Now?' he whispered urgently. 'Where? Where are they?' Eleazar had heard the accounts of my previous encounters with the shining men, but had never seen them himself. No one else in our company had. I was the only one afforded that privilege, at least up until now.

'There,' I jabbed my head in their direction. 'They are surrounding the ark.'

'Where?' he whispered again, squinting in concentration. 'Why is it I can never see them?' he grumbled. I didn't reply. What could I say? I had no idea why Yahweh chose to open my eyes to His messengers, despite my obvious weaknesses and unworthiness. Shaking myself out of my musings, I called Caleb, my second-in-command, and instructed him to tell the people to start crossing. Very soon, the jumbled sound of human voices meshed together with the bleating of frightened animals and the rumbling of cart wheels.

Yahweh's people were on the move again!

As I stood watching, Eleazar drew near again, whispering, 'Are they still there? How many are there?'

'Yes. They are standing guard around the ark. They bear its weight. There are . . .' I paused, counting under my breath, '. . . twelve. No, wait!' My gaze was drawn away from the magnificent creatures surrounding the ark, to the landscape all around us.

'Eleazar! There are hundreds . . . no, thousands of them! They're . . . *they're everywhere!*'

4

Shimmering Pillars

Columns of light appeared all across the landscape, materialising as it were out of nowhere; shimmering pillars that flickered, then took on the form of one of Yahweh's messengers. The heavenly host multiplied before my very eyes, like the swarms of fireflies that emerged on moonless nights.

'Where?' Eleazar grasped my arm. 'Where are they?'

'They are . . . everywhere,' I panted, breathless with elation. I didn't look at him, unwilling to tear my eyes away from the extraordinary beauty that lay before me. The new arrivals were not as large as the celestial warriors who stood guard around the ark. They carried no weapon and were clothed in simple robes tied at the waist with a linen belt, but they were no less magnificent.

'What are they like?'

'They . . . they are . . .' I stammered, blinking back the tears which threatened to overflow.

Wheels that had been wedged in a rut were released in an instant, lifted out with ease by unseen hands.

A frail grandmother struggling to walk through the mire of the riverbed found the strength she needed to continue, unaware of the men of light who stood either side of her, supporting and strengthening her.

A mother with a screaming baby and a cluster of overexcited children was somehow able to keep her little brood together. She couldn't see the three shining men who surrounded her children, thwarting their efforts to run amok, keeping them close by her side. I watched as one of the children looked up at the shining man by her side, wrinkled up her nose and smiled. She saw him, I was certain of it! He returned the little girl's smile and put his hand on her shoulder. The babe in his mother's arms stopped crying and stared, wide-eyed, at the shining man who leaned over to stroke his cheek, cooing at him.

Some of the shining men helped the flocks of sheep and goats that bleated in protest at being driven into a riverbed. Stroking them and speaking words of comfort, they kept them from scattering, leading them through the sandy pathway.

Others helped those who carried heavy loads, lifting their bundles while at the same time releasing strength into the carriers.

Many among us were fearful of walking across the riverbed. We were not a seafaring people and, having been born either in Egypt or in the desert, there had been little to no opportunity to learn how to swim. Countless shining men came to stand by these fearful ones, putting an arm around their shoulders, or placing their palms on the chest of their charges, over their hearts. The love and peace that flowed out of Yahweh's messengers seemed to take on physical form – shafts of light that penetrated, dissipating the smog of fear that had surrounded them. Those who had hesitated now found the courage to step forward, aided by their invisible shining helpers.

'What are they doing? Joshua, what do you see?' Eleazar urged, pulling at my arm. I glanced at him, blinking back the tears. How could I possibly hope to explain what I saw? An overwhelming sense of awe flooded my being, a surge of gratitude swelled within me. I told Eleazar what I could, but my words painted a woefully inadequate picture. We fell silent.

The shining men knew I could see them. For the most part, they focused on the task at hand but, every now and then, one of them would glance in my direction and smile or incline their head. It was one of the most humbling experiences of my life. I struggled to meet their gaze, such was the purity and devotion that shone from their eyes.

'*Why me?*' I wondered again. I could not fathom it. Why would Yahweh choose one such as I? My thoughts turned again to the harlot, adding more fuel to the angry fire of guilt that raged within me.

'What do your thoughts dwell on?' I looked up to see Eleazar studying me with curiosity. I hesitated, but thought better of trying to deceive him or brush it aside. Eleazar knew me so well and his powers of perception were finely tuned; there was no point in trying to hide the strivings of my heart from him.

'Yahweh spoke to me in the early watches of this morning.'

'And . . .?'

'He said . . .' I looked down. 'He said, "Today I will begin to exalt you in the eyes of all Israel, so they may know that, as I was with Moses, so I will be with you."'[3]

'That is a great honour, my friend, and yet I see only conflict within your eyes. What troubles you?'

I shook my head then looked up to meet his piercing gaze. 'How is it that I have found such favour in Yahweh's sight? How is it that He finds me worthy?'

Warm compassion flowed out of Eleazar's eyes. 'The very fact that you ask this question reveals its answer. Your humility makes a way for you, my friend; the Lord honours you for it.' He turned to gaze at the miscellany of humankind around us, a look of absolute longing on his face. 'To be able to look upon His shining ones – to see their form, look into their eyes – truly, that is the gift of God.'

It was.

It was *such* a gift, one of the greatest gifts Yahweh had ever bestowed upon me. I stood, hour after hour, watching the host of heaven minister to Yahweh's chosen people, desperate to preserve the details in my mind so that later, I might scribe what I had witnessed and capture it on papyrus.

'How?' I mumbled. 'I do not have the words.'

'Commander!' Caleb strode towards me, a broad grin on his face. Clasping me to himself, he gave me a tight embrace and slapped me on the back. 'Yahweh's arm is not short, *nu*? Look at this! The Lord has heard from heaven, and now all the earth will know that there is a God in Israel! But then,' he said punching me on the arm, 'you knew He would perform wonders this day, didn't you?'

I was grateful that Caleb didn't wait for a response, otherwise I would have felt obliged to tell him of my doubts and fears as to how this day would pan out. As a military leader, issuing instructions and making bold decisions had never been Caleb's struggle. Listening, however, was not his strong point. As he continued talking with fervour about the crossing, and how long it might take for all our people to cross over, my thoughts drifted back to the men of light.

---

3. Joshua 3:7.

The yearnings of my heart blotted Caleb's voice from my consciousness. I found myself being drawn into a place of cloistered fellowship with Yahweh.

A holy moment.

I felt His presence around me. It was tangible, pressing down on me ever so gently, wrapping me up in a fleece of warm peace. I looked up at the cloud of Yahweh's presence which swirled above us; velvety wisps floating in the heavens, soft tendrils dipping down here and there, as if to impart to us a taste of the flawless perfection of heaven. All thoughts of Jericho and Rahab lifted off me. A sense of awe surrounded me, a hush in the stillness of the moment.

I looked at the shining men nearby; they joined in with my adoration of Yahweh, glowing even brighter, until their bodies were like fire.

I gasped at the heat that rose up in my belly and flushed through my body. If I'd had the choice, I would have left the wretchedness of life on earth that very instant, and gone to be with Yahweh in the place where He dwelt. It was not to be. The euphoria of the moment passed and I came to myself, all of a sudden aware that Caleb had stopped talking and was staring at me.

'Forgive me, my friend,' I murmured. Caleb knew better than to press me for details, so he waited for me to speak first.

I couldn't.

I couldn't speak of what I saw. It was too much. My heart needed to hold onto it, preserve it as the priceless jewel it was. To speak of it would dispel its majesty.

But Caleb was waiting, so I stammered, 'This . . . the . . . this day must never be forgotten. Never.' I cleared my throat. Needing to escape Caleb's gaze, I said, 'I must speak with Phinehas. I will meet with you later, *nu*?'

I made my way to where Phinehas and his comrades still stood, in the middle of the riverbed, shouldering the Ark of the Covenant, and asked him how he fared. 'In truth,' he said, frowning and shuffling his feet, 'my strength has not waned. I know not how, but there is a power in me that belies understanding. I feel as though I could endure for much time still to come.'

An irresistible urge to tell Phinehas about the shining men rose up within me. Would it be prudent to tell him of the celestial guard that surrounded them? Should he know the reason for his great strength? The desire to tell him was too great to resist; I whispered to him the truth of the matter.

'The ...? Here? Where?' he asked, eyebrows raised in alarm. His arms started trembling. I put my hand on his shoulder.

'Do not fear. All is well.' Phinehas fixed his gaze on the landscape ahead of him, although I could tell he was desperate to see for himself the celestial warriors who had come to their aid.

The burly shining man nearest to him caught my eye and smiled; a smile of mutual understanding, of a fathomless treasure that we shared, a secret of inestimable value.

5

The Other Side

Gentle swells of waves topped with golden flecks rippled behind us as the sun dipped below the horizon with a gentle sigh. The waters of the Jordan River were flowing once again; the faint sound of rushing waters echoed in the warm night air as the first stars emerged from the deepening darkness, blinking a welcome.

Our people had crossed over safely.

We made camp on the west side of the river and this evening, for the first time, we would break bread in our promised homeland of Canaan.

'We are here. We are actually here, in Canaan,' I whispered to myself, surveying the surrounding landscape with a profound sense of awe.

'Is it as you remembered?' a quiet voice asked. I turned to see Joel watching me. Here was a man who I trusted with matters of the heart, not only because he was now the patriarch of our family, but because he and I had shared much over the years. My mind flitted back to when Joel was not yet twenty, a young man so traumatised by the brutality he had endured as a slave in Egypt that he found himself unable to embrace life, or even function as a free man after we escaped. I felt immensely privileged that Yahweh had chosen to use me to help Joel escape the claws of that pain and trauma. Now, forty years later, he stood before me, a quietly spoken, much respected elder of our people, and leader of our family.

'It is,' I replied. 'Nearly two score years have passed since we spied out this land, and yet, when I look upon it, I still feel like the man I was back then; eager for conquest, overwhelmed by the beauty of this land which Yahweh promised to us.'

Joel wandered over to me and crossed his arms. 'It is magnificent, isn't it?' he said, looking out over the land. 'To see so much green, after so many years of brown . . . it is a feast for the eyes, *nu*?'

Just then, Joel's wife, Alya, joined us. Slipping one arm through his, she cuddled up to him and sighed. Alya was a woman of few words but, when she did speak, I listened. She had very sharp senses and was much respected as an older woman in our culture, not only for her skills in midwifery, but also for the wisdom of her words and her abilities as a seer.

'We are here,' she whispered. 'Yahweh has been faithful to His people.' Looking across at me, her face broke into a smile. 'Joshua! We are standing on Canaan soil!' She turned to peruse the land with us. 'For so long I heard the promises but, Yahweh forgive me, I did not always believe that I would live to see their fulfilment. But . . . here we are . . . our feet are standing on the land of our forefathers, where Abraham himself walked.'

We stood like three sentinels, soaking in the goodness of that moment, guarding the priceless treasure of the knowledge that our God was good, and just, and true, and that what He had promised had come to pass.

After a little while, Alya drew her arm out of Joel's and said, 'Come, we are nearly ready to break bread.' Walking back towards the mats that were being laid out in a large circle around our communal firepit, she stopped and turned to beam at us. 'Our first meal in our new land. Yahweh is good!'

And what a meal it was! Our women had gathered an abundance of manna early that morning before the crossing, and a variety of warm herb bread and spiced manna cakes were laid out, along with dishes of olives, nuts and figs. A large cauldron on the fire contained a simmering stew of lentils and beans, and a goat had been roasted for this occasion – but my eyes were drawn to one particular dish which contained a pile of rosy, crowned fruit.

'Pomegranates!' I reached out to take one. 'Where did you find these?' I asked Alya, who laughed at my reaction.

'We found some pomegranate trees laden with fruit, this side of the river. Assuredly, this is a land of abundance!'

The question of whether or not the prostitute, Rahab, ate pomegranates passed through my mind. I winced at the absurdity of the thought, irritated at her uncanny ability to invade my thoughts, even at a family celebration.

Everyone found their places and sat on the mats in their family groups. I was given the place of honour at family mealtimes, with Joel and Alya on one side of me, and Yoram and Samina on the other. As patriarch, it was Joel's responsibility and right to pray a blessing before we ate but, today, he turned to me.

'Joshua, would you declare the blessing?' His soft sea-grey eyes fixed on me and a look of understanding flickered across his face as he saw me fingering the pomegranate's smooth skin.

I held the plump orb in my hand. I couldn't just pray one of our usual mealtime blessings – this was not a usual meal. I glanced at Yoram, who placed a reassuring hand on my shoulder. His presence was like a healing balm to me. He knew what I was thinking about, or rather, who. Yoram's father, Mesha, had been my closest friend since childhood. Although not my brother by blood, he was the brother of my heart and it nearly broke my heart when he passed away a short time before we crossed over into Canaan.

Mesha loved pomegranates. Of all foods, pomegranates were his favourite.

I cleared my throat to try to shift the lump that had formed there, before looking at the attentive faces of my adopted family gathered around. 'This day is a day of celebration, of thankfulness and . . .' my voice cracked, '. . . remembrance.' I paused to gather myself before continuing. 'Perhaps we could take some time to remember those who are close to our hearts, but cannot be here to celebrate with us.'

A succession of faces flashed before me – family members who I had loved and lost. Mesha, Azriel, Leora, Hareph, Shira, and the three men I had been fortunate enough to call father: Nun, Jesher and, more recently, Moses. Each face brought with it a stream of precious memories. I closed my eyes, savouring the richness of the reminiscence until, in the background, I heard the sounds of fidgeting, and children whispering. Opening my eyes, I saw lots of little faces staring at me. Clearly, the young ones were done reminiscing; they were ready to eat!

Grinning in response, I raised my head and prayed, 'Blessed are You, King of the universe, who has brought us safely through the waters and into this land that You have promised us. Blessed are

You, Lord God, who has led us to this land of milk and honey, and who bids us eat of the bounty of this land.'

Looking at each of the little faces watching me, I prayed, 'The LORD bless you and keep you; The LORD make His face to shine upon you, And be gracious to you; The Lord lift up His countenance upon you, And give you peace.'[4]

The little ones stared back at me, waiting for me to give the word.

'So, let's eat then, yes?' I roared, lifting my arms with a flourish. They responded with a shout of approval and a flurry of activity began. Voices 'oohed' and 'aahed' in appreciation of the tantalising new flavours that their palates were tasting, and the pomegranates disappeared within seconds. I chuckled to myself, thinking of how much pleasure Mesha would have had, watching us. Conversation turned to the day's events.

I had not told Joel, Yoram, or anyone else about the shining men. Only Eleazar and Phinehas knew. I couldn't talk of it yet. It was too soon, too precious. I needed time to let it sink into the deep places of my heart. I would tell them, but not yet.

Shallum, Yoram's youngest brother, talked about the first time Yahweh had parted the waters, at the Red Sea, after we had escaped from Egypt.

'I was too young to remember when we walked through the waters of at the Red Sea,' he told us, 'but I will never forget what happened today. Walking through the riverbank as Yahweh held the waters back . . . this will remain in my heart forever. My children's children will hear of how the hand of Yahweh was outstretched for His people.'

Murmurs of agreement resonated around the mat.

'I remember the Red Sea crossing,' Yoram responded. 'The memories of that day have not left me, all these years. The terror of being pursued by the Egyptians, then watching them die by Yahweh's hand. I have never forgotten the sound of their chariot wheels and whips, or their screams when the waters closed in on them. It still echoes in my mind, after all these years. But today, when we walked through the Jordan River, not fleeing in terror for our lives, but knowing that Yahweh is leading us into our own land, my memories of the Red Sea were washed away. Yahweh has

---

4. Numbers 6:24-26.

redeemed the fear of that day and replaced it with peace and . . . and joy!'

'Amen!' Joel shouted, and we all echoed his cry.

'Amen! Amen!'

'And soon we will have homes to dwell in. Our *own* homes! Think on that!' Joel said, turning to his wife. 'Think on that, my love!'

Alya laughed at the childlike excitement she saw on his face. 'I have thought about it – often – although we have lived in tabernacles for so long, I cannot hardly recall what it is to live in a house with solid walls!'

Joel grabbed her arm. 'I will build us a *magnificent* house! A house with walls, and a roof, and a door! No more tent flaps beating in the wind! No more wind whistling through the cracks or rain pelting on the hides!' Turning to Yoram and I, and the rest of the family in turn, he blurted, 'I will build one for you too, and for you. I will build homes for all of our kin!' We laughed at Joel's excitement. It was unusual to see our mild-mannered patriarch being so spirited. It reminded me of the vibrant young man that Joel had been in his youth, when he first discovered the joy of living a life full of purpose and creativity.

'It would be an honour to have Israel's finest craftsman build our homes,' I said, grasping his shoulder. 'But take heed: if you build them with too much skill, others might pursue you, demanding that you build them a home just as wonderful!'

Joel roared with laughter, ripped a cake of herb bread in half, and dipped it in a dish of stew to sop up the juices. 'A blessing on our new homes!' he shouted, hoisting his bread in the air.

'A blessing on our new homes!' we echoed in response. Talk turned to our prospective dwellings, and the night air filled with chatter as what had been mere dreams turned into actual possibilities. Joel leaned back to talk to his brother Naim and his wife about their preferences for the design of their home, while Alya bent forward to speak to me.

Leaning her forearms on her crossed legs, she said, 'Joshua, this day the Lord has exalted you in the eyes of our people. You have done what He asked of you. Look!' she said, gesturing at the myriads of families gathered around their campfires, for miles around. 'Look at your people! They have come home. You have brought them home. You did this!' She looked deep into my eyes, as if to ensure that I understood the magnitude of what had taken place that day.

I didn't know how to respond. I leaned over and squeezed Alya's hand. She returned the squeeze, then asked, 'So, what is next?'

I paused, looked over to the west, and said, 'Jericho. We are to take the city of Jericho.'

Joel and Alya knew how heavily this task weighed on me. She lowered her voice, leaning in more. 'And has Yahweh told you how we are to accomplish this?'

'No,' I replied, studying the mat in front of me. 'Not yet. Only that we are to take the city in His name.' I gave her a cautious smile. 'There is much to bring before Him, much that I need His guidance on.'

'And you will receive it,' she said with a firm tone. Conversations with Alya always left me feeling stronger and more peaceful. I loved that about her. She was a woman of faith and, right now, that was exactly what I needed.

'I heard an interesting story yesterday,' she said, probably trying to change the subject and lighten my mood. 'Nera heard it from her daughter, who heard it from Rae – something about two of our spies lodging with a harlot in Jericho, and the woman saving them from capture.' She laughed. 'I told them they should not believe everything they hear, especially when the story comes from Rae's lips, but th . . .' she froze when she saw the look on my face. Her eyebrows shot up into her forehead. 'Oh. Not just a story, then. Is it true?' she whispered. 'Surely, it cannot be true?'

I grimaced and nodded.

'A harlot?' Alya cocked her head. 'That is unexpected. I would not have thought our warriors could be so easily led astray by a woman like that.'

Feeling duty bound to defend my men, I whispered back, 'They were not . . . led astray by her – not in that manner. She offered them lodgings, but their presence was reported and the king's guards came to arrest them. The harlot . . .' I cleared my throat, '. . . Rahab, hid them and then helped them escape. In return for their lives, they pledged to spare her and her family.' I slapped my hands on my thighs. 'So, they must now be given sanctuary among us when we take the city.'

Alya couldn't have looked more surprised if I had told her that I had decided to worship the idols of Jericho myself.

'In truth,' I mumbled, rubbing my temple with one hand. 'My mind cannot fathom it. A harlot? Living among us? How can this be Yahweh's will? Why did He choose a woman like Rahab to deliver Beerah and Salmah? A Canaanite woman. A prostitute. Why?'

A curious expression cloaked Alya's face. 'Beerah and Salmah? So . . . the woman they were speaking of yesterday, when we brought your food, was this woman, Rahab?'

'It was. They seem to think she is a woman of great courage and . . .' I guffawed, 'wisdom. A courageous, wise pagan harlot – have you ever heard of such foolishness?'

Alya's expression changed to one of serious contemplation. 'You have told me often enough that Yahweh's ways are not our ways. You are right. Perhaps it is best not to render judgement on this woman until you have met her and talked with her.'

I grunted and looked away. Alya was a woman; of course she would say that. 'Meet her and talk with her' . . . that was precisely what I was dreading. I took a big mouthful of spiced manna cake and chewed hard. All thoughts of houses and celebrations were now forgotten. The sick feeling in my stomach returned, and my heart wrestled once more with the paradox of this pagan prostitute and her idol-worshipping family.

Perhaps Alya was right.

Perhaps I should keep an open mind and not judge the woman until I had talked with her.

'I will try,' I told myself.

But I still didn't like it – any of it.

6

Gone

My soul was glowing in the aftermath of the previous day's events. Our first Passover in this land, and it was the sweetest I had ever experienced! I shook my head, reminding myself again that we were here, in Canaan.

The cheerful chirping of desert sparrows, along with the gentle cooing of turtle doves, heralded the dawning of another day. I had always been an early riser, usually washed and dressed well before the dawn, but today I had decided to give myself the luxury of lying in. I rolled onto my back, put my hands behind my head, and closed my eyes, soaking in the exquisite decadence of doing nothing.

The sound of scuffling in the tent next to mine interrupted my contemplations. I heard Samina's voice. 'Yoram! Yoram, wake up!'

'I am awake, don't shout.' I heard Yoram groaning and pictured him sitting up, rubbing his eyes, and squinting at the bright light coming through the tent flap. Yoram was *not* an early riser!

'Hmph. For an awake man, you snore very loudly!' Samina retorted. I stifled a giggle, imagining Yoram's plump little wife standing with her hands on her hips, as she did when she scolded him.

'I wasn't snoring, I was meditating.'

'Meditating?'

'Yes, meditating.' She must have given him one of her 'looks' because the tone of Yoram's voice changed. 'But now I am finished meditating, and so I am getting up.'

Wise man, I thought to myself, still trying not to chuckle.

'Good,' Samina replied. 'I need you to go and fetch some manna.'

'For you, my beloved, anything. I will take Liron and Simha with me, *nu*?' I heard the smack of a kiss, then more discussions as Yoram roused his grumpy sons to go and fetch some manna. Although it had been our staple food for nearly forty years, I still marvelled at

Yahweh's miraculous daily provision of that wafer-like substance during these years of our desert wanderings.

I sighed, realising that the camp would come to life now that the dawn had broken. My time of relaxation was over. 'Ah well, it was good while it lasted,' I mumbled, pushing myself up to a sitting position with a hearty yawn. I took my time washing and dressing before joining my family outside. The younger men had already cleared the ashes out of the firepit, and a new fire was blazing cheerfully, in readiness for the women to bake manna cakes on the warm stones.

Joel was already positioned on the mats near the fire. I greeted him, plopped down next to him and crossed my legs, gazing into the flames.

'*Shalom*, Joshua. Did you sleep well?' he asked.

'I did,' I responded, giving another yawn and rubbing the sleep out of my eyes. The dried dung pats on the fire sizzled and popped, creating a flurry of sparks which flew up, pirouetting wildly in an exotic dance. Leaning forward, I rested my forearms on my legs and stared into the flames. The bustling noises of the women preparing food along with the giggles of children playing nearby waned as I succumbed to the fire's hypnotic allure. As always, when wooed by the mysteries of nature, my thoughts turned to deeper things.

'What do you think on?' Joel asked a little while later.

'Peace,' I replied with a smug, contented smile, still staring into the flames.

'Peace?'

'Mmm. There is peace in the camp. I can feel it.'

'Yes?'

'Mmm.' I turned to face him. 'For years, our people have been told of Yahweh's faithfulness. They have heard of His promises, but now, they have *seen* Him move on their behalf. He has done what He said He would do. We are *here*, in the land of our forefathers.'

'It still seems unbelievable, *nu?*'

'Mmm.'

Nestled side by side with that sense of peace was an undercurrent of excitement; it throbbed in the atmosphere. The huge city that loomed in the distance was a constant reminder to me of our next challenge.

Jericho must fall.

I knew it would have to be breached before we could continue in our quest, but I still had no idea how it would happen. Everyone was looking to me to lead them in this endeavour, but how could we possibly hope to break through the unassailable walls of that great city? That bleak thought was followed swiftly by the other thought that dominated my thinking.

Rahab.

Could she really be the courageous, wise woman that my spies declared her to be? Surely not? She was a harlot. She must have deceived them, used her womanly wiles to entangle them. I shuddered.

'Lord God, forbid that I should be seduced by her whoredom,' I prayed.

Was I obligated to meet with her, I wondered. Did I *have* to talk to her? Perhaps I could have her and her family housed in tents outside the camp and make sure their needs were met. As long as we spared their lives and protected them, had we not fulfilled our pledge? Surely that would suffice.

No.

It would not suffice.

Like it or not, my conversations with the spies had more than piqued my curiosity and, although I loathed the thought of meeting the harlot, I knew I wouldn't be able to resist seeing for myself if she was all they said she was.

My musing was shattered by the sound of yelling.

'*Ima! Ima!*' Simha shouted, running towards the tent, dodging people on his way. Heads turned in alarm to look at the boy as he sprinted up to Samina, panting and out of breath.

'Simha, slow down!' She held his arms and asked, 'What is it? What's wrong? Where's Liron, and your *abba*?'[5]

'They're coming,' panted Simha. '*Ima*, there isn't . . .' he gasped.

'What? Simha, there isn't what?' Samina demanded. 'Tell me!'

'Manna. *Ima*, there is no manna,' he blurted, eyes wide with trepidation.

'What do you mean, there is no manna? There is always manna. There must be manna. You must be mistaken. You did not look carefully.' Looking past him, she scoured the path for her husband. 'Where is your *abba*? Yoram!' she yelled out. 'Yoram!' By the time

---

5. *Abba* is the Hebrew word for father.

Yoram and Liron arrived, a crowd had formed. It was true, there was no manna. Nothing. Not a single piece. The growing crowds looked at each other in alarm.

'Why is there no manna?'

'What will we eat?'

'Where is the manna?'

'How will we make our bread cakes?'

Others had also had a similar experience; word spread throughout the camp like wildfire. Voices argued all around us, along with grumblings of dissent carried by the wind from other parts of the camp. Before long, the burble of voices turned into a rumble, then the crowd turned to demand a solution from their leader.

Pouring into our enclosure, they demanded to know what I was going to do about it. Staring at the chaos unravelling before me, my heart felt no fear; I knew what Yahweh would have me say. Climbing onto a rock, I raised my arms, and shouted.

'*Quiet*! Be still and hear me.'

I waited for them to quieten down before continuing.

'Do not fear, we shall not starve.' I smiled at them, wondering if this is how a father felt when he scolded his children. 'Have you already forgotten what the Lord God promised us? Look around you,' I said, gesturing to the land that lay before us. 'Our God is faithful and just. He protected us and provided manna for us to eat every day, while we wandered in the wilderness. Yahweh has fulfilled His promise and brought us safely into this land; do you think He will now abandon us? *No!*'

I noticed Eleazar standing on the outskirts of the crowd, watching me, a look of pride on his face.

'The manna has gone because we no longer have need of it,' I explained. 'Yahweh promised us a land of hills and valleys, a land that drinks water from the rain of heaven.' My voice rose in excitement. 'A land that flows with milk and honey, filled with olive groves and vineyards, fruit trees and pasture.' I swung around with outstretched arms. '*This* is that land. This is *our* land and, from this day forward, *we will eat of this bounty which the Lord God has given us.*'

The crowds erupted into cheers.

Eleazar grinned at me, nodding his approval.

The days of eating manna may have been over, but the days of feasting on the fat of this land were just beginning!

7

The Beast

Something was wrong. Why was she so quiet?

The air crackled with excitement as we broke our fast that morning. The absence of manna now seemed inconsequential, as talk turned to the different foods we might find in Canaan. Even the children found themselves being drawn into a tantalising new world of possibilities: grapes, pomegranates, barley bread, fresh vegetables, tomatoes, nuts, grains and beans.

There was one person, however, who was not taking part in the discussion.

'Alya, what troubles you?' I asked as soon as an opportune time presented itself. She glanced at Joel, who gave her a quick nod of encouragement, before replying. 'I had a dream last night which has caused me great distress.'

'I know well the angst that dreams can cause. What did you see in your dream?'

Alya hesitated. 'It would not be wise to talk of it here.'

'Come into my tent,' I said, wondering what kind of dream it must have been to prevent her from talking of it in front of her own family. I beckoned to Joel, who joined us. We sat down and I waited until she was ready; Alya was not a woman who responded well to being pressured or coerced. She closed her eyes, concentrating hard.

'I saw an enormous beast rising out of the ground before me – a foul creature with a thick hide, cloven hooves and a hairy snout. The beast had six limbs and five horns on its head, but its tail was that of a scorpion. It went and lay in the shadows, hidden from sight, unmoving, just waiting and watching until . . .' Alya shuddered and looked up at me. 'I saw our people laughing and making merry while the beast lay in wait for them, but my tongue clung to the roof of my mouth – I was mute, unable to warn them.

I couldn't move or speak. I could only watch as they drew near to where the beast lay in wait. It's tail curved upwards, quivering, then it plunged downwards, striking them in the back, one by one until all had been stung by its venom – and yet they did not know it!'

Her voice broke, and she started wringing her hands in her lap.

'The beast's attack was unseen by them – they had no knowledge of it.' Alya was normally so calm and peaceful, I found it unnerving to see her in this state. Joel reached out and took her hands in his. He said nothing but, when she looked at him, she seemed to draw strength from him. She breathed in and heaved a shaky sigh before continuing.

'They moved away from the beast, but were much changed, marked with iniquity. Their eyes were marred by the sting of the scorpion; they became unseeing, and a terrible darkness fell on them. The monster devoured many . . . so many fell prey to the poison in its sting.' Alya had gone pale; she trembled. 'Joshua, I am loath to say this. I know this is a time of celebration for our people, but I must speak what I know to be true: this dream is a warning. A vile evil inhabits this land – an abomination that would enslave us and fill the land with blood and desolation.' She grabbed my arm. 'Please, heed me in this!'

I put my hand on top of hers. 'Alya, I have always paid heed to your dreams and visions, you know this. Yahweh speaks through you. I will always listen to your counsel. Do you know what this beast is?'

Alya broke down, sobbing. 'No! No, I don't! I cannot think what it is. My heart fears for our people, but I cannot think how to prevent this from taking place. How can it be that I see such things and yet have no understanding of their meaning? It is folly! I must know. I must help them!'

Joel spoke up. 'My love, perhaps it is not given to you to know the meaning of the dream. Perhaps your part is to speak what Yahweh shows you and trust that He will give interpretation of the dream to another. It is often the way, *nu*?'

I voiced my agreement with Joel and thanked Alya for sharing the dream with me.

I knew what Alya's dream was about.

After they left, I stood at the entrance to my tent, eyes closed, listening to the sound of sparrows and the chattering of excited people. The cool morning breeze caressed my face with a fresh touch of hope and goodness. Gilgal, the place where we were camped, was blessed. Our presence there, Yahweh's presence among us, had brought blessing to this place. Yahweh had promised us that every place on which the sole of our feet would tread would be ours. This was to be our land, our home, the place where His name would be exalted among the nations, where righteousness would prevail and joy abound.

But it was not yet so.

For whenever I turned my gaze towards Jericho and to the land beyond, discomfort lay heavy on me. I sensed it the moment we crossed over the Jordan River and set foot in Canaan: a longing, a yearning that hung in the air around us, as if the land itself was begging to be redeemed, to be purged from the uncleanness that was rotting it, soil and leaf and bough.

'This land is troubled,' I whispered. 'There is a sickness that lies upon it.' I could smell it, hear it in the call of the wind, see it in the dark shadows on the horizon, sense it simmering beneath the surface, unseen by the human eye.

I couldn't sit down. I couldn't relax. My spirit was restless. Alya's dream was troubling – very troubling. I knew I could do nothing without first going to the Tabernacle to seek Yahweh's face. The cloud of His presence always brought solace to my disquieted soul. Eleazar would be there. I would discuss this with him, we would come before Yahweh, and seek His guidance. He would speak.

I was sure of it.

8

Dissipated

One look at my face told Eleazar all he needed to know.

'*Shalom*, Joshua. Is it well with you?' His greeting was rather redundant.

'*Shalom*, Eleazar. No. No, it is not well with me.' We made our way to the outskirts of the Tabernacle courtyard and, without pausing to exchange pleasantries, I launched straight into an account of the morning's events, recounting the details of Alya's dream. Eleazar sat down, gesturing to me to do likewise, and listened without interrupting, rocking and mumbling 'mmm' from time to time.

'What does your heart tell you regarding this beast?' he asked when I had finished. 'What does it signify?'

I needed no time to think on it. 'The idolatry which plagues this land. I know it, Eleazar. It is malignant, poisonous. We must cut the tail off this beast. It must not take our people into the dark places or rob them of their inheritance.'

'Mmm.' Eleazar's brow furrowed in concentration.

I shared with him what I sensed regarding the sickness that lay upon the land. 'Alya said that the beast rose up from the ground, which tells me that the very land we walk on is poisoned by its touch. It had a hairy snout and cloven hooves – Eleazar, its form matches that of a swine, forbidden to our people but embraced by pagan cultures.'

'Yes,' he muttered, 'and did she not say that the beast had five horns on its head? The horns speak of authority – this evil is not without power. I fear you are right; its hold over this land and its inhabitants is great.'

'The beast stung them in the back – Alya said they knew nothing of it. They were ignorant of their fate, unaware of the terrible evil that had inflicted them.' I hunched over. 'Eleazar, I fear for our people. They are like children. They have lived the simple life of a nomad for so long, they know little of the perils that await them, or the temptations they will face in Canaan. How will they resist? How can I protect them from what lies ahead?'

'You are right, much danger awaits us, but Yahweh has warned you of this already through this dream. He will show us what to do. He will not leave us defenceless.'

A question had been nagging me since Alya shared her dream, a question that I was loath to give voice to, but Eleazar was one of the few people who I knew I could trust completely. I had to ask him.

'Eleazar, there is . . . I must ask you,' I turned to face him. 'This beast. Does this great evil come upon us because of Rahab?'

'The harlot?' Eleazar's bushy eyebrows shot to the top of his forehead.

'Yes. The harlot. Have we sinned? Were we right to offer sanctuary to her and her family? Was it fitting for Beerah and Salmah to pledge their lives for hers, or is this Yahweh's judgement on us?'

He frowned. 'Yahweh's judgement on us?' Moments passed before he spoke again. 'No. I do not believe this is Yahweh's judgement on us for saving the lives of this woman and her kin. The Lord is just and righteous, but He is also merciful and full of compassion. From what I have been told, this harlot has heard of Yahweh and His wonders, and risked her life to save our spies. Yahweh rewards those who seek Him diligently. He does not do them harm.'

'Yes, but her words could have been a guise to save her life, and that of her family. A prostitute would be well versed in the ways of deception, would she not? Once safely living among us, she might turn back to her evil ways and lead our people astray.' I gasped. 'What if . . . what if *she* is the beast in Alya's dream?'

Eleazar flinched. 'Joshua, calm yourself. I struggle to believe that one prostitute could be responsible for wreaking such heinous evil on an entire land and all its inhabitants. The Lord will not forsake His people. He will show us how to cleanse this land, but,' he leaned in to get my attention, 'we cannot cleanse this land without first cleansing the soil of our own hearts. We must consecrate ourselves, search our hearts, see if there is any wicked way in us, anything that is not pleasing to Yahweh.'

He grasped my arm. '"Be strong and very courageous",[6] remember? Rid yourself of fear. Do not let your heart fail because of this dream. Yahweh has been faithful in warning us of what is to come, and He will show us how to cleanse this land and vanquish the beast, *nu?*'

I placed my hand on top of his. 'Forgive me, my friend,' I mumbled. 'My thoughts have been troubled of late.'

Eleazar smiled at me. 'Come, we will seek His face, yes? He will speak.'

I nodded and looked up to the canopy overhead, ready to soak in the peace that radiated from the cloud of Yahweh's presence.

Panic jolted my heart like a lightning bolt.

'No! No, no, no, no . . . !' I jumped to my feet, staring upwards, my thoughts scattering in every direction like seeds bursting out of a pod, to be swept away by the wind. 'This cannot be!' My heart started racing. No! Not now! Why? My breath came in short gasps. I felt dizzy.

'Joshua, what ails you?' Eleazar stood up, looking at me in concern.

'He . . . He is leaving us!' I stammered.

'Who is leaving us?'

'Yahweh!' I blurted. 'Yahweh is leaving us!'

'Yahweh is leaving us?' Eleazar repeated, confused.

'Yes! Look!' I pointed up at the cloud. 'Do you not see?' I yelped. 'Yahweh's cloud . . . look at it! Why is this happening? Why does He leave us? Have I sinned before the Lord? Is there iniquity hidden in my heart?'

Eleazar gazed up at the fading canopy. At first he looked alarmed but, as he continued to study the thinning cloud that shimmered overhead, his countenance changed to one of contemplation. 'Mmm.' He nodded his head, more to himself than to me. 'Joshua, Yahweh is not leaving us.'

'Then why is His cloud dispersing? Look at it! It is melting away in front of our eyes. Why, Eleazar?' I grabbed his arm. 'Why does Yahweh leave us? Why now?'

Eleazar's smile confounded me. It was full of tenderness, compassion and a touch of exasperation. He spoke to me as though he were chastising a child.

---

6. Joshua 1:7.

'Joshua, do you not remember the words you spoke to the people this very morning when they could find no manna?' Without waiting for my reply, he reminded me. 'You told them that the Lord is faithful and just, that Yahweh had fulfilled His promise and brought us safely into this land.' He pointed at me. 'Your exact words were, "Do you think He will now abandon us? *No!*" My friend, I exhort you to take counsel from your own words.'

Eleazar stared into my eyes, waiting for me to come to a place of understanding.

I didn't.

Fear had addled my senses.

'But . . . but His cloud has always been with us. Since we left Egypt, I have drawn strength and peace from it. Why must He take it from me now?'

'Because you no longer have need of it.'

'I do,' I protested. 'My need of Him is great – even greater now that Moses is not with me.'

'Your need of Yahweh is great, yes, but not your need of His cloud. He gave us His cloud and the pillar of fire to guide us in our wanderings, to show us where to go, when to make camp and when to move on.' He leaned forward, stared into my eyes, and spoke slowly and deliberately. 'Joshua, we have no need of the cloud now because we are here, in Canaan. Yahweh has brought us to the land He promised us – as you told your people. He is still with us, and He will still speak with you, but we have no need of His cloud to guide us because we have come home.'

A little smile played upon his lips as he raised one eyebrow, cocking his head.

I huffed, looking up at the fast-dissipating canopy overhead, to break eye contact with Eleazar. His gaze could be very piercing at times.

'I must know what He requires of me. I must know how to take Jericho. How are we to breach those walls? You have seen them – it is an impossible task. How are we to do this?'

'Joshua – ask – Yahweh. He has spoken to you for many years, and He will continue to speak to you. You *know* His voice. Seek His counsel. He will tell you His plans for breaching that city. He will speak to you, just as He always has.'

I nodded, saying nothing more. What more could I say?

We sat side by side in the Tabernacle courtyard, watching and praying. And my heart broke within me with wild desperation as the last whispery tendrils of velvety cloud dissipated, and Yahweh's glorious covering disappeared from our sight.

9

Foolishness

I strode out of the Tabernacle towards my tent, my face twisted in a deep frown. 'Attai!' I barked. 'Find Eleazar and Caleb. Ask them to come to my tent. Make haste!'

'Yes, Commander.' Eyes down, Attai asked, 'Gedaliah is asking to see you – can I tell him you will see him now?'

'No.'

'Forgive me, but he says it is important. The captains are asking about the battle plan for Jericho and he has been waiting for . . .'

'Not now! Fetch Eleazar and Caleb – and I do not want to be disturbed when I am with them.'

'Yes, Commander.' Attai darted off to call Eleazar and Caleb. I could see he was puzzled, probably wondering what had happened in the Tabernacle to put me in such a bad temper. What indeed! My conversation with Eleazar yesterday had helped to bring me back to a place of peace. I had spent the rest of the day praying and seeking Yahweh about Jericho, and about Aya's dream. First thing this morning, after we had broken fast, I went back to the Tabernacle to seek His face.

Yahweh had spoken, but I didn't like what He had to say.

In my tent, I poured myself a drink of water and drank deeply. I paced up and down, muttering to myself, then stopped and hurled the cup on the ground, shattering the earthen vessel. 'Aaagh!' I roared, sinking into my chair, holding my head in my hands.

A short while later, Eleazar arrived. He paused in the entrance of my tent and gave me a tentative greeting. '*Shalom*, Joshua. You asked to see me?'

'*Shalom*, Eleazar. Yes, come in. Sit, please.' I gestured to a bench and Eleazar sat down, waiting for me to make the first move.

'I have sent for Caleb also. I will wait until he comes, so I only have to say this once,' I snapped.

Just then, we heard footsteps, and Caleb's mop of curly hair appeared around the tent flap. '*Shalom*, Joshua. You sent for me?' he asked and, seeing Eleazar, he greeted him. 'Ah, *Shalom*, Eleazar.'

'*Shalom, Shalom.* Come, sit,' I said.

Caleb stepped inside and, seeing the smashed pieces of pottery on the floor, glanced at Eleazar. Out of the corner of my eye, I saw Eleazar shrug. The two men sat in silence, waiting for me to tell them what had angered me so much that I had smashed a goblet.

'The Lord has spoken to me,' I blurted, staring at the floor, tapping the ends of my fingers together.

'Yes?' Eleazar said.

'About Jericho.'

Silence.

Tap, tap, tap.

The tension was palpable.

'What did He say?' Caleb asked.

Tap, tap, tap.

'Yahweh gave me the battle strategy for taking Jericho. He said . . . He said that . . . *eiysh!* I will tell it to you just like He spoke to me.' Leaning forward, I drew a deep breath and spoke with an impassive tone. 'He said all our men of war are to march around Jericho. Seven priests are to march with us, blowing rams' horns, followed by priests carrying the Ark of the Covenant. Armed guards will surround the priests carrying the ark.'

I paused to look at them but, seeing blank expressions on both their faces, I looked down and continued before they could comment or ask questions. 'We must march around the outskirts of the city of Jericho once. We are not to say anything or do anything else, just march in silence and return to the camp. For six days, we must do this. On the seventh day we must march around the city in the same way, but seven times, not just once. Then the priests are to blow their horns with long blasts, we must all shout with a great shout, and the walls of the city will fall down.' I lifted my head and glared at them, daring them to respond. 'That is it. That is what Yahweh has instructed me.'

Tap, tap, tap.

Eleazar held my gaze.

Silence.

Tap, tap, tap.

'So, we are taking the Ark of the Covenant to Jericho?' he questioned.

'Yes.'

'And we will not unsheathe our swords?'

'No.'

'We will blow rams' horns and shout?'

'Yes.'

'But not raise our swords or weapons?'

'No.'

'Aah.' Eleazar looked away, stroking his greying beard.

Tap, tap, tap.

Caleb said nothing. The silence was agony.

'Why don't they say something?' I thought to myself. Both of them sat like dead men, staring into space, just waiting. For what? For me to do something? What? What could I do, when faced with such a ridiculous plan?

'How am I to tell my captains?' I blurted out. 'I have trained these warriors for years and led them into many battles. We have fought bravely and won many victories for our people, and now I have to tell them . . . this?' I said, waving my hands in the air. 'They will think my mind has gone, that I have lost my senses.'

Silence fell again.

The bustling sounds of camp life echoed outside as each of us wrestled with our own thoughts. Caleb avoided my gaze altogether. Clearly, he thought this was a situation that Eleazar would be better at handling. He was probably right. Eleazar was a man of wisdom, and good with words. Caleb fixed his eyes firmly on the floor and waited for Eleazar to respond. Eleazar closed his eyes, rocking gently and muttering intermittently in prayer. I had a great love for this man of God and respected his wisdom. Normally, I would have appreciated his prayerful stance.

Today, I found it irritating.

I slumped back in my chair, staring glumly at the walls and ceiling of the tent. After some time, Eleazar spoke.

'Do you remember what happened at Pi Hahiroth?'

'Of course,' I grunted. 'Being pursued by the armies of Egypt is not something you forget easily.'

'What happened?'

'You know what happened,' I snapped. The last thing I needed now was an inconsequential stroll down memory lane. 'We all know what happened; we were there. Our people walked through the Red Sea on dry land, then the waters came back and the Egyptians drowned.'

'Yes. And before that? When we were camped at Pi Hahiroth, how did Yahweh stop the Egyptians from reaching us?'

'He sent the pillar of cloud and fire.' I glowered at him, tapping my fingers on the wooden bench. Reminding me that the cloud had gone was not helpful.

'Yes! A pillar of cloud and fire. Joshua, think back to that time! Why a pillar of cloud and fire?'

'I know not,' I growled, 'but I am sure you are about to tell me.'

Undeterred, Eleazar continued. 'Why did He choose to hold back the waters of the Red Sea so that our people could cross there? He could have led us from the north, so we would have no need to cross the great waters, but He didn't do that. He took us through the Red Sea and we watched Him perform miracles and destroy our enemies. He did it again at the Jordan River. Why, Joshua? Why?'

'I don't know!' I bellowed, hoisting myself up to a standing position, knocking my seat over in the process.

'Exactly!' Eleazar thrust his arms in the air victoriously, unperturbed by my outburst. 'We do not know the ways of Yahweh. We cannot perceive His thoughts, and it is not ours to understand His ways, but to obey His commands.' Pointing his finger at me, he stressed, '*That* is when we see His victory.' Eleazar leaned forward in his chair. 'We are not to question His ways, Joshua. If Yahweh has decided that we no longer need to follow His cloud and fire, then we no longer need them. If this is how He has told us to attack Jericho then this is what we must do.'

'But...blowing trumpets and shouting?' I squinted in confusion. 'How will that cause us to breach the ramparts?' I picked my chair up and thumped it back into place.

'Hmm. Assuredly, it has never been done before,' he said, scratching his beard, 'but Yahweh will show us.'

I grunted. 'It is foolishness.' I tramped to the other side of the tent. 'The day we crossed the Jordan River, Yahweh told me that He would begin to exalt me in the eyes of all Israel, so they will know that He is with me, as He was with Moses. *Is this His way of exalting me?*' I raved, gesticulating. 'By making me look like a fool in front of my people, in front of my own warriors?' I crossed my arms in an effort to calm myself.

It didn't work.

'He saves our spies from capture.' I glared at them. 'Through a woman! Not just any woman, no! A Canaanite woman – a *harlot*! And now I must meet this harlot and talk with her, and she must live among us with her family, and bring about who knows what kind of evil in this camp. Why?' Both of them looked at me with curiosity. I shut up, stomped back to my chair, and sat down.

We sat for a while, saying nothing. This time, it was Caleb who broke the silence. 'Do you remember your first battle?' he asked me.

'Of course,' I snorted. 'I still have the scars,' I said, pulling my robe back to reveal several jagged scars on my upper arms.

'So do I,' Caleb grinned at me. Pausing for a moment, he continued. 'What do you remember most about that battle?'

'What do I remember most?' I repeated. *Another* unwanted walk down memory lane? I breathed out and paused to reflect. 'It was my first battle. I was terrified. The Amalekites were many in number, ferocious, and their weapons were sharp and plentiful, compared to ours.'

'What else?' Caleb probed. 'Do you recall how we gained victory over them?'

'I don't think any of us would have forgotten that. Our warriors were brave men; peace be upon them.'

Eleazar smiled and nodded his head in acknowledgement.

'Do you remember how the battle raged on, while Moses held his staff above his head?' Caleb persisted. 'When his hands dropped, our losses were great, but when his arms held the staff aloft, we were victorious.'

'I remember it well,' I said, starting to feel calmer. 'It was remarkable. Once Moses realised it, he did not lower his staff. Aaron and Hur held his arms up until the evening, and we won the battle.'

'Won the battle?' Caleb protested. 'Joshua, we *crushed* them. Our inexperienced, unarmed army of men *slaughtered* them – they ran in terror from us! Do you not remember that?'

'Yes. Vividly.' I looked at him, curiosity getting the better of me. 'Why do you speak of this now?' I asked, rubbing my temple to try to ease the ache that throbbed there.

Caleb came to sit next to me. 'Because we should not have won that battle. Our warriors were novices, our weapons were crude and few in number. But we *did* win it. We listened to Yahweh and we obeyed Him. *That* is why we won, and *that* is how we will defeat Jericho.'

Eleazar joined us. 'What Caleb says is true. Yahweh uses things that seem like foolishness to us, to bring about victories that we could never achieve in our own strength or by our own devising.'

'Yes, but blowing trumpets?' I guffawed. 'Why would Yahweh have us march in silence and then blow trumpets when He could easily raze the city to the ground Himself? His arm is not short.'

Eleazar paused and then his face broke into a broad grin. 'No, it is not. He *could* do that, yes. But where would be the fun in that, *nu*?' He continued to watch me, waiting expectantly. 'Just think on what could happen when we blow our trumpets and shout! Think of what it will be like when those mighty walls crumble and fall before our very eyes. Just think of it, Joshua!'

I stared at him, utterly confounded. He believed it! He actually believed that this senseless, foolish plan would work! I glanced over at Caleb. There was no doubt in his eyes; he believed it too. The fight went out of me. I groaned, closed my eyes, and shook my head.

Sighing, I rested my head in one hand and opened my eyes slowly to see both Eleazar and Caleb watching me, smiling, and nodding in anticipation.

'Hmm?' Eleazar raised his eyebrows and inclined his head.

'*Eiysh*. I surrender.' I lifted my hands, a wry smile forming on my face. 'You have prevailed. I will obey Yahweh in this matter, despite how foolish I feel.'

'Of course you will.' Eleazar stood up resolutely and walked towards me. 'Remember what Moses said to us at Beth Peor: "Hear, O Israel: Today you are on the verge of battle with your enemies. Do not let your heart faint, do not be afraid, and do not tremble or be terrified because of them; for the LORD *your God* is He who goes with you, to *fight for you* against your enemies, to save you."'[7]

---

7. Deuteronomy 20:3-4, my italics.

I stood up and shook my head. 'Ay, ay, ay! I am getting too old for this, Eleazar.'

'Never! Do I have to remind you *again* what Yahweh said to you at your inauguration? Do you not remember it?' Eleazar wagged his finger in my face. 'I remember. I remember it well. "Be strong and of good courage; do not be afraid, nor be dismayed, for the LORD your God is with you wherever you go."[8] Yahweh was with Moses and He is with you, Joshua. And so are we.' Eleazar pointed to the entrance of the tent. 'So, meet with your captains and instruct them in the ways of the Lord.'

'How? What am I going to tell them?'

Eleazar looked at Caleb, who stood up, reached out, and pulled me to my feet. Putting his hands on my shoulders, Eleazar drew himself up to stand tall and straight.

'We tell them together. All three of us. Now.'

---

8. Joshua 1:9.

10

The Man

It went better than I thought it would. Yes, there were blank stares from most of the captains when I told them Yahweh's glorious battle plan for taking the city of Jericho. However, thanks to the united front demonstrated by Caleb, Eleazar and I, they accepted the word of the Lord, and we finished the meeting in unity, if not altogether in high spirits.

'You see?' Eleazar said to me when the men had all left, leaving only he and Caleb in my tent. 'I told you it would go well, *nu*?' He grinned and slapped me on the back.

'Well . . .' I said with a grimace. 'I was unsure at the beginning, especially when I told them that we had to march in silence.'

'I can understand why that would discourage them.' Caleb took a fig from the dish on the table, popped it in his mouth, and looked at us with a cheeky grin. 'Some of us do not find it easy to stay silent. We are made for noise, not for quiet!' Caleb threw a grape at me. I caught it and popped it in my mouth, laughing. It felt good to laugh. There had been too much solemnity in recent times.

Caleb turned to me. 'Come! Shall we go through this battle plan that Yahweh has given you and discuss the details?'

I heaved a big sigh and thought for a while. 'We will have need of that, yes. But I think right now, I would prefer to go for a walk. I need time to think.' I turned to them and smiled. 'Just because I have accepted the plan that Yahweh has given us does not mean I *like* it!' I shrugged. 'I need some time to think it through. I still cannot see how it will work.'

Eleazar started to speak, but I cut him off, lifting my hands in surrender. 'I know, Eleazar! I know. It is not given to me to understand the ways of Yahweh. But I would at least like to try to come to peace with the plan before we march into battle holding only our trumpets, *nu?*'

Eleazar and Caleb said their goodbyes. I put my outer robe on and walked out of the tent. 'Attai,' I said, 'I am going to walk for a while, but I will be back after midday.'

'Yes, Commander. Shall I come with you?'

'Not this time, but thank you.' Remembering how I had treated him earlier that morning, and knowing he must have heard our conversations from his position outside my tent, I felt a twinge of regret. 'Attai,' I called, swinging around to look at him. 'You serve me well. Thank you.'

He smiled and inclined his head, obviously relieved that my calm demeaner had returned. I pulled my head covering down over my eyes and disappeared round the side of the tent, staying away from the main pathways that wound their way through the camp. I walked for quite some time, struggling to reconcile what Yahweh had told me with what I knew from my experience as a warrior. The rays of the sun beat down on me, now that Yahweh's canopy had lifted, so I took my outer robe off and tied it around my waist, using it to wipe the sweat off my face and neck.

Finding myself by a hill, I strode up to the top and looked out over the plains, towards the city of Jericho. Hands on hips, I stood for a while, letting the wind blow the sweat from my brow, and the cobwebs from my mind. I frowned, trying to imagine what it would look like – thousands upon thousands of warriors walking around the outskirts of that city without saying a word or drawing their swords.

I wondered what Rahab would think of such absurdity. I pictured a red cord hanging from a window near those huge city gates.

I growled in frustration. Rahab! Always Rahab! Why? Why did this infernal woman continue to dominate my thoughts?

All of a sudden, the hairs on my arms stood up, and my legs started to shake. I turned around slowly, putting my hand up to shield my eyes from the glare of the sun, which was nearly at its peak. Although I couldn't see clearly, I could just make out the vague outline of a Man standing a short distance away, watching me. The Man was tall in stature, well built, and He held a long sword that glinted in the sunlight. Instinctively, my hands went to pull my sword out of its scabbard but, to my dismay, I realised I had been so consumed with thoughts of the ludicrous plan to take Jericho that I had not buckled my sword belt on before coming out.

I was utterly defenceless.

My heart rate increased as I weighed my options. Should I run? No, the Man was so tall, he would in all likelihood outrun me in no time at all. Should I look for rocks to throw? Not enough time. The Man was only a few feet away. By the time I was able to pick some up, He would be upon me. I would certainly not be able to wrestle Him to the ground, that much was certain.

My military training told me to stand my ground and not run, so I stood, my heart in my throat, ready to move at any moment. I stared at Him from behind the cover of my hand, but couldn't see His facial features because of the glare of the sun, so I couldn't read His expression.

The weight of silence continued. 'Who are you?' I thought. 'Why don't you move, or say something?'

Still the Man stood.

He didn't attack and He didn't retreat. He just stood there, watching me.

'Is he a spy from Jericho?' I wondered. 'Or an assassin hired to kill me?'

Still the Man stood.

Finally, I could bear it no longer.

'Are You for us or for our adversaries?' I shouted.

The Man didn't respond immediately but, when He did, my knees went weak and I found myself bowed low on the ground without knowing how I had got there.

'No,' the Man said. 'As Commander of the army of the LORD I have now come.'

The power in the Man's voice was unmistakable. His tone was rich and resonant, His air of authority silencing any opposition. I worshipped, face down in the dirt, not daring to lift my eyes or gaze upon Him. Instead, with a voice trembling in fear, I asked, 'What does my Lord say to His servant?'[9]

The voice spoke again.

'Take your sandals off, for this is holy ground.'[10]

---

9. Conversation from Joshua 5:13-14.
10. Verse 15, paraphrased.

I reached down with trembling hands and untied my sandals, hurling them as far away from my prostrate form as possible. I stayed in that place, bowed down in worship, for an inestimable amount of time. My heart pounded within me in reverential fear, yet my spirit sang out the purest of songs from the depths of my being. As I lay on the ground, worshipping, a voice rang out in my consciousness.

'Be strong and of good courage; do not be afraid, nor be dismayed, for the LORD your God is with you wherever you go.'[11]

A mighty strength flooded my being; deep conviction and resolve rose up from my spirit as I received the fulfilment of what the Man had spoken over me: *courage*!

---

11. Joshua 1:9.

11

Conquest

'How many battles have you fought thus far?' I asked Attai as we strode through the camp.

Beads of sweat dotted his brow. 'One, Commander.'

My head jerked around to look at him. 'One?'

'Yes, Commander.' His eyes focused on the path ahead. 'I was not of an age to go to war when we fought against the Amalekites, but I fought in the Battle of Hormah against King Arad and his men.'

'Yes. I remember it well. So, this will be your second battle?'

'Yes, Commander.' He didn't look at me. We continued walking in silence. The sun was still rising and the dew damp upon the ground, as Attai and I approached the assembly point.

'Attai, I would have you stay by my side at all times today.'

Attai stopped and turned to face me. 'Commander, I am not afraid to fight.'

I stopped to look at him. 'Of that, I have no doubt. I remember well your zeal during the battle at Hormah, but I may have need of you to relay a message. You would serve me best by staying at my side.'

The slightest hint of suspicion flitted across his narrowed eyes but, after a short pause, he replied, 'Of course.'

Attai was not required to go to war.

A manservant's responsibilities lay in the ordering of his master's day and his service to him, not in the taking up of arms, but Attai had insisted on coming. He walked by my side, a scabbard hanging from his leather belt, the handle of his sword poking out of it in a bizarrely comical manner. His helmet was tucked under his arm but that, too, looked odd. Too big for his head, as if he were a child playing at war. Attai was small of frame, slender, and at least a foot shorter than me. I knew he had undergone army training, as all our men had during our years in the wilderness, but I didn't realise he had only fought one battle.

One battle, and now he must face the onslaught of the armies of Jericho.

Caleb and Eleazar welcomed me when we arrived. 'Eleazar,' I said, clasping him to me, 'you are still determined to march with us, my friend?'

'Where the Ark of the Covenant goes, I must go,' Eleazar replied.

'We have the best of our warriors guarding the ark. Do not fear.'

'I am not fearful. Yahweh is with us, and you are leading us. What is there to fear?' he said. His smile put me at ease; it overflowed with confidence and trust. 'I have been pondering the words spoken by the diviner, Balaam.'

'Balaam?' All I remembered of that strange man was his inability to curse Yahweh's people, despite being promised great riches by the Moabite king who hired him. Why was Eleazar thinking about the words of a man like Balaam at a time like this?

'Which words do you speak of?' I asked.

'The shout of the King is among them . . .'[12] Eleazar said, his eyes twinkling with excitement.

'Mmm.' I struggled to see the relevance of his words. My focus was on the march and, in truth, I was eager to discover whether or not we would find a scarlet cord hanging from the harlot's window. If there was no scarlet cord, we would be released from our pledge, and I would be absolved of the burden of dealing with the troublesome prostitute.

'"The shout of the King is among them",' Eleazar repeated, obviously hoping I would understand his meaning. I stared blankly at him. '*The shout of the King,* Joshua. Yahweh's instructions to you were that, on our seventh day of marching, after we had circled the city seven times, we were to lift our voices and *shout* – that is when the walls would fall, yes?'

'Yes.'

'Perhaps the Lord did speak through Balaam after all. Perhaps it is our voices raised in a victory cry to our King that will bring down the walls of Jericho. Think on that,' he said, peering at me before taking his place among the priests.

---

12. Numbers 23:21.

I nodded and turned to my faithful general. Like me, Caleb was dressed in full battle armour, sword and shield at the ready, even though Yahweh had forbidden us to use them. I felt naked without them. Caleb interlocked his right arm with mine in a warrior's greeting. I put my other palm on my chest, 'Strength and courage!'

'Strength and courage!' Caleb responded.

I smiled at him. 'It is good to have you at my side.'

'It is good to be at your side. Come, we have hungered for this day long enough. Jericho awaits us!' he said with a wicked grin. I grinned back and turned to face Jericho when the hairs on the back of my neck stood up. My legs felt a familiar trembling. I swung round.

He was there.

The Man.

He stood a short distance away, beams of light radiating from his body, even though the sun had not long risen. He drew His sword and thrust it heavenward.

Turning to face the multitudes of warriors that stood before me, as well as the priests who marched with us, I brandished my sword, roaring the words I had heard time and time again out of the mouth of my master.

'Rise up, O LORD!

Let Your enemies be scattered,

And let those who hate You flee before You.'[13]

---

13. Numbers 10:35.

12

Just March

It was done!

The first day of our march around Jericho was over! It happened just as Yahweh had said it would. The men of Jericho didn't attack us as we marched, and we suffered no casualties or losses of any kind. The sense of relief among the troops was palpable. Attai had stayed by my side, as requested, without having unsheathed his sword. I released the men to return home, with instructions to be ready early the next morning.

The family waited for the warriors among us to return to them, anxious to hear what happened. It was nearing midday and the sun was high in the sky, so we sat under the shade of our tent awnings drinking water and munching on fruit as we talked.

'Did the men of Jericho attack you?' asked Joel's grandson, eyes wide with anticipation.

'No, Reuben,' I replied. 'They were hiding inside their city, too scared to come out and face us!'

'So what did you do?' he asked.

'We marched,' I told him.

'You marched?' he said, screwing up his face. 'You didn't fight?'

'No, we marched, because that is what Yahweh told us to do, and we must obey Yahweh, yes?'

He nodded, but didn't look very impressed.

'When will you fight them, *Abba*?' little Reuben asked his father, hoping for a more exciting answer than he got from me. As an elder of our people and a master craftsman, Joel no longer served in the tribe of Benjamin's army, but his eldest son, Joash, had served for many years.

'Well, we will march around the city each day for six days – can you show me six fingers?' Joash asked Reuben, who dutifully counted out six fingers. 'Good boy. We will march in silence and not make any noise, and then...'

'No noise?' Reuben looked at his father, appalled at the thought of having to be silent for so long. 'For *six days?*' His little face scrunched up in horror.

'That's right – we will not speak a word while we march,' Joash said, putting a finger on Reuben's lips to emphasise the point. 'Then, on the seventh day, we will march around the city seven times. The priests will blow their rams' horns, we will all shout as loudly as we can, and the walls of the city will fall!'

'How, *Abba?*' Reuben moved closer to his father, leaning right into his face. 'How will the walls fall down?'

'We don't know yet,' Joash chuckled, pulling his son into a hug which turned into a wrestling match, 'but Yahweh has declared it to be so, and we believe His words. Your *ima* can bring you to the edge of the camp on the seventh day so you can shout with us, and watch the walls fall down. You would like that, *nu?*'

Joash's wife, Jana, gave him a disapproving look and shook her head. 'No, Joash. I don't want Reuben anywhere near the battle.'

'Why not? He is a brave boy, and Yahweh is with him, yes?'

'Yes, *Abba!*' Reuben said, jumping up. He grabbed a stick and proceeded to start a mock swordfight with two of his cousins, who rushed off to find their own 'swords'.

'What did the men of Jericho do when they saw you?' Joel asked me. 'Did they retaliate?'

'No,' I replied. 'They just watched from the ramparts – hundreds of them, fully armed. In truth, I think they were confounded by our silence.'

'Mmm. I too would be confused – it is a very unusual battle strategy,' he said, chuckling.

'They didn't shoot arrows or spears from the walls?' Alya asked.

'No. We marched just out of range of their weapons,' Yoram answered as I took a big bite of a juicy orange.

The fact that Jericho had locked its city gates when we crossed the Jordan River was a great advantage to us. The fields surrounding Jericho were full of barley, ripe for harvest, and their citrus trees were heavy laden with fruit. No one had entered or exited the city since we set up camp at Gilgal, which gave us plenty of opportunity to harvest their produce without fear of retaliation. Each day, we sent out squadrons of soldiers to reap the fruit of the land, and they returned with carts laden with oranges, lemons, barley, almonds, apricots and, of course, pomegranates. Most of their vines were not yet ready for harvesting, but we found a few that had an early crop of grapes, which we sampled with abandon. I found a bizarre sense of pleasure in knowing that we were reaping the fruits of our enemy's hard labour, while all they could do was look on.

Our second day of marching unfolded the same way as the first but, by the third day, the Jerichoites had grown familiar with our routine, and began mocking us while we marched.

'Come closer, Israelites!'

'Come and fight us, you mangy dogs, or are you too scared to face us?'

'Why do you not speak? Have your tongues been cut out?'

'Do you not know how to use those weapons? Come, let us show you!'

'Has your God deserted you?'

'Has He lost His power?'

'Is He fearful of these great walls?'

I impressed upon our warriors the importance of staying silent and not reacting to the heathens' taunts. For many of them, it was challenging, but none more so than Caleb who, by the end of the fourth day, was bursting for a fight. His face was red with rage as he stomped up to me at the conclusion of our march.

'I cannot do this, Joshua. I cannot stay silent and listen to them mock us and revile the name of our God!'

'You must. There is no other way. We must obey Yahweh. Only two more days, and then you can unleash your anger on them.'

'Two more days? Aaaaaagh!' he bellowed through gritted teeth. 'I cannot endure it.'

'You can, my friend, and you will,' I said, slapping him on the back with a grin. 'It will be worth it when their walls fall, and we watch their mocking smiles melt in terror at the sight of us, *nu*?'

Caleb shook his head. 'Two more days. Two more days. It is beyond endurance,' he mumbled as he tramped off to his longsuffering wife.

Not reacting to the Jerichoites was the least of my worries. As the days went on, my thoughts focused more and more on what would happen when we lifted up 'the shout of the King' on the seventh day. A few weeks after Moses had died, Yahweh took me into a vision where I saw the walls of Jericho fall. It was to this vision that I returned. I replayed it over and over again in my mind but, try as I might, all I could see were the walls crashing to the ground, and never what had caused them to fall.

My frustration grew, coupled with a deepening sense of foreboding each time I thought about my impending meeting with the harlot to whom we might soon have to give sanctuary.

12

Taking Jericho

This must be his first battle.

Even in the murky haze of pre-dawn, I could see the lines of anxiety that creased his smooth, beardless face. He re-tied his belt, fiddling with his sword and leather scabbard with shaky hands. From under his furrowed, wispy eyebrows, head still lowered, he threw a brief glance at the warriors standing around.

There were many like him in our company. Young men still warm from their mother's embrace, eager to taste of the perils of battle, terrified of what they might face.

He drew his sword, clenching and unclenching his fist around the hilt. Running his hand over its blade, he stared at it with grim fascination. Before this day, he had used this weapon only to spar and train. Today, he must plunge it deep into the body of another man and end his life.

He sheathed the blade and wiped his sweaty hands on his robe.

I looked away.

It was time.

Best not to keep them waiting.

'Caleb,' I called out. 'Call the men to fall in.'

We set off just as we had done on the previous six days, marching in silence, our faces grim but fixed on the task ahead. I grunted to myself when I saw the thick scarlet cord hanging from the prostitute's window near the city gate.

'So,' I muttered. 'The harlot is to be saved. So be it.'

There were fewer warriors on the walls of Jericho today; it seems they had become bored of watching us march around their city day after day. The soldiers and curious citizens who were on the walls still shouted abuse at us as we marched but, today, instead of riling our warriors, it seemed to spur them on.

The first circuit of the city was completed with surprising ease. Second, third, and fourth circuits followed in steady succession. Our strength did not wane. As we approached the end of our seventh orbit of that towering monument to idolatry, a surge of anticipation rushed through my body.

I lifted my right arm, hand in a tight fist.

The signal to halt rippled through the ranks; each man readied himself. I glanced across at Eleazar, who stood by the Ark of the Covenant. He locked eyes with me and gave an indiscernible nod.

Raising my arm high, I took a deep breath and bellowed, 'The Lord has given us this city. *Now shout!*' The piercing call of rams' horns blasted across the plains of Jericho, mixed with the roars of thousands of hardened warriors. Heads back, mouths wide open, eyes blazing and neck veins protruding, they gave themselves over to raising a battle cry for their God.

A blinding flash tore through the air.

Shockwaves rippled down my back as thousands of shining men appeared, armed and dressed for battle. Rays of sun reflected off their breastplates as they took up their positions by the wall, surrounding the city in a glistening halo of light. Each shining man lifted his foot and brought it down with a thud, then another, and another.

Shafts of light pierced the ground as they stamped.

Thousands of glowing feet rose and fell, stomping in a wild, warlike dance. Leaping, bending, whirling, spinning, they shouted and whooped, joining their voices with ours in a jubilant war cry.

We heard it before we felt it.

It started out as a low grumbling which crescendoed into a roar of crashing and rumbling. The ground shook, convulsing in response to the shining men's pounding call. Small segments of wall fell away, then larger cracks appeared. The walls of Jericho writhed, crumbled and hurtled to the ground with a deafening thumping and thudding.

A wall of dirty brown and grey clouds billowed outwards from the city. We pulled our headscarves up to protect our faces from the limestone dust that reached out to choke us with pale, chalky fingers.

A few more stubborn echoes rumbled backwards and forwards over the plains of Jericho, then it was over. For a few seconds, there was absolute silence.

Sinister.

Eerie.

The smell of dust and limestone lingered in the air.

Hearing the pattering of falling pebbles, I squinted through a gap in my scarf. I could see nothing but a ghostly, quivering curtain of dust. I blinked, wiped away the tears that defended my eyes from the chalky powder, and peered through the crack again. The dust-ridden clouds started to diminish; I could see faint outlines through the haze.

The throngs of shining men were gone.

But so were the walls of Jericho.

Those once proud walls now lay in ruinous mounds of stone, rocks and wood. All that remained was one small section of wall that stood upright, undeterred by the desolation that surrounded it. It was marked by a stubborn scarlet cord that fluttered from a stone window in the midst of the dust and debris, where a small group of shining men stood guard.

I turned to Beerah and Salmah, standing nearby.

'Whatever happens, make sure that you get her and her family out before it's too late.'

I stepped forward, unsheathed my sword, and roared, 'Attaaaaaaaack!'

Beerah and Salmah, accompanied by a small squadron of soldiers, leaped into action, sprinting towards the section of wall that was still standing. Our warriors drew their swords and swarmed towards the mangled remains of what had once been a lofty, impregnable structure.

I tightened my headscarf, coughing in protest at the swirling plumes of dust kicked up by the stampede. I watched until the last of our warriors disappeared into the dusty cauldron of blood and rocks.

Ear-splitting shrieks soon overshadowed their battle cries.

Shrieks of terrified men.

The screams of their women.

The clash of blade meeting blade.

The thump of weapon on shield.

Then, through narrowed eyes, I saw a shrouded figure emerge, stumbling out of the ruins through the gloom of the smoggy haze.

14

A Prostitute's Abode

Her hooded cloak prevented me from seeing her face, or indeed much of her form at all. I watched from a distance through a slit in my head covering, as Beerah and Salmah heralded Rahab and her family out of the ruins. Their squadron surrounded the little group, then they set off for Gilgal.

I waited until they had moved away, then pulled my headscarf down and strode towards the murky ruins, Attai by my side. The hellish screams of humankind meeting their end ricocheted among the ruinous remains. Our warriors knew their mandate: none could be spared.

'None but that foul woman and her family,' I thought.

I did not relish the taking of life. I never had. It may have seemed incongruous to some for a veteran warrior to recoil from slaying, but it was true, nevertheless. I did what I had to in obedience to Yahweh, as an example to my men, and to protect my family and my people, nothing more. I took no pleasure in it; it was the way of war. The death the Jerichoites would receive by our hands would be far more merciful than that of the nations surrounding us, who raped captured women and tortured their men until they begged for death.

We paused at the entrance to the city. Its massive wooden gates now lay in splintered pieces on the ground, covered by boulders and dust. The corpses of two Canaanite soldiers were strewn across them, trickles of blood seeping out of the gashes in their still-warm bodies.

I looked across at the stubborn section of wall that stood staring at me in defiance. Curiosity demanded that I go into Rahab's home to see what her life had been like, but an irksome sense of honour held me back. It felt like a betrayal and yet I had no idea why. She was a harlot – surely she would have encountered far worse forms of betrayal than someone inspecting her abandoned home.

Attai watched me in silence for a while before speaking out. 'Many would consider it prudent to enter her home, Commander. There is no telling what we might find. What we discover could be helpful in our dealings with the pagans.'

'Mmm.' I thought on it for a few moments, then started walking towards Rahab's home. I paused outside the door, looking down the streets either side at the mounds of rubble that, less than an hour ago, had fronted doors just like this one. It looked incongruous – one lonely door, one defiant house standing firm against a backdrop of chaos and destruction.

The door was closed, its wood stained with age, but, when I lifted the latch and pushed, it opened with ease. The comforting, woody aroma of herbs filled my nostrils as soon as I stepped inside. Cardamom, thyme, cumin . . . the fragrance was homely, welcoming.

Odd.

To the left of the entrance was a door to a room separated from the rest of the home. It was closed. To the right, a dividing wall with an entranceway covered by a thick, colourful drape which led to an airy living space. The balmy aroma of herbs was coming from the far corner of the room, where bunches of plants in varying stages of drying hung from timber beams. Beneath them, neatly stacked, were various cooking pots and utensils, a large jug and a washing bowl. A wide woven mat covered the floor, providing an unexpected burst of colour.

'She must be a weaver of flax,' Attai said, bending down to run his hands over the patterned surface of the mat.

'Yes. This is skilful weaving. Helah would be pleased with this workmanship,' I replied, picturing the beautiful designs which my sister-in-law wove into her creations.

Clay lamps had been hung from the beams. They had been filled with oil, and the wicks were new – the twine had not yet been lit.

A rough-hewn table stood against the wall on the other side of the room. On it was a clay jug painted with mottled, swirling designs of pink, green and brown. It was filled with freshly cut flowers which I believed to be the blue, white and pink blossoms of the flax plant.

Why?

Why would you display fresh flowers in a home that you were about to leave forever? Why go to the trouble of filling the lamps with oil, and trimming new wicks, in a home that would never again be occupied, whose lamps would never be lit?

I don't know what I had expected, but it wasn't this. I glanced around the room, hands on my hips. This home bore the imprint of a woman who took pride in her surroundings. This was the home of a woman who cared, who loved, who was mindful of subtle touches like flowers and colourful woven mats. The floors and surfaces, even the lime-washed walls, had all recently been cleaned.

Everything was in its place.

It was neat and clean. Simple, but homely.

This was not the home of a prostitute.

Surely?

I could see no idols, nor were there any of the alcoves that were so common in pagan homes, to suggest that an idol had been housed there. Walking over to the shelves hollowed out into the wall on the other side of the room, near the cooking implements, jars of spices stood in neat rows next to two piles of dishes and platters. I took one of the jars, pulled the stopper out, and sniffed. The sweet smell of cinnamon filled my nostrils. I frowned. Cinnamon was an expensive spice, much sought after. Why had she left this behind?

'Cinnamon,' Attai said with an air of authority. 'My wife uses it in her cooking, but sparingly. It is a costly spice,' he said, frowning at the same unanswered question which hung in the air.

Why?

The more I discovered about her, the more of a mystery this woman was becoming to me. I put the stopper back and replaced the jar, turning it until it was perfectly aligned with the other jars. 'As if that matters,' I thought to myself, irritated at my need to keep everything as I had found it.

Both sets of windows in the living space had shutters which had been flung open. I leaned out of the larger of the two, noting the crimson cord tied around the outside of the timber frame. I pulled the cord in, fingering the smooth, firm plaited strands of flax. This cord had saved the prostitute's life. It was a sign of her obedience, her desire to leave behind her past and turn towards a new life. Or was it just a devious ploy by a cunning woman who wanted to avoid death? I untied it and handed it to Attai.

'Have this given to the harlot. She may yet have need of it.' Curiosity filled Attai's face, but he knew better than to question me. He twisted the cord around the length of his hand to elbow, then secured it over his shoulder.

Two doorways led out of the open living space. One had stone steps extending upwards, which I assumed led to the roof. The other was covered with a thick drape made of different coloured stripes of material sewn together. I hesitated, steeled myself for what I might find in that room, then pushed it aside.

There was nothing there but some rather unremarkable bed pallets, now empty of their bedrolls. More lamps hung from the beams, all containing fresh oil and new wicks. *Why?* I huffed to myself, frustrated at my inability to discern the answer. Some woven baskets stood on the floor, along with a simple wooden box. Attai opened the box. It was empty. Whatever had been there had been removed. Why would the harlot have deemed the contents of this box worthy of taking, when she left valuable spices like cinnamon behind?

This woman was fast becoming an enigma.

Attai and I walked out of the room and climbed the steps which led up to the roof. We found it just like the rest of the harlot's home – swept tidy and devoid of debris, although it was now covered with a thick layer of lime dust. The pallet of flax stalks which Beerah and Salmah had hidden under was still there, with an abundance of flax drying out, ready for peeling and soaking . . . to what end?

A modest firepit occupied one side of the roof, away from the flax stalks and under the covering of some timber roofing. It was swept clean; fresh dung and wood had been laid, ready for use. I grimaced. The only fire this pit would see would be the one my warriors would light, when we laid waste to the desecrated remains of this unholy city.

Walking to the edge of the roof, I crossed my arms and stared into the distance at the retreating forms of a squadron of soldiers surrounding a small family group.

'This . . . uh . . . home,' Attai said, coming to stand next to me, '. . . is not what I expected to find.'

'No. I am of the same mind,' I said, glancing down at him. 'There is one more room to search,' I added, remembering the closed room near the entrance to Rahab's home. Without further ado, we made our way back down the stone stairway, through the living space, towards the closed door. I grasped the handle and pushed. My heart was pounding.

The door opened to air that was stale, overpowered by a sickly-sweet odour.

Incense.

The room was a fair size, dominated by one piece of furniture: a sizeable bed pallet. Unlike the pallets in the other room which had been stripped of their bedrolls, this one was still made, albeit carelessly. A sheepskin rug covered the wooden pallet, falling to the floor on one side. On it were various linen covers in shades of crimson and purple. I shuddered. This must be where she plied her trade. This was where a never-ending stream of men came to spend their ill-gotten gains on carnal pleasures and debauchery.

A small table held an ornate bowl of incense. The only other piece of furniture in the room was a wooden chest.

'Shall I . . . ?' Attai asked, pointing to it. I nodded and moved closer to see what was inside. The chest was filled with exotic robes, veils, belts and jewellery. A few small vials of perfume lay on top. It reeked of decadence and the excesses of the flesh.

'Have these burned . . .' I muttered to Attai, slamming the lid shut.

There were only two small oil lamps hanging from the rafters in this room. Both were almost empty of oil and their wicks were burned out and stale. The window was shuttered. I didn't open it. I had no desire to shed light on the sordid circumstances of this chamber. This room seemed completely disconnected from the rest of the house; dark, dusty and neglected. We walked out and I closed the door quietly behind me.

Walking back into the living area, I closed the shutter in the living area, taking care to lock the bolt into place, although I had no idea why. Taking one last look at the jug of fresh flowers and pristine surroundings, I sighed and turned to leave.

An immense sense of sadness filled me as I stood outside Rahab's house. I closed her front door and placed my hand upon it, fighting the urge to pray a blessing over this conflicted home.

I had come here to find answers to the questions that had troubled my mind for weeks, but all my visit to Rahab's home had done was fill my mind with even more unanswered questions.

13

The Harlot

I peered through a slit in the thick curtained inner wall of my tent at the woman who had bewitched two of my most trusted spies.

'You will not bewitch me, woman,' I murmured. 'I will not fall prey to your charms so easily.' Eleazar, Joel and Alya paused their conversation and turned to look at Rahab as Caleb ushered her in.

She was very beautiful, there could be no denying that. Unveiled, but then I would have expected nothing less from a pagan. Even through the layers of paint and adornments, I could see that her natural features were striking. Her cheekbones were high, skilfully enhanced with powders to give them a rosy hue, like ripe pears on either side of her pert nose. Her lips were full and luscious, painted a deep shade of red, pouting with displeasure as she looked around my tent.

Her form was full bodied and shapely; her silken robe did little to mask her physical assets. It was a burned orange shade with scarlet threads running through it, cut low in both front and back. It offset her mane of glossy, dark hair to perfection.

Rahab's body dripped with jewellery which clinked and jingled as she walked. Bracelets of silver and bronze adorned both wrists and ankles, and her slim arms were encircled with banded armlets. Ornate rings decorated her fingers, and her headdress was held in place with a linen band of gold and cream, woven together with a thin chain from which dangled a selection of coins.

Her most noticeable jewels, however, were the necklaces that draped her body, emphasising the length of her proud neck. The longest of them led the eyes on a downward journey to where an amber pendant nestled between the plump rise of her breasts.

Warmth flooded my body. My heartbeat increased. I looked away. 'Curse you, woman,' I muttered. After a few moments I turned back to the slit and watched as Caleb left her in the centre of the room and went to greet the others. Rahab waited, watching them, her eyes flickering from one to the other. Lighting upon Joel, she turned towards him and bowed her head.

'My Lord, I am . . .'

'Oh! No!' Joel stretched out his hands to stop her. 'No, please, I am not Joshua.' Alya, standing at his side, lowered her head, stifling a smile.

Rahab blushed and shifted her gaze to Eleazer, who stepped forward before she had time to speak. 'I am not Joshua either,' he said firmly, 'but he will join us presently.'

Conversation was halted; an awkward silence filled the room. Even Attai, who stood at his usual post by the tent flap, studied the ground with great concentration. Much though I found it amusing watching their discomfort, I knew I could delay no longer. It was time to face this troublesome woman. Straightening my head covering and tugging my belt, I took a deep breath and pushed aside the heavy curtains. Ignoring Rahab, I greeted the others, walked over to the ornate seat at the front of the room (which I would normally avoid with great fervour), and sat down. Placing my arms on the armrests, I gestured to the benches on one side of my tent.

'Sit, please,' I said, smiling at Caleb, Eleazar, Joel and Alya.

Rahab stood before me, hands by her side. Her eyes looked me up and down. I met her imperious stare.

Silence.

'Say something,' my thoughts chided me, cursing the paralytic awkwardness that always seemed to overcome me when it came to dealing with women outside of my family. I cleared my throat.

'You are Rahab?'

'I am.'

She was not as young as I had expected. I estimated she must have seen close on thirty winters, and wondered how long she had been plying her trade of harlotry. She shook her head to shift some strands of hair that dangled in front of her eyes. The coins on her headband jingled, and her hair swirled around her neck like a cloud of dark silk. I wondered what the weight of her thick tresses would feel like in my hands.

The heady scent of her perfume filled the tent.

It was intoxicating.

I forced myself to look away from her and glanced across at Eleazar, Caleb and Joel – they all seemed as fascinated as I was. Turning back to Rahab, I was met with a look of smug disdain.

'My men have given an account of their time with you, but there are some questions I would ask of you,' I said with a gruff voice.

She dipped her head in acquiescence but said nothing.

'Did you know that my men were Israelites?'

'I did,' she replied. 'I watched them from my window as they approached the city gates. I am well acquainted with the ways of men,' she said, pausing to see the effect her words would have on me. She ran her hand down the side of her gown, smoothing it against her thigh. She was trying to distract me.

It worked.

My hands itched to stroke the silken material that clung to the contours of her body, to feel the softness of the linen, and the firmness of what lay beneath. I stared back at her, my face like flint. A flicker of a smile crossed her face, then she continued.

'Their manner and clothing were unusual. I knew they were not of our people, and suspected they might be Israelites, but it was only when I spoke to them at the city gates that I knew without a doubt who they were.'

'Did you approach them?'

'I did.'

'Why?'

She paused, studying my face. 'To offer them lodging for the night.'

'Is that the only reason?'

Silence. Doubt flickered in her eyes. I thought I saw a flash of fear, but it disappeared as soon as it had arisen, replaced by a cold aloofness. 'No.' She waited for me to respond.

I didn't.

She continued. 'I wanted to speak with them.'

'Why?'

She squared her shoulders and lifted her head before responding. 'I wanted to find out more about your God and your people, and your plans for Jericho.'

'To what end?' I asked, wondering if perhaps she was in the employ of the king, tasked with finding out information from the men who frequented her lodgings.

She glanced over at her audience to the side, trying to get the measure of them.

'I'd heard stories,' she said, looking at us one by one. 'We *all* heard the stories about your God. What He did. Bringing you out of Egypt. Parting the Red Sea. The cloud and fire. Stories from Egypt about plagues and death. But they were stories from another time, another place, which need not concern us – until you crossed over the Jordan River.' She stared at me with a sardonic smile. 'Even the strongest of our warriors who came to me to find comfort could not ease their fears. Their hearts melted in terror of you and your God.' She paused and looked down, murmuring, 'But it was not so in my heart.'

'No?' I said, leaning forward, despite my efforts to appear calm and aloof.

'No. The stories which brought such dread to my people did not do the same to me.' A wistful expression flickered over her face. She folded her arms around her torso and looked away. 'The more I heard, the more I wanted to know. Your God, He worked miracles. He was not a god of myth and mere tales, an impotent idol sculpted by the hands of greedy men. He worked wonders. He was . . . alive! I wanted to know how . . . who He . . . I wanted to know more.'

She looked up at me and the softness disappeared. She smirked, almost daring me to disbelieve her.

I didn't.

Whether she meant to or not, Rahab had just given me a brief glimpse into her heart. I knew her quest to know about Yahweh was true. What I didn't know, however, was her motive.

I cleared my throat. 'And did you?'

'Did I . . . ?'

'Find out more about our God and our ways.'

'I did, later on,' she said with a smug smile, 'although it came at a cost. I hadn't realised that we had been seen at the city gates.'

'Mmm. The king's guard. Beerah and Salmah told me of your courage and . . . uh . . . shrewdness.' I grimaced inwardly. Why did I say shrewdness? Why not wisdom, as they had said to me? I knew why: because I could not, or would not, attribute the virtue of wisdom to a painted harlot.

She tilted her head, holding my gaze. Her eyes were green, with flecks of golden brown. They held sway over me, drawing me into their depths. No! I would not let myself be captivated by this prostitute. I would not fall under her spell, as so many before me surely had.

'Rahab,' I said, standing up to break the enchantment. 'Why did you save my men? Why not let the king's guard take them, and be done with it?'

A hardness came over her. Her voice was sharp and cutting as she replied, 'I wanted to escape Jericho. I needed to leave behind the . . .' I thought I heard a trembling in her voice, but the expression of her face was emotionless and hard to read. 'I had to leave. This was my opportunity and I seized it.'

'They said you risked much to save them – that your life could have been forfeit if they had been discovered.'

She laughed in derision. 'Never! I know the captain of the guard well. I have had many . . . dealings with him.' She peered at me to see if I understood her meaning. I did. 'He is a spineless fool who couldn't see past the tip of his own nose. I know how to deal with men like him.' Her eyes narrowed. 'They are weak creatures, as dough to be moulded in my hands.'

Although I knew she meant it as a direct challenge, I found myself becoming aroused by her words. Her glossy hair spilled over her shoulders in dark, curling waves, coming to rest at the peak of her cleavage. She smirked at me, clearly waiting for some kind of rebuff, probably expecting me to retaliate in defence of my sex. I said nothing. I would not be drawn into a contest of wills with this pagan whore.

Silence fell.

The tension in the room grew and, out of the corner of my eye I saw Caleb and Eleazar look at each other. Joel and Alya did likewise. I ignored them, continuing to scrutinise the harlot. She, in turn, met my challenge with a cold stare. I wondered what could have happened to Rahab to cause her to walk the path of whoredom, and cause such a hardness to come upon her. An unexpected and unwelcome strain of compassion touched my heart.

'Whatever your reasons,' I said, 'I thank you for saving the lives of my spies. They are good men and I would not be without them.' My thanks seemed to disarm Rahab. She opened her mouth to reply, but must have thought better of it because she closed it and instead, inclined her head to me.

'I am your servant, my lord. Whatever you would have me do, I am yours to command.' I studied her, feeling sure that she spoke with more than a hint of sarcasm and a definite air of scorn. I walked towards her and waited until she looked up at me. I stood nearly a foot taller than her.

'Rahab, you are not a servant, to me or to any of my people. We did not bring you and your family out of Jericho in order to enslave you. We delivered you because you saved the lives of my men, and so we will do likewise. You and your family are free to live with us here in peace and safety.'

She bit her bottom lip to try to stop it from quivering. The veneer of disdainful arrogance cracked; I saw in her eyes both pain and fear. I could feel myself being drawn to her.

No!

I stepped back, breaking the invisible cord that sought to bind us.

'However, there is one thing I must ask of you,' I said. She froze. Her eyes narrowed in weathered distrust, as if she knew well the question I was about to ask, and had heard it a thousand times before.

'I must ask your permission to have my men search your family's belongings.'

The look of distrust evaporated, replaced with bemused curiosity. 'My permission? You seek my permission to . . . ?' Her eyes flicked from side to side, searching mine, then she gave a slight bow and replied, 'We are your servants, my lord. Do to us as it seems good to you.'

'As the Lord lives, no punishment shall come upon you or your family.' I locked eyes with her. 'We do not seek your harm, but the commandments of our God are clear. No pagan idols or accursed items can be permitted in the camp, which is why we must search your belongings.'

'I understand, my lord Joshua.' Rahab's eyes were starting to glaze over; I realised how exhausted she must be. The fight had gone out of her; it was time to bring our meeting to a close.

'We have set up tents for you on the outskirts of the camp, near the watchman's tower. Food and water have been placed there for you. Our watchmen stand guard in the day and throughout the night watches, so no harm will come to you. Return to your family and we will talk more tomorrow when you are rested.' Motioning to Caleb, I said, 'Caleb will escort you to your tent. Your family await you there.'

'Thank you,' Rahab whispered. I ushered her towards the tent flap, listening to the enticing jingle of her anklets as she walked. Alya went to Rahab and, while she spoke kind words to her, I took the opportunity to speak to Caleb.

'Instruct the watchmen to keep a close watch on Rahab and her family and report back to me daily on their movements,' I whispered. 'I would know their coming in and going out.'

Caleb raised his eyebrows and nodded his understanding before disappearing into the darkness with the infamous woman of the night.

16

The Smell of Death

His efforts to hold it in were heroic. I watched him gagging and retching for some time as he picked his way through the bloody carpet of dead bodies, but the sight of an engorged vulture ripping out the eyes of a young man of similar age to him was too much. Bending over, he tore his head covering off his face and spewed the contents of his stomach onto the blood-soaked earth, his lithe young body heaving in protest.

I knew Hamul's parents. They were good people, and he was a son they could be proud of; well-spoken, honourable and brave. Like most young men, Hamul couldn't wait to turn twenty, eagerly anticipating the glories of warfare. He had fought well in the conquest of Jericho and I was heartened to hear that he had survived that battle with only a few minor scratches and bruises.

The glories of war were spoken of with great zeal, mostly among those who were yet to experience them. The aftermath of a battle, however, was hardly ever spoken of. There were no words to describe the putrid stink of death that hung over the pitiful remains of a battlefield, or the nauseating scenes that greeted the soldiers who were unlucky enough to be tasked with returning to clean up in the days that followed.

I walked over to Hamul and put my hand on his back. He jerked upright.

'Commander!' he blurted, wiping the sick from his mouth on his sleeve while trying to stand to attention.

'Be at peace, Hamul,' I said, grasping his shoulder. He was still retching; there was more to come. 'Get it all out,' I said. 'There is no other way. An empty belly is the only way to accomplish this task.'

Hamul doubled over before I had even finished talking. I stayed with him, holding him steady while he convulsed. After some time, the spewing turned to retching, then he stood to his feet, swaying.

'The first time is always the worst. It will get easier,' I reassured him, patting his back. 'Next time, ask your mother to give you some herbs to bind to the inside of your face covering. Breathing their scent will help.'

I smiled at Hamul, squeezed his shoulder and left him to gather himself. There was no way to prepare for this particular task other than to just do it. It was the same for every man the first time he witnessed the sickening sight of flesh being ripped off a corpse by vultures. Jericho was a large city; this was a banquet of gargantuan proportions for the vultures that had descended, hissing and rasping as they fought over the choicest carcasses.

The city that had stood proudly for centuries as the first defence of the land of Canaan was now just a heap of stones, its inhabitants fodder for wild beasts and the fowl of the air.

I wrapped my headscarf twice around my head to protect my nose and mouth from the foetid odours that threatened to suffocate me. The air reeked of decay. I wiped the sweat from my brow; the heat was intense, even at this early hour of the morning. Hamul was not alone; many of the men were gagging and retching in protest against the nauseating stench that surrounded us. This day would not be a pleasant one.

'Have the men been given their instructions?' I asked Caleb.

'They have. The captains have their orders, and they have instructed the men under them. Each troop has been designated a section of the city to search.'

'They must know without a doubt to abstain from things that are accursed. *Nothing* must be touched or taken from this place, except the gold, silver and vessels of bronze, which are to be consecrated to the Lord and placed in the treasury.'

'That has been made very clear, Commander. There can be no doubt in their minds about this.'

Attai and I watched our warriors file into Jericho, picking their way through the rubble and bodies, grim-faced and tight lipped. I turned away, pointing to a path which led to the centre of the city where an extensive, now dilapidated building stood perched on a hill, surrounded by rubble.

'This way. We will have a good view of the city from there.' Attai fell into step behind me. I could see why Jericho had been called the City of Palm Trees. An abundance of palms lined the streets, many with tantalising clusters of dates hanging from their fronds. It would have been pleasurable to partake of its fruit, but Yahweh said we were to destroy everything, so that is what we would do. The fruit would remain where it hung, to be burned along with the rest of the city.

Shrines to various gods were abundant. On street corners, in clearings, by trees and in homes, everywhere I looked, crude idols crafted from wood or metal which had probably stood in prominent positions now lay on the ground, their feckless existences terminated, just like the lives of those who had worshipped them.

'Truly, this land must be cleansed from such evil,' I said to Attai as we passed yet another idol, a grotesque, twisted creature with two heads made out of clay, displayed in an alcove on the street corner.

Attai said nothing, but I could sense his agreement. He was a man who did not waste words, only speaking when it was warranted. It was one of the things I liked most about him. He threw the idol on the ground and brought his sword down, smashing the image to pieces.

'One less idol for our warriors to destroy, *nu*?' he said.

We grinned at each other and continued on our way. I focused on the derelict buildings, trying to avoid looking at the bodies that lay strewn along the pathways. I couldn't help but notice the revealing clothing worn by the Canaanite women, or the flimsy material of their robes. An image of Rahab wearing the silken dress I saw her in yesterday flashed through my mind.

'How does a man remain pure among all this corruption of the flesh?' I grumbled as I tramped on. I knew the answer to that question before I had even finished asking it: he didn't, not in Jericho. No man could remain chaste in Jericho.

'These heathens know nothing of purity,' Attai responded. 'Their women are shameful. It is an abomination to all that is holy.'

That fact was driven home to me a hundredfold as we reached the site of the building on the hilltop. The wide steps leading up to its entrance, the ornate pillars, now smashed on the ground, and the vastness of the structure's interior led me to believe that this was the infamous temple to their moon god, Yarikh, and his heinous counterparts, Ashtaroth and Chemosh.

I dragged my feet up the steps, not wanting to go any further, dreading what I would find, but unable to stop myself. Leaning against the remains of an opulent carved pillar at the entrance, I paused to steady my pounding heart. Attai locked eyes with me. We squared our shoulders and braced ourselves before stepping into the cavernous enclosure.

Beams of sunlight streamed down through the gaping holes in the temple roof, revealing broken floors littered with limestone boulders, torn wall coverings that must once have hung proudly, and the smashed remains of what had been elaborate furnishings.

The morning sunbeams seemed inappropriately cheerful.

My gaze shifted upwards; what I saw made my skin crawl. I stared with morbid fascination, unable to look away from the debauched scene that unfolded before me. The bodies of several men lay scattered throughout the temple, some of them half-clothed, some naked, many of them wearing gaudy priestly robes – but it was not them that my eyes were drawn to.

Numerous temple prostitutes, some wearing flimsy transparent garments, but most of them completely naked, lay sprawled on the steps leading up to a rough-edged stone altar. Each of the prostitutes were pierced through, killed by a dagger to the heart. My warrior's eye knew that their deaths had not taken place by another's hand, but by their own. The shafts of the daggers that ended their lives were ornate, encrusted with jewels, with gold and silver circlets around the handles. Their deep-seated cultic practices and rituals would have demanded that they take their own lives, rather than be slain by another. I looked at the faces of the girls, horrified to see that some of them were still children, not yet women.

I heard Attai gasp, then moan. Following the direction of his gaze, my heart stopped in horror. On the stone altar lay the body of a small child. The child lay in a pool of stale blood, staring with wild, unseeing eyes. The glossy folds of her robe which had once been the purest white were now splattered with blood, ripped to pieces by sharp sacrificial blades. A dainty garland of flowers lay on the floor next to the altar, its white blossoms wilted, their dry, crinkled tips turning brown.

A surge of bile rose in my throat; I turned away, heaving in revulsion, clasping my hand to my mouth to try to contain it.

Enough!

I had seen enough. I could take no more. What devilry was this? How could humankind stoop to such degradation, such . . . I could not find the words; it was too much. At that moment, I believe I understood why Yahweh had commanded us to cleanse this land, to destroy it all – and I was ready to do so. I couldn't get away from that vile place fast enough. Attai and I hurried towards the outskirts of the city, neither of us looking at each other or saying a word, until we came upon Caleb.

'The fires have been laid,' he said, joining us. 'When you give the word, they will be lit, starting with those in the centre of the city and moving outwards.'

I nodded.

'Burn it. Burn it all. As soon as the men are out, give the signal to light the fires.'

A short while afterwards, I stood watching the first wispy tendrils of smoke rise from the middle of the ruined city. I could not rid my mind of the image of the child upon the altar, or the blood-soaked bodies of the girls on the altar steps. Attai came to stand with me; we still had not spoken. To speak at that moment would have been ill-considered. We stood apart and watched as the fire spread and the flames rose higher and higher.

A flock of vultures flew upwards, scattering in different directions as a new section of the city burst into flames. The roar of the blaze filled the air, along with the sounds of cracking, popping and spluttering, as the inferno unfurled its scorching wings. The flames burned with a savage temper, ravaging this once proud city, as if eager to be rid of the foul evil that had stained it for so long. We stood some distance away but, even there, I could feel the blistering heat of the blaze reaching out to sear my face. Tears welled up in unbidden response; I blinked, peering through narrowed eyes.

Never before had I encountered such a monstrous firestorm.

We moved further away to safety before turning to gaze upon the city once more. Many of the warriors stood with us, silent witnesses to the tragic, sanctifying justice of a holy God. Billowing clouds of black smoke rose upwards and outwards, filling the sky with a smoggy haze, masking the sun. By now, the fire had taken over the whole city, but the section that blazed with the most fury was the highest point: the temple on the hill which had become a tomb.

I could watch no longer.

A surge of rage, coupled with an unquenchable grief, stirred in my belly. 'It is finished,' I said to no one in particular. Turning to the warriors who stood with us, I shouted, "Cursed be the man before the LORD who rises up and builds this city Jericho; he shall lay its foundation with his firstborn, and with his youngest he shall set up its gates."'[14]

There were no cheers in response, only some sombre 'amens'. The warriors left to return to Gilgal. I stayed on for a while longer. Attai kept watch with me.

For better or for worse, Rahab's home would soon be gone. The city where she had been born, spent her childhood years, and turned to the business of prostitution, was now a glowing edifice of smoke and flames. My thoughts turned to the jug of flowers on her table, the newly filled lamps, and the colourful woven rug, now blackened and turned to ash.

I realised that the column of smoke permeating the skies would be seen from far off. The rest of the inhabitants of Canaan would soon know that Jericho had fallen, and that the God of the Israelites was unstoppable. By morning this would all be gone, leaving only a heap of smouldering ashes to remind us that Jericho had stood there. The grimy smell of burning, however, would linger on, as would the memories of what we had seen that day.

The cleansing of this land had begun.

---

14. Joshua 6:26.

17

Rising Smoke

I needed to bathe. More than anything at that moment, I longed to wash the grime and sweat off my body and, with it, the toxic stench of all I had witnessed that morning. Attai walked with me to a fast-flowing stream near the camp. I removed my outer robe and headscarf and waded in, crouching down to submerse my whole body under the water.

'Cleanse me, Lord God,' I prayed, letting the cool waters flow freely around me.

Images of the temple prostitutes flashed through my mind; their bloodstained bodies slumped over on the steps leading up to the altar. I scooped up handfuls of water and rubbed them over my arms, watching the splatters of blood and dirt being swept away by the flow of the water.

'Cleanse me from iniquity.'

The altar child's dead, unseeing eyes pierced my thoughts. Her long hair was matted with blood. I lay backwards, lowering my head into the water, running my fingers through the tangled threads of my hair.

'Purify my soul before You.'

An image of Rahab filled my mind, standing in her silken robe, her luxurious head of hair flowing in the breeze.

'Wash me until I am clean before You.'

The fragrance of her perfume filled my senses. Her lingering green eyes bore into me with an air of challenging defiance.

'Cleanse my heart. Make me clean before You.'

I plunged down, drenching my whole body in the cool flowing waters, rubbing it vigorously with handfuls of sand until every last stain of filth was gone from my skin. The purging waters of the stream absolved me from the wretchedness of that morning. I lay on my back in the stream, staring up at the sky, longing to see the cloud of Yahweh's presence again, grieving its loss.

After a while, I waded out of the stream and sat on a rock, letting the warmth of the sun dry my wet tunic. Attai hovered nearby, saying nothing about what we had experienced that morning. His ability to discern when I needed quiet and when I desired conversation was invaluable. Today, I was in need of silence, and I was grateful that he recognised that.

I stared up at the blackened sky to the west and realised with a jolt that Rahab would be able to see the fire and smoke – the destruction of her home – from her position on the west side of the camp. It must be grievous to her, I thought, although she had shown little fondness for Jericho when we talked yesterday. In fact, she seemed to indicate a strong desire to leave it. Why?

'Why should you care?' an inner voice accused me. 'She's just a harlot, and a Canaanite one at that.'

But I did.

I did care and it infuriated me to know that the thought of her heart being aggrieved troubled me. I deliberated within myself about the best course of action, then decided to pay her and her family a visit. After all, I had said I would speak with her again today. I released Attai to go to his family and went to ask Alya if she would come with me to see Rahab. It would not be wise to go alone and a woman's company would be useful when dealing with a harlot.

It was mid-afternoon when Alya and I arrived at Rahab's tent. She was sitting outside her tent, arms wrapped around her drawn up knees, staring at the burning heap that used to be her home. A look of overwhelming sadness shadowed her face. She scrambled to her feet as soon as she saw us and stood straight-backed, fists clenched, like an animal caught in a trap.

Her orange robe was gone. Today she wore a robe of pale green. It matched her eyes well. I looked away, berated myself for noticing such fleshly, mundane details.

'My lord Joshua,' she said with a slight nod.

Alya smiled and greeted her. '*Shalom*, Rahab.'

Rahab seemed unsure of how to respond but, with an encouraging smile from Alya, she replied, 'Uh . . . *shalom*.' It seemed wrong to greet a pagan prostitute in that holy manner but, now that Alya had done it, I felt duty-bound to do the same.

'*Shalom*, Rahab,' I muttered.

Rahab stood, looking at the ground like a convicted prisoner awaiting sentence.

'Is it well with you?' I asked.

She looked up, startled. 'Yes. Yes, my lord Joshua. I am . . . well.'

'And your family?' Alya asked her, looking around at the other two tents. 'Is it well with them?'

Rahab flushed. 'They are well, but . . . they are in need of much rest. They grieve for what has been lost.' Alya nodded in sympathy, her brow furrowed with concern. 'They have left much behind,' Rahab continued, then hesitated, looking into our eyes as if seeking permission to say more. She found it. 'My brother, Alu, did not come with us.' Tears filled her eyes; she blinked them back and gave an angry toss of her head. 'He did not believe my words and would not be moved. He refused to stay in my house and, when the walls fell, he and his family . . .' She looked away and wiped her eyes with her sleeve.

All I could think of was the mass of bodies I had walked through that morning.

Taking a deep breath, Rahab stood up straight and faced me. 'My lord Joshua, we thank you for honouring your pledge to us, for giving us these tents to dwell in, and food to eat. I fear I am undeserving of your kindness, but one day I will repay you, I swear it.'

This woman was so confounding! I couldn't determine whether she was genuine or merely feigning gratitude. Her words were honouring, but her tone was harsh and sounded more like a challenge than appreciation. I decided to give her the benefit of the doubt.

'There is nothing to repay. You saved the lives of two of my men. It is done.' She gave me a lukewarm, rather suspicious smile. 'We must take our leave. There is much to do and you must rest.' I motioned to Alya. 'Alya will tell you where to find water and explain . . . our ways . . . while I talk to the watchman.' I made to go, but then wheeled around and blurted, 'Should you have need of anything, seek me out.' I cringed inside. Why did I say that? '*Shalom*, Rahab,' I muttered.

'*Shalom*, my lord Joshua,' she said, bowing her head to me, somehow making an act of submission seem almost arrogant and hostile. I left her with Alya and went to talk to Nosson, who reported that no one had come to see Rahab or her family, and that none of them had ventured from their tents since arriving last evening. He also told me that Rahab had been sitting outside her tent, alone, staring at the ruins of Jericho, since early that morning when we began the burning.

Alya and I walked back through the camp together. 'Beerah and Salmah were right, she is a brave woman,' Alya said, 'and strong.' She glanced at me. 'Is she what you thought she would be?'

'I am not sure what I thought she would be,' I said with a grimace. 'In truth, I cannot fathom her. Her words say one thing, but her manner shows another. I have always thought of harlots as being foolish women with too much jewellery and too little sense, but I am not sure that Rahab is like that.'

'No,' Alya chuckled, 'she is not. But then,' she gave me a sly smile, 'this wouldn't be the first time you have misjudged a woman, would it?'

I stopped and swung round to face her. 'Do you mean . . . ?'

She raised her eyebrows and shrugged. I was speechless! She was right, though, I could not deny it. In their youth, Alya and Joel had fallen deeply in love, unbeknown to either of their families. When their betrothal was deemed impossible, due to Alya already having been promised to another, they planned to run away together. Their plan was discovered just in time and a turbulent few months followed. However, whether by chance or by Yahweh's making (to this day I still don't know which), Alya's betrothal was annulled, and she and Joel were joined in marriage.

When I first met her, I expected to see a brazen seductress with all the charms necessary to lure a fine young man like Joel from his family. Instead, I found a modest young woman with a wise heart and a strong sense of nobility. I realised with a start that Rahab reminded me somewhat of Alya in her youth. What? Impossible! Rahab was nothing like Alya.

Was she?

Although Alya was now a grandmother and much older than Rahab, I could already see a bond forming between them. Perhaps that was why Alya had so much compassion for Rahab – one misjudged woman to another?

'Humph,' I grunted, feigning disapproval. We continued walking. 'So, she isn't what I thought she would be, but even so . . . a harlot?' I grimaced. 'I cannot fathom why Yahweh would use a harlot to save our spies.'

'As you have told me many times, His ways are not our ways.' Alya tucked a strand of greying hair behind her ear, pulled her scarf tighter and flung the ends over her shoulders. 'I believe there is purpose in Rahab coming to be with us. In truth, she could be very helpful in gaining knowledge about the surrounding kingdoms.'

'Mmm.' Alya had a point. That had not occurred to me. It should have, but my mind had been so preoccupied. My thoughts turned to what we found when we searched Rahab and her family's possessions.

'My men found nothing accursed when they searched her belongings. Her clothing is very . . . pagan . . .' I glanced at Alya. 'She will need some help with this if she is to continue living among us, but there were no idols or accursed images in their bundles. The only thing they found among Rahab's possessions which seemed strange, was a doll – a child's doll – and yet there is no child among them.'

18

The Attack on Ai

It felt as though I had been holding my breath for days. A black smog hung over the plains, an incessant reminder of the iniquitous barbarity that had taken place in that city. However, a few days later I was heartened on waking to find a clear sky with no trace of smoke or fumes.

I could breathe again! I held my arms out sideways, put my head back, and drew in a deep, strong breath.

'*Shalom*, Joshua,' a cheerful voice called out, cutting short my celebration.

'Ah. *Shalom*, Caleb,' I replied, lowering my arms as he strolled towards me, grinning like a fox that had just caught a rabbit. Hoping to cut short any jokes he would make at my expense, I invited him to sit with me in the shade of my tent awning, and launched straight into a discussion about which town we should target next.

'Mmm. I was talking to Uri about this very thing, yesterday,' he replied. 'Ai is not far from here, near Beth Aven. It appears to be small and not well defended; we should be able to take it with ease.'

I had heard similar reports regarding Ai; it seemed good to me. 'Send four men to spy out the town and report back to us,' I said, 'but not Beerah or Salmah. They have been away from their families often in recent weeks, *nu*?'

Caleb agreed and, the following day, four warriors left to spy out Ai. Within the week they returned with a good report. The town was indeed small and its defences seemed weak and sparse.

'Commander,' the leader of the team said with a flourish. 'This town is ripe for the picking.' He recommended taking only three troops of a thousand, saying, 'They will fell the men of Ai with ease, crushing them like ants under their feet.'

After dismissing them, I turned to Caleb. 'What are your thoughts on this matter?'

He shrugged. 'I agree. There seems no point in tiring many men if only a few are needed.'

'Mmm. Which troops would you send?'

Caleb thought for a while. 'Some of the newer captains have been eager for conquest.'

'Which ones?'

'Alon and Manasses. They are young, but strong. They plundered many in Jericho and have earned the respect of their men.'

'Who is their commanding officer?'

'Yoram,' Caleb replied with a grin. 'He has never been one to turn from a battle, *nu?*'

'True. Choose two more captains of a thousand and inform them of the plan. We leave in two days' time – that should be sufficient time to prepare,' I said, standing up. 'I will speak to Yoram. We will lead the assault together.'

'You will go to Ai with them?' Caleb asked, standing up.

'Yes. Should I not?'

Caleb pursed his lips. 'It is always good when Israel's commander marches with his troops, but there is much for you to do here in camp, many plans to be made. You might be of greater value here. Yoram is an experienced warrior and Ai is just a small settlement. Perhaps you should let Yoram lead this attack.'

He could be right. A thought flitted through my mind: if I was to remain in camp, I would be able to check on Rahab. I brushed the thought away as I would an irritating fly.

'Very well,' I said. 'Tell Yoram that he has command of this mission.'

Yoram, Ishbah and Hanoch left with their troops early the next morning, slipping away without fanfare or ceremony. I spent the day with Caleb and Attai, mapping out the territories nearest to us and scribing what we had learned regarding each town or city. Thanks to our competent team of spies, we now had knowledge of most of the nearby settlements, their rulers, the extent of their kingdoms, and the state of their fortifications. The following day, we would plan the sequence of our advance on the Canaanites.

My sleep was troubled that night. Not only were my dreams many, but they were chaotic and made little or no sense. I woke exhausted and went straight into my meeting with Caleb. He was of the opinion that we should divide our troops and send out small detachments to subdue the lesser towns and villages, as we had with Ai, so as not to weary our warriors without cause. I was eager to hear Yoram's report of the conquest of Ai, to know whether he agreed with Caleb's proposal.

Midday came and went, and still Yoram had not returned. The afternoon wore on. I stood outside my tent, hands on hips. Should I set out to meet him on his return? Ishbah and Hanoch rounded the corner. Finally! As they approached, I noticed their demeanour was not that of conquering heroes. Quite the opposite. They were dishevelled and downcast and, when they drew near, they did not look me in the eye.

'*Shalom*, Ishbah, Hanoch. How did you fare at Ai?' I asked, already knowing the answer to that question.

They glanced at each other then Ishbah, the older of the two, focused on the neckline of my robe and said, '*Shalom*, Commander. We . . . the . . . the battle was . . .' he stuttered. He lifted his head and looked me in the eye. 'We were vanquished, Commander. We led an attack on the gates of Ai but they fought valiantly and we were forced to flee.' He gulped and cleared his throat. 'Thirty-six of our number were struck down.'

A chill swept over me as I saw the fear in his eyes.

Time stopped.

All words and thoughts hung in the balance.

My heart started racing.

No! No . . . it could not be!

'Where . . . where is Yoram?' I rasped.

'Commander,' Ishbah's voice cracked. 'Yoram was . . . slain.'

My heart seized. 'Slain?'

'Felled by the city gates. An arrow to his heart.'

A primitive cry burst out of my mouth, a bestial howl such as I had neither heard nor uttered before.

Attai was by my side in an instant. He waved Ishbah and Hanoch away and led me into my tent. I couldn't walk properly; my limbs felt paralysed. I leaned on him, stumbling inside. Attai sat me on a bench and crouched in front of me. I couldn't breathe. The pain was too intense, a hammer blow to the gut. I grunted and groaned, gasping for breath, staring at Attai in wide-eyed panic. No words came, only a flood of guttural noises that gushed out of my mouth.

'Breathe, Commander. *Breathe!*' Attai urged me, taking deep breaths in and out himself, entreating me to copy him.

At that moment, Joel and Alya entered the tent, drawn by the noise of my cries. Their eyes widened with shock at the sight of me, but one word from Attai was all that was needed for them to understand what had happened.

'Yoram.'

They froze in heart-stopping realisation for a moment before springing into action. Joel knelt in front of me, while Alya sat beside me. 'Joshua, you must breathe,' Joel said, placing his hand on my shoulder. *'Breathe, Yoshi, breathe!'* Joel said, inadvertently reverting to the affectionate name which Yoram had called me from his childhood. Far from getting better, my inability to breathe grew worse. The retching and heaving increased until some unseen force rose within my body, causing a jet of vomit to spew out of my mouth.

I vomited, gagging and trembling, until nothing was left but the bitter taste of bile. Now I breathed; shallow, ragged breaths. Joel and Alya supported me, one on either side, while Attai stood to the side, his eyes so full of pain you would have thought it was his kin who had been slain.

When I could speak again, I turned first to Joel and then to Alya. 'Yoram,' I panted. 'I killed him!'

19

Accursed

I had killed him, just as surely as if I had shot the arrow into his heart myself.

I had committed the very sin which Moses had warned me of, not so long ago. I could still picture the severe expression on Moses' face as he pointed his finger at me and said, 'Never forget what I am about to tell you. Mark my words well. *Never* go to war unless Yahweh has instructed you to do so, for if you go without His blessing, it will not go well for you.'

Never forget.

I forgot.

I sent my men off to war without Yahweh's blessing, to fight a battle that should not have been fought. It had not gone well for them. Thirty-six of our valiant warriors had perished because of my pride and foolishness.

Yoram had perished.

Because of me.

'Forgive me, Yori, I beg of you, forgive me . . .' I sobbed, crouched on the floor of my tent. Joel released Attai to relay the message about our defeat at Ai to the elders. Knowing better than to try to convince me that I was innocent in this matter, he and Alya waited as I put on a sackcloth robe, and witnessed me tearing the bottom section with a gut-wrenching cry.

When Mesha died, I promised to look after his family.

I had failed him.

'Joel, forgive me. Forgive me,' I wept. 'I have robbed you of your closest friend.' Joel said nothing. He drew me close and we lamented together for the gentle, brave soul that was Yoram ben Mesha. Sometime later, when our grief was spent and we sat in subdued silence, Attai returned and whispered in Joel's ear. Joel nodded, then turned to me.

'Yoshi, the elders have assembled at the Tabernacle to pray and seek Yahweh. They await you there.'

Yoshi. He called me Yoshi again.

Joel had never called me Yoshi before today – it was Yoram's name for me, not his – but somehow it felt right now, as though Yoram lived on through that name

'I asked them to meet you at the Tabernacle,' he murmured. 'I thought it best that no one come to your tent today.'

I thanked him and stood up. It was time to put aside personal grief and deal with matters of state. Joel and I walked to the Tabernacle, barefooted, dressed in our mourning tunics, and knelt down on the ground with the other elders and priests. Throwing dust on our heads, we lamented before the Lord, hour after relentless hour. As afternoon gave way to evening, so our prayers regressed from an outpouring of grief into a wretched display of complaining and self-pity.

'Lord God,' I wept, lying prostrate before Him. 'I cannot comprehend Your ways. Why did you hold back the waters of the Jordan River and bring us into this land, only to deliver us into the hands of the Amorites? Is it Your wish to destroy us?' I hit the ground with my fist. 'This land of milk and honey has become to us a curse, and death to Your people.'

The others joined in my weeping, throwing more dust on their heads, and wailing in their grief.

'What will your enemies say when they hear of our ruination? How great will their rejoicing be when they hear how we have been brought low. How will Your great name be magnified if we are cut off from the earth? Speak, I beg of you,' I implored the Lord, 'for we are undone before You.'[15]

A fresh deluge of sorrow erupted, voices crying out in desperation and confusion.

'*Why do you grovel before me in this way?*' a voice thundered, cutting through the weeping and wailing. '*Stand up!*' Yahweh's voice boomed with indisputable authority.

No one moved. Fearful eyes looked around the tent, waiting for someone else to make the first move. It had to be me. I stood to

---

15. Joshua 7:7-9, paraphrased.

my feet, trembling with trepidation. Eleazar was next to stand, then Joel. Yahweh waited until every man had stood to their feet before speaking again.

'My people have sinned.' The deep tones of His voice echoed, bouncing off the thick walls of the tent. 'They have transgressed My covenant and taken the accursed things of which I said they should by no means take. They have stolen and deceived. That is why they could not stand before their enemies.'[16]

My mind blurred. I put my hand on my chest, trying to calm the frantic beating of my heart. How could this be? Was I not clear in my instructions to our warriors? I raked my hand through my dirty, matted hair. I *had* been clear; I was sure of it. Caleb assured me there could have been no doubt as to Yahweh's commands regarding the accursed things.

Who had taken them? What could these accursed things be?

A dagger entered my heart.

My knees buckled.

Rahab!

Was it her? Was she the accursed thing?

'Neither will I be with you anymore, unless you destroy the accursed from among you.'[17]

'*No!*' My mind shrieked in response. 'I cannot lead this people without You! I cannot do it!'

'Sanctify the people,' the voice thundered again. 'In the morning, bring them out tribe by tribe. The tribe which the Lord chooses shall be judged, family by family, household by household, then man by man.'

The air crackled with fear.

Rahab's sumptuous form and flawless features flashed before my eyes. What if it was her? What would happen to the guilty person?

As if in answer to my unspoken question, Yahweh said, 'The man found to have the accursed things shall be burned, with all his possessions, because of his disobedience and sin before the Lord.'

Silence.

The only sound, the pounding of my heart.

I didn't look at anyone.

No one spoke.

---

16. Joshua 7:10-15, paraphrased.
17. Joshua 7:12.

'Leave me,' I told the elders, fixing my gaze on the ground. 'Relay this message to the people. We will begin at first light tomorrow. Eleazar, stay.'

I waited for the shuffling of feet and swish of robes to finish.

'Eleazer, what if . . .' I looked up. 'What if the accursed thing . . . is Rahab?'

'Rahab?' his brow crinkled. 'How could that be? You sought the Lord concerning the woman, did you not?'

'Yes.'

'And He gave you leave to redeem her and her family?'

'Yes. I think so. Unless . . . ? Was I mistaken?'

Eleazar's eyes peered at me from under his bushy greying eyebrows. 'You have never misheard Yahweh before now. Why should this be any different?'

'I don't know. It is only that . . .' I shrugged. 'You saw her. Her manner of dress, her jewels and necklaces. Perhaps . . . ?'

Eleazar looked troubled. 'You had her belongings searched, yes? And those of her family?'

I nodded. 'We found nothing of concern. There were no idols or amulets. There were none in her home at Jericho, either,' I said, recalling the cosy home which Attai and I had inspected. 'But perhaps she brought something out with her. She could have buried it in the ground, or hid it on her person. Or could it be that her jewels and adornments are accursed? Perhaps it is she herself who is cursed?'

A horrifying image of Rahab's smouldering body lying on a burned pyre of her possessions, ripped into my thoughts. I shuddered.

Eleazar's gaze pierced the thoughts and intents of my soul. I gulped and looked down.

After a while, he spoke. 'There is only one way of knowing. We must do as Yahweh has commanded. We will bring each tribe before him, according to their families and households. If the wrongdoer is not found among our own tribes, then we will look to the stranger among us.'

20

Achan's Plunder

'Could you be the one?' I wondered, studying the dishevelled man wiping sweat from his brow, despite the cold dawn that had smothered the camp in swathes of mist. He stood alone, a little apart from his brethren. The man exhaled a cloud of mist through his pursed lips, shifted his feet again and fiddled with his headscarf.

The crowd was grave-faced; a hush lay over the assembled men.

'Neither will I be with you anymore, unless you destroy the accursed from among you.' Yahweh's words rang in my mind with relentless persistence. This was a day of reckoning. We must root out evil and purge it from our midst. But, like a throbbing toothache, another thought would not stop tormenting me: what if I was the one who had brought the evil among us, and caused the death of our men, of Yoram?

'We will judge the tribes camped to the north of the Tabernacle first,' Eleazar's hushed tones jolted me out of my musings, 'beginning here with the tribe of Dan, then making our way east, south and finally west.'

I nodded, not trusting myself to speak.

Eleazar stepped forward, drew the two stones of judgement, Urim and Thummim, from his high priest's breastplate, and held them out. A brittle silence fell. A few moments passed, then Eleazar spoke out.

'The accursed things have not been taken by one from the tribe of Dan.'

A communal gasp of relief pulsated through the gathered crowds. The Danites embraced each other and a buzz of chatter arose. The dishevelled man's face relaxed and he loosened his white knuckled grip on his belt. Not waiting to celebrate or confer with those around him, he slipped away on his own. As Eleazar and I strode on in silence to meet with the next tribe, I wondered what the man must have done to have made him so fearful of judgement.

'Neither will I be with you anymore, unless you destroy the accursed from among you.' The weight of Yahweh's words hung over me as we approached the men of Asher a short while later. Their elders and leaders waited for us, the same fear mirrored on their faces. Within minutes, it was over.

The transgressor was not from the tribe of Asher.

The tribe of Ephraim would be one of the last to be judged, as they were camped on the west side. A thought swooped down out of nowhere, an arrow of fear that pierced with intent. Would I have to stand with my tribe and be tested? Surely, as leader of this people, no one would expect me to. No one would suspect *me* of being guilty of such a crime.

What if I did have to be tested with them?

What if I was chosen?

What if it *was* me who had sinned, by bringing Rahab into the camp?

What if she *was* the accursed thing?

'She cannot be, surely,' I argued with my fears as we moved on to the tribe of Naphtali. 'Yahweh permitted us to fulfil the pledge that Beerah and Salmah made with her . . . didn't He?'

My chest tightened. I could feel my heart beating erratically. I felt clammy, dizzy. Eleazar's hand shot out to steady me when I tripped over a stone on the pathway and stumbled. He said nothing, but I could see out of the corner of my eye that he was watching me.

As we approached the tribe of Naphtali, I felt sure that the fear in their eyes was mirrored in my own. I avoided looking anyone in the eye, deferring leadership to Eleazar. My stomach knotted when he declared the tribe of Naphtali's innocence. My desperation to find one of my own people guilty was superseded only by the shame in my heart at my duplicitousness.

Turning eastward, we made our way to the tribe of Judah's camping grounds. By now, quite a crowd had formed behind us, mostly made up of those who had been declared innocent and were curious to find out who the guilty party was. Caleb stood with his tribal elders and greeted us personally before returning to stand by their side. Eleazar held out the stones. I lowered my head, waiting to hear the words: 'The accursed things have not been taken by one from the tribe of Judah.'

They didn't come.

Instead, I heard Eleazar declare, 'The man who stole the accursed things is among the tribe of Judah.'

My head jerked up. The tribe of Judah? The guilty man is here? 'It's not me! I'm not the guilty one.' A babble of chaotic conversation burst out from the crowds, but the relief I felt vanished when I looked at Caleb, who tightened his jaw and went to stand with his family.

The clan leaders were brought before Eleazar one by one; I stood by his side, thankful that Caleb's family was one of the first to be judged. The tension was unbearable. Caleb stood tall when his clan was called, but I saw the veins in his neck pulsating. The relief on his face when his clan were declared innocent was unmistakable. Eleazar moved on to the next clan.

The family of the Zarhites, led by an elderly man named Zabdi, stepped forward next. My heart was stirred by his bravery. He had obviously seen many winters and needed the aid of a stick but, despite his stooped frame, he stood with head held high. Zabdi's frame did not stoop when his son's name was called out, but when his grandson, Achan, was named as the thief, silent tears trickled down Zabdi's cheeks.

Eleazar put the stones of judgement back in his breastplate and turned to me to announce the sentence. My heart broke for Zabdi. What would I do if one of our family was taken in sin?

What would I do if it had been me?

I couldn't imagine the pain Zabdi was enduring, but my desperate need to obey Yahweh was stronger than my compassion for Achan or his family. There could be no room for mercy today. Blatant disobedience to Yahweh's commands could not – would not – be tolerated. This land must be cleansed, and the cleansing had to start within our own camp. Moses was not here with me today because he had disobeyed Yahweh. I swore to myself that I would not make the same mistake. There was too great a price to pay.

'Neither will I be with you anymore, unless you destroy the accursed from among you.' Yahweh's words rang in my mind, as clearly as they had when He had declared them the day before.

'Achan,' I said, stepping forward to speak to the young man, who was trembling. 'You have been found guilty of possessing accursed objects. Tell me what you have done. Hide nothing from me.'

Achan fell to his knees, confessing his theft of an ornate robe, 200 shekels of silver, and fifty shekels of gold. He had taken them on the day we plundered Jericho and buried them under his tent, out of sight – or so he thought. Two of my trusted captains went with some of the leaders of the tribe of Judah to find Achan's plunder. They returned, forbidden items in hand, shortly afterwards.

By now, my relief at knowing that I was not guilty of this crime was dissipating, replaced by a sickening dread of what I knew must now happen.

'Did I not say that you were to abstain from the accursed things by all means, lest you become cursed when you take of them, and trouble this people? Why have you sinned against the Lord? You have brought great trouble on our people.'

Achan fell to the ground, begging for mercy. I turned away from him, my heart in conflict. Through this man's greed and disobedience, thirty-six warriors had died. But then, who was I to condemn Achan? If I had but enquired of the Lord as to whether we should war against Ai, we could have discovered Achan's sin earlier and no lives would have needed to have been lost.

Yoram would be here, standing with me.

Justice was effected without delay. The longer we waited, the worse it would be. All Achan's possessions, his tent and livestock, along with the accursed items, were taken to a nearby valley. The leaders and elders took up rocks and stood ready, waiting for me.

The one who declared the sentence threw the first stone.

I closed my eyes, picturing the beast from Alya's dream, its venomous, quivering sting plunging into the backs of my people. The images of the atrocities in the temple of Jericho were still fresh in my mind. No! It could not be! We *must* cleanse this land. We would vanquish the beast that stalked us. It would *not* take my people. Hardening my heart to the frantic cries of Achan and his family, I raised my arm and hurled the rock.

It was soon over. Achan's body, his possessions and the accursed things would be burned.

More smoke.

More fire.

More burning.

The smell of it turned my stomach. I walked away, leaving the elders to supervise the closure of Achan's sentence. Calling Eleazar and Caleb to my side, I walked a little way from that valley of trouble where a great heap of stones would soon be raised over Achan's bones.

'I give you my pledge,' I said to them, 'that from this day hence, I will *never* send my men into battle without first seeking the counsel of the Lord.'

I never did.

21

Grieving Yoram

I had to get away.

Being surrounded by family at a time like this should have been healing for me. It wasn't. Each time I looked into the faces of Yoram's wife, Samina, or his mother, Helah, all I saw was pain. It was torturous. I longed for them to shout, hurl accusations, scream at me for what I had done. That I could have borne, even embraced.

But they didn't.

They bore their pain with quiet resilience, and their looks of concern and love only served to heap coals on the fuel of my heart's guilty fire. I couldn't look at them. I started eating my meals in my tent, and stopped admitting visitors or meeting with the elders, as our mourning rites permitted.

I welcomed the solitude, but even that wasn't enough at times. I needed space. I paced up and down inside my tent. I needed to breathe fresh air. Waiting until it was nearly midday, when I knew most of the camp would be resting, I set off on a walk, escaping the confines of the camp as fast as I could, my headscarf pulled down over my face. Attai was resting with his family and would not have expected me to leave my tent, so I managed to evade even he, my faithful shadow.

I decided to make my way to the cooling waters of the stream where I had washed on the day of the burning of Jericho. There would be no one there at this time of day. I could be alone with my thoughts – not that my thoughts were pleasant to be alone with, at the moment.

As I rounded a grove of palm trees, I saw the figure of a woman kneeling by the water's edge. My first thought was to flee and hope I had not been seen but, as I veered to the left, a flash of colour caught my eye. The woman's robe. It was a pale-green colour.

I stopped, wondering if my eyes were deceiving me, when the woman, probably sensing my presence, turned around.

My eyes weren't deceiving me. It was Rahab.

I was caught!

She looked equally as unenthusiastic as I did, but there was nothing to be done now except to acknowledge each other's presence. I gave her a cursory greeting, which she returned, an uncongenial look on her face. I shuffled towards her, cursing her inwardly for preventing me from bathing, and for ruining my much-needed time of solitude. Then I noticed she had a large pitcher with her.

'You have come to draw water?' I questioned her.

'I have,' she replied, her disparaging tone indicating that the answer to my question was obvious.

'In the heat of the day?' I asked, confused. 'Why now? Our women draw water first thing in the morning, or in the evening, when it is cooler.'

Rahab smirked and lifted her eyebrows. 'It seems your women do not welcome the company of someone like me when they draw their water or wash their clothes,' she said, glancing at me sideways to see my reaction to this revelation.

Initially, I was both shocked and angered by her disclosure, and not a little embarrassed. However, my conscience reminded me of my own feelings towards this woman. How could I blame them for not wanting to be in the company of a woman like Rahab, when I despised the very sight of her?

Rahab, clearly sensing my awkwardness, sighed, and sat back, drawing her legs up to her chest. Her lips twitched into the beginnings of a sad smile.

'I understand why they despise me. I cannot say I blame them.' She shrugged and reached out to pluck some blades of grass. 'It is just easier to come at midday, then I don't have to see the disdain on their faces, or hear their mocking comments. In truth,' she said, looking around her, 'I like solitude. I welcome the quietness. Time to sit, to be alone, to think . . .'

'Until an unexpected visitor intrudes on you,' I said, unable to stop a smile from forming.

She smiled in response – a genuine smile. It was the first time I had seen her smile, really smile. It was beautiful. And disarming.

I looked away, studying the bubbling waters of the stream. Putting a stern expression on my face, I said, 'I will instruct Alya to ask one of our women to come with you to draw water and do your washing. These women will be told of your deeds of bravery in saving our spies, and they will treat you accordingly.'

'That is not necessary,' she replied, looking at me in suspicion. 'I am content to come in the heat of the day. It is no great hardship and, as I said, I like the solitude.'

I grunted. 'If you are sure. In truth, I share your desire for solitude,' I admitted.

'You do?' She didn't look convinced.

'Why would you think otherwise?' I asked. Who was this woman to question me?

She stared up at me, studying the expression on my face before answering. 'You have a loving family and, from what I have seen, faithful friends who stand with you and honour you. Why would you wish to be away from them?'

I moved a few feet away from her and sat on a flat rock which protruded into the stream. I took off my sandals and dangled my feet in the water. It was cool and cleansing, just as I knew it would be. Would that I could lower my whole body in. Another time. If we had been in camp, or in the company of others, I would not have felt the liberty to do so. However, sitting here by the edge of a babbling stream in the heat of the day with a cool breeze blowing on me, in the company of this beautiful woman, somehow it felt right. I felt comfortable just being myself, with my official rank and responsibilities stripped away – although why, I could not imagine.

I glanced at Rahab. She was still staring at me, waiting for a response.

'You are right about my family, they are a great blessing, a gift to me. They are not my blood kin – my family died in Egypt,' I explained, wondering why I was trusting a harlot with the intimate details of my life. It didn't stop me. 'My *abba*, before he died, gave me into the care of his closest friend, a man named Jesher. He became my father. His family became mine and, in truth, I have thought of them as my kin for so long now, I forget they are not of my blood.'

'That is a rare gift,' Rahab said with an understanding look.

'Mmm. It was an honour to join my life with theirs, one that I am deeply grateful for. But sometimes, even the company of those you love so well can cause pain, instead of healing. Sometimes you just need to be alone, to think.'

'Do you speak of your grief at the death of the warrior, Yoram?'

I swung round in accusation and barked, 'How do you know of such things? Who told you?'

'Forgive me.' Rahab lowered her gaze. 'I mean no offence. I heard fragments of conversation about some warriors who had been killed at Ai. I asked Alya about it and she told me only that Yoram was much beloved in your family, and an honoured captain in your army. Forgive me, I did not mean to intrude on your grief.'

Once again, I questioned myself as to why I would share the deep issues of my heart with a Canaanite harlot. Some inner sense told me I could trust her. My mind told me otherwise. Trust her? A woman such as Rahab? Why would I do that?

Pagans could not be trusted.

Women could not be trusted.

Harlots could *definitely* not be trusted.

I stayed silent.

She continued staring at the stream. 'My Lord Joshua, I am . . . well acquainted with grief. I know the pain of loss. It is like a dagger to the chest that will not be dislodged. Instead of pushing its way out, it becomes embedded within you.' She placed her hand over her heart, pushing against her chest. 'It becomes part of you, a pain you know so well that, after a while, it starts to feel like an old familiar friend. Instead of spurning it, you begin to embrace it. You cling to the pain. It sours within you as time passes, but you don't let it go, because it has become all that you have left of the one you lost.'

I stared at her, stunned by her response. She knew! She had put into words exactly what I had endured, not just with Yoram, but many times over the course of my life. How did a wanton woman such as Rahab know of such deep things?

'One thing I have learned,' she said, continuing her discourse to the stream, still avoiding my gaze, 'is that the longer we hold our pain close and welcome it, the harder it becomes to embrace life. The anguish of grief can only truly be broken when we let it go – when we pull the dagger of torment out of our heart and choose to embrace a different pain; the pain of living life without our loved one.'

I wanted to tell her.

I wanted to tell her about the grief that was swallowing me up, of the anguish that had threatened to burst out of me when we laid Yoram to rest, and the tormenting guilt that crippled me whenever I thought of his cold, dead body lying in the ground outside our camp.

I wanted to tell her that I could no longer look at Samina or Helah, or Yoram's children, or any of the family, lest my guilt overwhelm me.

I wanted to tell her of the agony that filled my heart when I heard the wailing of their death lament, of my longing to hold them close and comfort them. Of the paralysing guilt that stopped me from doing so.

I wanted to tell her.

But I couldn't.

Instead, I nodded like a dumb mute and studied the flowing waters of the stream as they meandered past my feet. After a minute or so, Rahab stood up and lifted the heavy pitcher onto her shoulder.

'I will leave you to your solitude,' she whispered, the folds of her pale-green robe rustling as she slipped quietly away, like a fleeting angel.

22

Victory

It was an irrefutable victory. We followed the battle plan that Yahweh gave us, drawing the men of Ai out from their city by pretending to flee before them, then ambushing them on the plains. They were vastly outnumbered and, at the end of the battle, not a single man of Ai was left standing, and not one of our soldiers had lost their lives.

'I have avenged you, Yori. Be at peace,' I murmured, looking at the devastation that surrounded me. 'Rest with your fathers now. Be at peace.'

Although I had never revelled in killing, even heathens such as these, I found that the conquest of Ai brought a sense of closure to my grieving heart. This victory couldn't vindicate me from the sin of not seeking Yahweh's counsel the first time we fought them, but the fact that I had avenged Yoram initiated a restorative process within me. For the first time since his death, the heaviness that had weighed me down started to lift.

In truth, although I was reluctant to admit it, I believed the change started the day I spoke with Rahab at the stream. I tried to block that thought out of my mind. It was ridiculous! How could a few words spoken from the mouth of a prostitute effect such change within me? It was foolishness.

But it was true, nevertheless.

Being away from camp, from family, from everything that reminded me of Yoram, even for a few days, had been helpful. I welcomed the rough functionality of the life of a soldier, the physical demands and rigorous disciplines that only warriors truly understood. Out there, I was not required to engage in deep or meaningful conversations. We talked only of strategy and numbers and weapons. That, I could do.

I was surprised, therefore, when after just a couple of days, I felt impatient to get back to Gilgal.

'Why?' I muttered as I stood watching our men plunder the remains of Ai. The answer came in a flash – the image of a beautiful woman dressed in a pale-green robe with flowing hair and piercing green eyes.

'*Eiysh!*' I exclaimed. The very fact that Rahab had trespassed on my thoughts irritated me. It irritated me a *lot*. I tried to banish thoughts of her from my mind, turning my focus towards the burning of Ai – without success. Something had shifted in my grieving on the day we spoke, at the stream. Being seen and understood, without having to endure any long, draining conversations about Yoram, had been healing.

I wanted to thank her. But how?

'Enough! I will tolerate this invasion of my thoughts no longer!' I told myself as I strode towards Ai. Something glinted on the ground. I bent down and picked it up. An arrow. Not one of ours; it bore the markings of the Canaanites on the arrowhead. I picked it up and turned it over in my hand. An arrow like this one had ended Yoram's life. Perhaps this very one – after all, I was standing in front of the city gates, where the original attack had taken place.

A familiar wrench of pain ripped into me. I closed my eyes, breathing hard in resistance to the guilty sobs that threatened to arise. Then I remembered her words.

The prostitute's words.

'It is like a dagger to the chest that will not be dislodged . . . It sours within you as time passes, but you don't let it go, because it has become all that you have left of the one you lost . . .'

My fist tightened around the arrow, knuckles white with the strain. I would take the arrow back to camp with me, keep it as a reminder of how Yoram's life had ended . . . of my guilt. Rahab's words rang once again in my consciousness.

'The anguish of grief can only truly be broken when we let it go – when we pull the dagger of torment out of our heart and . . . choose to embrace a different pain; the pain of living life without our loved one.'

My shoulders slumped; my hold on the arrow relaxed.

'Very well, woman,' I mumbled. 'I will heed your words. Just this once.'

Kneeling on one knee, I dug a shallow grave for the arrow and placed it in the ground with a sense of reverence. Covering it with clots of soil, I patted it down and laid my palm upon the small mound. No words came, but I knew as I stood to my feet that I was one step closer to finding release from the pain of Yoram's death.

I turned my face towards Ai. It was time for the burning.

The following morning, we left to return to Gilgal, arriving mid-afternoon. On the march home, my thoughts strayed again to my conversation with Rahab at the stream and, more specifically, to what she told me about the scorn and rejection she was subjected to by our women. I thought about moving Rahab and her family's tents into the camp, where we could watch over them more closely, but that was impossible. It was not permitted for foreigners to dwell in the camp. The laws of Moses clearly stated that all *goy*[18] were to pitch their tents outside the camp.

The family gathered round to welcome me on my return home. This time, I didn't avoid them or try to escape their embraces. No one spoke of Yoram by name, but I felt it in the way their arms held me, the way they looked at me. Acceptance, peace, love. Forgiveness.

I updated them on what had happened at Ai, leaving out my musings about Yoram and the arrow. As soon as I could do so without drawing attention to myself, I asked Alya for an update on Rahab and her family. She reported that all was well with them.

'Good,' I responded, trying to sound blasé. 'They will need more food and supplies. Attai and I will visit them to find out what they have need of.'

'It is kind of you to think of them, but there is no need for you to do that. Salmah, Iru and Serah have been attending them, and I visit Rahab every day. They have everything they need – indeed, they are being very well looked after.'

'Salmah and Iru? I knew nothing of this,' I responded, trying to keep the irritation out of my voice.

'Yes. Caleb asked Iru to watch over them while he was with you at Ai, and they thought it prudent to involve Salmah, as he knew Rahab from his mission in Jericho. Iru takes Serah with him when they visit. It is good for Rahab to have the company of a woman closer to her own age, *nu?*'

---

18. Goy is a Hebrew word for a non-Jew.

'Ah. Yes. Good. So . . . there is nothing that they have need of?'

'No, no. You need not trouble yourself, Yoshi. Rest. You must be tired after your journeying.'

I couldn't think of another excuse for visiting Rahab. It was probably a good thing. The more distance between us, the better, I told myself. I thanked Alya and went to my tent to rest, all the while knowing full well that rest would be far from me.

23

Covenant

She was easy to spot, even among the multitudes that gathered by Mount Ebal and Mount Gerizim. None of our woman wore glossy robes of emerald green and, even if they had possessed such a gown, they would never have worn it to a solemn reading of the Law of Moses. I could imagine their disdain at seeing Rahab doing so, the condemnation in their eyes at such a blatant act of vanity.

All twelve tribes were assembling on the mountains for the reading of the law and commandments, to witness the burned offerings and to worship Yahweh, as instructed by Moses before he left us. This was a day of consecration, of covenanting ourselves afresh to the God of Israel who had delivered us from Egypt and brought us into our homeland of Canaan.

And Rahab was among us, shining like a jewel among pebbles.

Despite the fact that she had worn a scarf to cover her head – thanks to Alya's wise input – she still stood out in the crowd. Alya, Salmah, Iru and Serah walked with her but, even though she was in the company of well-respected men and women, she was given a wide berth. Rahab would have had to have been blind not to notice the outraged stares of the people around her, or the way they turned their backs on her when she drew near.

I felt ashamed of my people for treating her like that, but a voice in my head screamed, '*Hypocrite!* You have scorned her and turned your back on her many times in your heart.'

It was true. I had. So why was I struggling when others did what I myself had done? Had my opinion of her changed?

Yes.

It had. That was the truth of the matter. Yes, I was still wary of her, as she undoubtedly was of me. I hated the fact that she was a harlot and still despised her pagan ways but, the more I got to know her, the more my curiosity was piqued, and the more I wanted to know about her. I still knew so little about her past.

She was a mystery to me, and I didn't like mysteries.

I watched as Alya ushered the harlot to a clearing, surrounded by Salmah, Iru and Serah. Rahab held her head up high and walked with confident, some would say arrogant, steps. Part of me despised the fact that she was here among us on such a sacred day, but the other part of me could not help but admire her resilience in the face of such ostracism. She must have known this was the reception she would get, but she came, nevertheless. She showed much courage.

Or was it arrogance, or rebellion?

However, despite their obvious loathing of her, Moses had made it clear all those months ago when he gave instructions for this day, that the strangers among us were to be included.

I just had never dreamed that one of the strangers would be a Canaanite prostitute.

For some reason, I found the irony of that fact comical, and had to put my hand to my mouth to try to hide the smile that crept out, unbidden. Although they had also been invited to join us on this day, Rahab's family had not come with her. Alya reported that although they were grateful to be among us and seemed content on the whole, they were not yet able to let go of their old life or embrace new ways.

Eleazar, Phinehas and their brethren offered up peace offerings and the whole congregation worshipped the Lord together, following the lead of the priestly choir.

'Give thanks to the Lord,' the priests sang. We echoed their words. 'For He is good and His mercy endures forever.'

I glanced across at Rahab and was intrigued to see an expression of amazement on her face. I was so used to hearing the rich tones of the male voices that led our worship that I hardly noticed the beauty of their chorusing any more. Seeing the almost childlike wonder on her face gave me cause to listen more closely and appreciate anew the deep, earthy beauty of their worship.

After the worship came the reading of the law.

'This book of the law shall not depart from your mouth, but you shall meditate upon it day and night.'[19] I declared to my people the

---

19. Based on Joshua 1.

same words which Yahweh had spoken to me when I took over leadership of His people. This was the key to our cleansing of this land. They *must* know this. They *must* walk in obedience to Yahweh if they were to prosper and flourish. I continued to read out the laws that Yahweh had given us.

After a while, I paused to drink from my waterskin. I couldn't help but glance across at Rahab, and was startled to see an expression on her face of fascination mixed with what looked like admiration.

Admiration?

For whom?

For me?

My heart started thumping. Was it true? Did this beautiful woman admire me? I pushed the thought to the back of my mind and focused on continuing to read the Mosaic laws. Her fascination (if that is what it was) would not last, of that I was sure.

The reading of the law would continue for the rest of the day. I knew that, at first, the multitudes would listen carefully, responding when required. However, as the day went on and they grew tired, their attention would wane. Most of them would stare around them, bored and stiff from sitting for so long, and many would doze off during the readings. Rahab would not last very long before she grew bored, of that there could be no doubt.

I was wrong.

Her face was filled with rapt attention and, during some of the breaks, I saw her talking to Alya and Salmah in an animated fashion. Her focus was fixed on me, and on the words I shared, for the entire duration of the day. Not once did I notice her dozing off or looking bored.

That night, around our mat, Alya spoke to me as we broke bread. 'Yoshi, Rahab was much impacted by today's events.'

'Mmm? That is good,' I replied. 'Surprising, but good.'

'Yoshi, she is hungry to learn our ways.'

'Yes?' I took a big bite of bread.

'Yes.' She paused, waiting until I had finished my mouthful. 'She would like to become one of our people. Rahab would like to become an Israelite.'

24

To Be an Israelite

Why? Why would a beautiful woman like Rahab willingly submit to having her hair shaved off, her nails cut, her jewellery and clothes taken from her, as well as having to spend months, possibly years, studying the law and learning our nation's history?

'Alya has told me of your desire to turn your back on the gods of Canaan and become one of our people, a follower of the One True God. Is this so?'

'It is.' There was no hesitancy in Rahab's tone. She stood tall and looked directly at me. A frown crossed her face; a familiar defensiveness shuttered her eyes.

In truth, her request had confounded me. Ever since Alya had told me of it the previous night, I could think of nothing else. My mind was a whirl of questions, accusations and possibilities. I had never heard of a stranger who lived among us relinquishing their previous life and becoming one of us. There were plenty of non-Israelites with us, Egyptians and those from other people groups who had either come with us when we left Egypt or joined us along the way. Our laws demanded that they be allowed to travel with us, living outside the camp under our protection, but none of them had forsaken their heritage in order to follow our ways. Rahab was the first I knew of who had asked to become an Israelite.

I was not convinced she understood what she was asking, or what would be required of her.

'It is not a simple thing that you ask,' I told her. 'Our ways are as different to the ways of your people as our God is to your idols. Much would be required of you. You would have to study our laws, learn our ways and undergo a time of purification in order to become one with us.'

'I understand,' Rahab replied.

I glanced at Alya, who stood on one side of the tent along with Eleazar, Joel and Caleb. She stepped forward. 'I have explained to Rahab the laws of Moses regarding the cutting of her hair and nails, the purification rituals, and the atonement offerings...'

'And you would endure all this,' I asked, 'to become one of our people?'

'I would, my lord Joshua,' she replied, meeting my eyes with a steady gaze. Her eyes flashed, daring me to deny her request.

'Rahab,' I said, leaning forward in my chair. 'You need not fear, we will keep our vow to you. You and your family will be free to dwell with us for the rest of your lives, should you desire to do so. As long as you don't worship other gods or lead our people astray, no harm will come to you, I give you my word. There is no need for you to go through the purification rites. It would be a great hardship for you. It would mean turning your back on your people and your customs. Everything you know would change.'

'I understand what is required of me.' She lowered her eyes. 'I know it would be a hardship, but it would be nothing compared to what I have endured thus far.' Glancing first at Alya, she looked up and spoke in low, measured tones. 'My lord Joshua, we cannot choose the manner of our birth but, if we could, I would not have chosen to be born in Jericho. It may be the city of my birth, but it has never been the city of my heart.'

'How so?'

She thought for a moment. 'Our family did not have the means to live near the centre of the city like the rich landowners, but we were happy in our home on the city walls, and it was only a short walk to the fields outside the city walls where my father laboured each day.' Rahab's face softened; a gentle smile played upon her lips. 'We didn't have much, but we had each other, and we were happy.' The smile disappeared and bitterness covered her countenance. 'Until the day of the choosing.'

'The day of the choosing?'

She paused, her eyes flicking from side to side before meeting my gaze.

'The choosing of the child to be offered up to Chemosh at the festival. They . . . my . . .' She took a deep breath in to steady herself, and breathed out before continuing. 'She had seen just six winters. Her whole life was ahead of her – but they liked them young.

The little ones didn't have the strength to fight back like the older children did.'

A stunned silence filled the room. Surely, she couldn't mean . . . ?

Rahab's arms hung by her sides. The fingers of her right hand started tapping on her leg and she focused on the walls of the tent behind me. 'They came to our home on the afternoon of the festival to tell us the news: she had been chosen. I remember hearing the sound of revelry and celebration in the streets, and wondering what was happening, why everyone was so happy. We were playing outside when they arrived, five of them, to take one small child.'

She shook her head and her eyes narrowed.

'It was always a closely guarded secret. No one knew who had been chosen until the day of the festival. They said it was to "preserve the honour of the family".' She gave a cryptic laugh. 'It had nothing to do with honour. None of it had anything to do with honour. The only reason they waited until the last moment to tell the family was so they couldn't run away, or hide the child.'

Silence hung heavily in my tent. My breathing sounded loud. *Please, say no more*, I silently pleaded with Rahab. I didn't want to hear it. I could not bear to watch the desolation that was settling upon her.

I had to.

'They filled her head with stories about what an honour it was to be chosen, talking of the wreath of fresh flowers that would adorn her head, the beautiful white robe she was to wear, how all the people would be there to cheer for her . . .' Rahab flinched in distress. 'I was not two years older than her. I had no understanding of what was going to happen.' Her voice broke as she cried out, 'I was *envious* of her. I hated that she had been chosen and not I.'

Alya gasped, then covered her mouth with her hands, her eyes wide with trepidation. Rahab didn't even notice. Her face had turned to stone, her body stiff and unmoving. She spoke in a dull tone, staring ahead of her.

'They took her away. It all happened so quickly. I never got to say goodbye. Three of them stayed with the rest of us while we readied ourselves for the festival, and then they escorted us to the city gates, where the procession started. We were given the place of honour, as the chosen child's family. The crowds were shouting and laughing, dancing in the streets behind the bronze idol of Chemosh as it moved through the city.'

Rahab still stared, unseeing. A single tear rolled down her cheek. 'I danced along with them. I didn't understand why my mother took my hand and pulled me close. I didn't know. I didn't know that...' She looked back at me, her eyes dark pools of fear, wild and raw. 'The closer we got to the temple, the louder the multitudes shouted. I covered my ears, but I couldn't block out their cries. The noise of the trumpets, the pounding of the drums; it went on and on, louder and louder, until we reached the steps of the temple.'

I knew those steps.

I had walked up them, dragging my feet just as Rahab must have done.

'I begged to be taken home, but I was denied.' Her face twisted in bitterness. 'As the chosen child's family, we were *highly honoured* and, as such, were expected to watch the ... the ...' Rahab clasped her hands in front of her, pulling them into her belly and rocking backwards and forwards. Everything in me wanted to go to her, to hold her, to protect her from this torment.

I couldn't.

So, I sat in my chair and watched as waves of pain and agony poured out of her.

'They led us into the temple and we climbed the steps until we reached the high place, where all the priests were gathered, waiting. The noise was unbearable. The drums ... like thunder ... echoing, bouncing off the walls of the temple, louder and louder. Then, all of a sudden, it stopped.' Rahab froze. Her eyes glazed over. 'Everything ... just ... stopped. So quiet. So still.' She frowned, tilting her head to one side. 'And somehow, the silence was far worse than the noise had been.'

I held my breath.

'Then I saw her,' Rahab whimpered. Her fingers toyed with the scarf that hung around her shoulders, pleating and releasing it over and over again. 'They led her out and presented her to the crowds. She was such a happy child, so full of joy and laughter, but she didn't look happy. She looked ... drowsy ... confused. I found out years later that they had given her something to drink to dull her senses. They were right about the robe and the flowery wreath, though. It was like a crown of white on her head. Her hair flowed from it like the softest golden cloak down her back. She was beautiful. So beautiful. So perfect.'

Please stop, I begged Rahab silently. *Please, just stop.*

'They chose only beautiful children. Those that were perfect, unblemished. As a child, I remember seeing little girls with scarred faces. I wondered what had happened to them. When I was older, I found out. Their own mothers had defaced them to save them from being chosen. An act of such cruelty, and yet such love.'

A spasm of pain pierced my chest. I forced myself to stay seated. I bent forward, bracing myself for what I knew was coming.

'She didn't know what was happening. Right until the end, she didn't know. They led her to the altar,' her voice shook, 'and laid her on it. It was only when the priest lifted the knife and started praying to Chemosh that she realised. She screamed, fighting against the priests who held her down, but they were grown men and she was so little.'

Rahab's words were unfettered, as was now her heart, her anguish laid bare for all to see. 'The crowds started chanting, calling out to Chemosh, and the drums started pounding again, and she screamed and screamed and screamed. They couldn't hear her, but I heard her. She cried out, not for Mother or Father, but for me. She cried out *my* name. She called to *me* for help, and I couldn't help her. I couldn't get near her. I tried to go to her but the priests held me back. I saw the terror in her eyes and I could do nothing ... nothing ... except watch the ...'

Rahab's face contorted with grief. She collapsed to the ground, sobbing in agony. Every atom of my being strove to reach out to her, to hold her and comfort her, but it wouldn't be seemly. I motioned to Alya, who rushed forward to do what I could not.

We waited as wave after wave of agony and grief poured out of her. I stood up and turned away, grateful for the opportunity to gather myself. Alya joined her tears with Rahab's, holding her in her arms and rocking her, as she had done with her own children when they were babes, frightened by night fears. I stood up and walked to the other side of the tent in an effort to stop my hands from shaking. I was a man of war. I had seen my fair share of death, and encountered much hardship and loss over the years – but not like this. Never like this. The image of the child lying on that altar in a pool of her own blood, eyes frozen in unseeing terror, would not leave me.

After a while, when Rahab had recovered, Alya helped her to rise and stood by her side, her arm around her.

'Forgive me,' Rahab mumbled. 'I have not spoken of this since that day and . . .'

'Please, no forgiveness is necessary,' I replied, walking back to my chair, and sitting down again. 'I am thankful that you are able to rid yourself of this terrible burden. It takes much courage to pull the dagger of torment out of our heart, to bring into the light that which has held us in darkness for so long.'

Rahab stared up at me, astonished. The vulnerability in her eyes acknowledged my reference to our private conversation about grief. 'Yes. Many years have passed, and yet I can still hear her screaming my name.' She shuddered. 'I hear her often in my dreams, sometimes even in my waking hours, calling me, over and over.'

No one said anything. What could we say that would possibly help to heal the trauma that had scarred this beautiful woman's heart for so long? We stayed silent, each of us wrestling with our own thoughts. Alya stroked her shoulder, speaking gentle words to her and, after a while, when her vacant stare had been replaced with a look of hopeless exhaustion, I asked Rahab a question.

'What was her name?'

My question jolted Rahab out of her stupor. She stared at me, clearly confused. Her brow furrowed but she said nothing.

'Your sister,' I repeated. 'What name was she know by?'

'Her name? Her name . . .' Rahab's voice cracked, '. . . was Ayna. In our tongue it means little flower.'

'That is a beautiful name.'

'She was a beautiful child. Chemosh did not deserve her.' Bitterness clouded her countenance as she went on. 'We were not permitted to grieve or mourn her loss.' She baulked. 'There was no grave to go to, even if we had been allowed to do so. They burned her body on the altar of Chemosh. All I have left of her is her doll.'

Alya and I glanced at each other, remembering the child's doll that was found in Rahab's bundle of belongings.

'We were instructed only to speak about what an honour it was to have been chosen, nothing more. One year, we heard of a chosen family who had done otherwise. They could not hold their tongue, and shared the depths of their grief with their friends and neighbours. They disappeared one night shortly after the festival. The whole family, gone. We were told that they had travelled north to live with relatives, but it seemed strange that they told no one of their plans beforehand, and said no farewells to their friends before leaving.' Rahab shuddered and gave a weak smile. 'So we smiled and said how grateful we were to be so honoured, and we tried to keep on living, when our very hearts were shrivelling and dying inside of us.'

25

Becoming a Harlot

Ayna's sacrificial death was not the only tragedy to befall Rahab's family.

Her father had an accident a couple of years later which left him lame and unable to work. A merchant's cart, loaded with heavy bolts of cloth for his marketplace stall, had knocked him over and rode over his legs. He was no longer able to work in the fields and there was no other work suitable for a cripple, so he and Rahab's mother made the decision to move the whole family into their sleeping quarters, and they rented out their best room to travellers.

Rahab's task had been to go and stand by the city gates each day, to spot travellers and invite them to lodge with them.

'We offered lodgings and simple fare to travellers who needed a bed for the night. Salmah and Beerah saw our home,' she told us, giving me a searching look. I think she suspected I had also seen it, but said nothing. 'It wasn't big, not like the inns and taverns in the middle of the city, near the temple. They did a thriving business, especially at festival times when men became sodden with too much wine, and their purse strings loosened. We couldn't compete with them, but we managed to get by on what our lodgers gave us . . . for a while.'

She looked away, in the direction of where Jericho had once stood, wrapped her arms around her body, and murmured. 'The winters were the worst. Not many travellers came asking for lodgings during those wintery months.' Rubbing her arms, she continued, 'Food was hard to come by. Many times we had nothing to put in our bellies; my brothers and sisters and I had to take to the streets to beg for scraps. Then my little brother became ill; my mother feared it would be unto death.'

Tears filled her eyes. She blinked them away, but I noticed her hands were trembling. She stared up at me with a look of desperate defiance. 'That's when I did it.' Rahab searched my eyes as she spoke, looking for signs of condemnation or disapproval.

'I saw the way men looked at me and, although my father never told me himself, I knew they enquired after me. I heard them. So, that night, as my brother lay fighting for breath, I went up to our lodger's room and offered myself to him – for a price.'

Her tone once again became dull and lifeless, as if telling a well-known story that had been rehashed too many times over the years.

'In our culture, women were not shamed for giving themselves over to a man. Among many, it was encouraged. The temple priestesses were paid handsomely and revered for their services.' The memory of the beautiful young girls lying dead on the temple steps, and the ornate daggers that killed them, flashed into the forefront of my mind.

'Every parent of a pretty young girl strove to have her accepted into the priesthood from as early an age as possible.' Rahab flashed me a look of anger and bitterness. 'Priestesses were protected from being chosen. It was a position much sought after by our young women. But not by me. It is not the life I would have chosen. To have your body used in such a manner is . . .' Rahab's lips moved, but she spoke no words.

Heat crept up my neck as rage filled me. I struggled to compose myself. To treat women thus was abhorrent. Even though Rahab was not my woman, or even of my kin or my people, I could not abide the thought of her, or any young woman, being subjected to such abasement. My thoughts turned immediately to the young women in our family. What would I do, should one of them be treated with such contempt? I stared at the ground, not wanting Rahab to see the conflict that raged in my heart.

'My parents were distraught when they found out what I had done, but by then it was too late. It was done.' Sarcasm rung out in her tone. 'I was soiled and could never reclaim my maidenhood. I became a woman soon afterwards, but my mother was wise in the ways of women and kept me aside at the appointed time each month so I never had to bear another's child. I became known, not only among the travellers, but also among the men of Jericho.' She sneered. 'They said I was . . . different from the rest of the women they frequented. I made sure they paid more for me. My earnings never kept us in a style of abundance, but we never went without food again.'

Looking around the room with an glare, Rahab said. 'It is not a path I would have chosen, but I would do it again if I had to. Because of the coins I earned, my brother lived, and my family was saved from starvation.' Her glare softened and the look of hopelessness returned. 'That is why I wish to become one with you; to leave behind all that has befallen me up until this time, and to become a worshipper of Yahweh.'

Rahab turned to me, expecting a response.

I couldn't give her one. My heart was too full; I had no words.

Interpreting my silence as disapproval, she blurted, 'Have I said too much? Forgive me. I do not wish to offend, but I cannot withhold from you the truth of the path I have trodden. I must rid myself of all lies and deception, if I am to embrace a new life as an Israelite – if . . .' she hung her head, 'if you find me worthy.'

I cleared my throat and rasped, 'It is not for me to find you worthy. It is Yahweh who you will bow your knee to, and it is He who will receive you or reject you.'

Rahab's anxious expression stirred my heart. I stood up and smiled through the rage I was feeling. 'Yahweh is a good God. He is compassionate and kind, unlike Chemosh or your moon god, Yarikh. I will seek His face on your behalf, but I believe you have nothing to fear.'

'Thank you, my lord Joshua.'

As Joel and Alya prepared to escort Rahab back to her tent, I remembered what I had seen in Rahab's home in Jericho. The same questions that had dogged my mind then came back now to haunt me. If this woman was to become one of us, I needed answers to those questions.

'Rahab?'

She swung round to face me. 'My lord Joshua?'

'There is something I would ask you. It concerns your home. Your home in Jericho.'

Her brow furrowed with anxiety. 'Yes?'

'After Jericho fell, before we lit the fires, we searched your home . . . to ensure that no one had hidden there.'

The corners of her mouth lifted slightly. She lowered her head. 'Indeed.'

'While we were there, we noticed some items of worth which had been left behind.' Her eyebrows lifted. 'Uh . . . spices, cinnamon, robes, jewels . . .' I couldn't continue. Her eyes bore into me. I felt exposed, but I had to continue. I had to know the answers to my questions.

'Yes?'

'Why is it that you left behind items of such value? Would they not have been . . . useful to you? Were they left in haste, or by design?'

Rahab's expression softened. She thought for a moment before responding. 'They were a part of the life I was leaving behind. I wanted to take nothing with me into my new life that would remind me of the life I had led there.'

Our eyes locked.

'I see. Forgive me, but . . .' Despite the awkwardness of this conversation, I had to finish my questions. 'Your home, it was . . . cleaned and swept. There were fresh flowers, new oil and wicks in the lamps. Everything was as if you planned on returning. Why?'

She spoke softly. 'That is how I wanted to remember it, as the place of peace and love that it once was.'

'And do you?' I asked.

The sweetest smile lit up Rahab's face. 'Yes, my lord. I do.'

My eyes fogged over at the simplicity of the answers to these questions that had mystified me for so long. I cleared my throat. 'Go now. Alya will accompany you back to your tent, and I will send word to you as soon as Yahweh speaks.'

I motioned to Alya and, when she came near, whispered to her, 'Stay with her until she is . . . recovered. Ensure her family have all they need. You and I will talk more on your return.'

Alya led Rahab from my tent, followed by Eleazar, Joel and Caleb. No one spoke, except to bid each other farewell. I instructed Attai to leave me, and closed my tent flap.

The evening was drawing in. I didn't light the oil lamps. I sat alone in my tent as the dim fingers of darkness swallowed up the last vestiges of daylight. Slumped in my chair, I wept, sickened by the hideous evil that the beast had wrought in this land, and the terrible desolation that one woman had endured because of it.

26

Purification

'Yahweh has decreed you are to do according to all that is in your heart.'

Rahab stood outside her tent, listening to me with a confused frown on her face. She jerked her head round to Alya, asking for her help in discerning my meaning. Alya smiled in response.

'Yahweh has found you worthy, Rahab.' Grasping the younger woman by the shoulders, she whispered, 'You are to become an Israelite, one of Yahweh's chosen people.'

Rahab gasped and covered her mouth with her hands, eyes wide open in disbelief. I couldn't help but smile at her childlike response. I had thought to ask Alya to relay the message, but was glad I was here to see Rahab's reaction; it delighted my heart to see expressions other than defiance or defensiveness adorn her face. Her smile was like the rays of the morning sun that shone, even as we talked.

I waited while they embraced before saying, 'Your time of purification starts today. Alya and Serah will attend you and explain what must be done.' I coughed, clearing the phlegm that seemed to have emerged out of nowhere. 'When your purification is complete, we will move your tent inside the camp. You will be under my protection and you will dwell with my family.'

Alya looked at me, clearly surprised. I realised that, although I had been thinking on it for a long time, I had forgotten to speak to her and Joel about it.

'Uh – that is, of course, if you should wish to do so, and if Joel gives his blessing. Yes. Since you were not born into one of our tribes, you may choose where you dwell ... but, if you would like to, you may ... uh ... dwell among us.' I could feel a familiar heat flushing up my neck and into my face. At times like this I despised

145

my own weakness. Why must this awkwardness always assail me when I dealt with women? It was a curse. 'I will not see you or speak with you while you are in your time of purification but, if there is anything you need, please ask Alya or Serah.'

I wheeled around with military precision and marched off. Stopping in my tracks, I turning to gaze upon this unfathomable woman who I had despised with such fervour.

'The Lord bless you,' I said. 'May His footsteps be your pathway, and may you be blessed with an abundance of peace.'

'Amen,' Alya said.

'Thank you, my lord Joshua,' Rahab said, an unfamiliar vulnerability gracing her face.

I nodded and continued my walk but, as I reached the edge of the camp, before I disappeared around the corner of an outlying tent, I paused to look back. It would be some weeks before I would see Rahab again. An inexplicable sense of loss filled me at the thought. I gazed upon her willowy form, soaking in the sight of her luxurious hair and pomegranate-red robe before turning to make my way home.

That evening, I plied Alya for information about the first day of Rahab's purification. My greatest concern was her reaction to having her head shaved. How could a woman as beautiful as she endure having her beauty cut away like that? I held a whispered conversation with Alya during our evening meal.

'Did it cause her distress when you . . . when her hair was shorn?' I enquired, concentrating hard on the piece of fruit I was peeling.

'No.' Alya paused, also looking down at her dish. 'She shed no tears and didn't even flinch when the blade met her scalp. In truth,' she said, sounding bemused, 'she seemed to welcome it. It was as if each lock that fell was a cleansing to her soul. Her countenance was one of peace.' She glanced at me. 'I did not expect that.'

'No.' I didn't say it, but that was the last thing I had expected, although I was glad that she had borne it so well. 'And her clothing?' I asked. 'Was she loath to part with her robes and headdresses? Her jewellery?'

'Again, no,' Alya frowned. 'She has the prettiest clothes I have ever seen. Silken fibres, the colours so vibrant, and her veils and headdresses . . . oh!' Alya put her hand to the base of her throat. 'So beautiful! And yet she spoke not one word of protest or regret when we took them away. In truth, she had them all folded, ready to be taken.'

'Mmm?' Rahab might not miss those robes, but I would. Especially the pale-green one that she had worn that day by the stream. 'Well, that is good news,' I said, putting a cheerful smile on my face. 'It is a good start to her month of purification, *nu?*'

Alya spent much of her time with Rahab over the next few weeks, updating me regularly on her progress. She spoke to me of Rahab's fervour, of her newfound love of prayer, how she repeated the prayers after Alya with due diligence, and her insatiable appetite for stories about our ancestors and their encounters with Yahweh. Apparently, Rahab could hardly wait to start her lessons with the priests in order to learn about the laws of Moses and the commandments.

The days crawled by. I never knew time could pass so slowly. It was not like I had nothing to do – far from it. Each day was filled with planning and mapping and plotting, as well as several missions to conquer some nearby settlements. But underneath all the activity that took place, there was a steady pulse that beat in my heart and mind.

Rahab. Rahab. Rahab.

I berated myself for thinking so much on one woman – after all, she was just a pagan prostitute and not worthy of my thoughts.

Wait!

It dawned on me: when I saw her next, Rahab would no longer be a pagan prostitute. She would be a woman of Israel; consecrated, sanctified and set apart for Yahweh. I could not reconcile that thought in my head, it was too bizarre.

Rahab, a woman of Israel?

The day finally came when her purification was complete. The atonement sacrifices had been offered, all the purification rites were fulfilled, and it was time to bring her tent and all her belongings into the camp of Israel. She had chosen to come and live with my family, close to Alya, much to my secret delight and Alya's evident joy!

Attai and I walked to the west side of the camp, where her family's tents were pitched. My stomach was in a tight knot; I felt like a nervous youngster. As much as I chastised myself for being so foolish, I couldn't shift the heightened sense of expectation which increased as we neared the site. I could feel my heart beating with such intensity, I feared Attai would hear it as he guided the oxen that pulled the empty cart. We rounded the corner. Salmah and Uri were already there, dismantling Rahab's tent, while Serah helped pack Rahab's belongings into bundles. We greeted each other and exchanged brief pleasantries.

Then I saw her.

She turned to look at me. The woman who I saw before me now was unadorned and unpainted. She wore a simple robe with no jewellery of any kind, and the beginnings of her new hair growth were swathed under a modest scarf. Her attitude was one of humility and contentment; I sensed no fear or defiance.

She was as beautiful as she had ever been – in fact, more so, to my eyes. Whereas before, her beauty had been enhanced by accessories and paints, it now flowed from a sense of peace and serenity which highlighted her flawless skin, the exquisite contours of her form, and the deep pools of her eyes.

She was perfection in all its natural comeliness.

Rahab rose gracefully to her feet and stood before me, blushing as she looked up at me.

'*Shalom*, my lord Joshua.'

27

Persecution

Having her nearby, being able to see her every day and share meals with her, was an absolute joy, not only to me, but to all our family. Rahab settled very quickly into our Jewish way of life, taking great pleasure in the things which we took for granted. Routines that had been part of our day-to-day life since birth, such as our morning blessings, prayers before mealtimes, even our manner of greeting each other, were a source of delight to Rahab.

'*Shalom*, my lord Joshua,' she would say, her eyes lighting up with pride when I responded in like manner.

I began to see our people and our traditions with fresh eyes, and I wasn't alone in that. Rahab quickly became an intricate part of our family life. Her tent was pitched next to Joel and Alya's but, whereas before she had spent most of her time hiding away, she now revelled in being part of a large, nurturing family.

Alya told me a little about Rahab's relationship with her own family. Apparently, although her parents understood why she had chosen the path of prostitution and were grateful for the funds that Rahab had been able to provide, a sense of guilt had soured their relationship over the years. Her father lived with the shame of not having been able to provide for them, for being the cause of Rahab's harlotry, and Rahab's siblings did not understand or appreciate the sacrifices she had made. Being among us, therefore, was a fresh start for her and, although she still visited her blood family regularly in their tents outside the camp, to my mind, she always looked relieved to be back 'home' with her Hebrew family on her return.

The children adored her and would rush to be the first to hug '*Doda* Rahab'[20] each morning, or when she returned from fetching

---

20. Hebrew word for auntie.

water or visiting. She had a natural rapport with them and loved nothing better than to cuddle the youngsters in her lap or listen to their stories. It seemed to me that her relationship with our little ones was redemptive. Many a time when she held them in a tight embrace, I would see tears sparkling in her eyes. I knew she thought of her lost sister, Ayna.

Evening meals had always been a special time for our family, but Rahab joining us had brought a fresh vibrancy in our breaking bread together, especially our storytelling times. Rahab seemed to have a never-ending supply of questions about our Jewish history; she devoured stories like tasty morsels, gobbling them up with gusto. As head of our family, Joel was our principal storyteller. Like his grandfather, Jesher, he had a particular talent for doing different voices, and used gestures to full effect, acting out the stories for the little ones . . . and for Rahab.

I had always enjoyed watching Joel when he told stories but, these days, I found greater pleasure in watching the expressions of wonder and astonishment on Rahab's face as she listened. She always had at least one child in her lap and, although we pretended that the stories were told for the little ones, we all knew without a doubt who Joel's most enthusiastic listener was.

Sometimes, Joel would play his reed pipe – a skill he had been blessed with since his youth – and we would dance and sing. The youngsters joined in, some of them playing pipes and drums, or shaking percussion instruments. Rahab held hands with the little ones, dancing in a circle or clapping her hands in delight at their antics. The evidence that she had pulled the dagger of torment out of her heart was right there in front of us; she blossomed more and more with each day that passed.

However, it seemed that not everyone was as pleased as we were at the miracle of Rahab's conversion and our decision to welcome her into our family.

'Where is Rahab?' I asked one evening as we sat down to break bread together. Rahab always sat next to Alya but, tonight, her place was empty. 'Is she unwell?'

Alya gave me one of her looks – the one where she was trying to decide how much information to divulge.

'Alya?' I said, locking eyes with her. 'Tell me. Why does she not join us around the mat?' Something was wrong, I knew it. My heart started thumping. What would cause Rahab to stay away? She loved our family times and looked forward to them with great anticipation. So why was she not with us? My mind started skimming through a list of possible reasons. Our women withdrew and ate in their tents during the time of their monthly outflowing, but that could not be it. It was not Rahab's time, not so soon – her time of cleansing had ended just a few days ago.

I flushed, embarrassed and irritated at myself for knowing the times of an unmarried woman's cycle. It was not seemly. I cringed, admitting to myself that there wasn't much about Rahab's daily life that I *didn't* know. It was true that nothing was private among tent dwellers; tent walls made very poor guardians of privacy. That aside, I would not be comfortable with anyone knowing that I was aware of Rahab's womanly cycle.

'Alya, tell me!' I demanded. 'Is she unwell?'

'Yoshi, please, keep your voice down,' she replied, a familiar zeal flashing in her eyes, quickly replaced by a convincing smile. 'Let us talk after we have broken bread, and I will explain to you what happened.'

'What do you mean, what happened? What *has* happ . . .'

'*After* we have broken bread, Yoshi, *nu*?' Alya said, giving me the same stare that she gave her grandchildren when they became unruly. It never failed to produce the desired result with them.

It did with me, too.

I blanched and glared at her. 'Very well,' I snapped, huffing to myself. There were not many members of our family who had the courage or audacity to challenge me, but Alya was very hard to resist. It would be pointless to persist, or risk making a scene.

I hardly spoke at all during our evening meal. My mind was a whirl of worry. I must have eaten, but I couldn't tell you what, or how much. The meal seemed to drag on and on and, when the children began asking Joel to tell them a story, I could bear it no longer.

'Come!' I whispered to Alya.

Realising she would not be able to delay the inevitable any longer, she rose to her feet, whispered something to Joel, and followed me to my tent. I didn't even wait for her to close the tent flap.

'Tell me,' I demanded. 'What has happened?'

Alya walked over to one side and sat down on the bench, while I stood, arms crossed, in front of her. 'Sit, Yoshi,' she said, tapping the bench. 'I cannot concentrate when you are looming over me like that.'

I grunted but complied. Anything to hasten her response. 'So?'

'Rahab is not unwell as such, but . . .'

'Then why did . . .' There it was. The look. I lifted my hands in acquiescence.

'She had an . . . encounter . . . with some women on her way to the stream this morning, whi . . .'

'Encounter? What kind of encounter?'

'If you will just keep silent, I will tell you,' Alya snapped. I frowned at her, but obeyed. She was hard to oppose at the best of times, even more so when she was in one of her 'determined' moods. 'A group of women accosted Rahab this morning when she went to the stream to get water.'

I opened my mouth to speak but, seeing Alya's warning expression, closed it with a snap.

'I asked her who they were, but she refused to name her assailants,' Alya told me. 'She does not want to cause any more trouble fo . . .'

'Assailants?' I barked. 'How many were there?'

'It seems there were a few, but, as I said, she will not give me any details.'

'She must name them! They will be dealt with. I must see her! I must speak to her. Now!'

Alya sighed. 'Yes, I think you're right. Clearly, I will have no peace until you do.' I bristled, but rose to my feet and made to leave. Alya stood. 'Come with me.'

I waited outside Rahab's tent while Alya went in to tell her that I wanted to see her. I heard muted voices and muttered words, then the tent flap opened and Alya came out. 'Yoshi, you must prepare yourself,' she said, peering at me to ensure I understood her meaning. 'Rahab is very shaken by what happened. She is not herself.'

28

A Woman in Israel

She was hunched over in the far corner of her tent, knees pulled up to her chest, her back to me. A dish of food lay on the floor near her, untouched. Her scarf was pulled low over her face. She didn't turn to face me when I entered.

'Rahab?' I stood just inside the entrance.

'My lord Joshua.' Her voice was dull, lifeless.

'Rahab, Alya told me what happened to you. I cannot tell you how this grieves me. Please, tell me what happened. Tell me what I can do to ease your suffering.'

'There is nothing to be done,' she snapped.

'Nothing to...? No! I must do something. Let me help you, please.'

'You cannot help me. No one can. I have decided to leave.'

'Leave?' I blurted, stepping towards her. 'And go where?'

'To live with my family outside the camp.'

'No! You cannot leave.'

'*I must!*' she shouted. 'I cannot stay here. I do not belong here,' she cried, jerking round to face me. I gasped when I saw the angry welt that lined her cheek. The purple discoloration of bruising was already forming around the wound, and her eyes were red and swollen.

'Who did this to you?'

She winced and closed her eyes. 'The women.'

'Which women?'

'I cannot say.'

I glanced at Alya, who shrugged and shook her head.

Rahab gave a cynical laugh. 'You would think such injury would be caused by men, yes? No. It was women who did this to me.' Her voice dripped with bitterness. 'I know how to withstand the reproaches of men. The sly looks they give me, the lustful glances,

153

muttered suggestions.' She looked up at me. 'I have endured their lecherous groping my whole life. I know how to deal with them, even here, in your camp.' She flashed me an accusatory glance. 'But *women*? Never have I endured such hatred from my own kind.'

'But . . .' my mind was whirling in confusion. 'But why did they do this to you? Did you give them cause them to attack you?'

'Did I give them . . . ?' Rage burned in her eyes. 'You assume this was *my* fault?'

For a moment, I thought about asking her to lower her voice, but decided against it. It would only antagonise her more and, besides, what was the point? The whole family could probably hear our exchange. If they weren't already aware of what had happened, they soon would be.

'I did *nothing*!' she raged on. 'I said nothing, I did nothing. I was walking to the stream to draw water, I greeted them, and they set upon me.' My thoughts went back to the day I met Rahab by the stream, and the reason she gave me for drawing water in the heat of the day. Why had I not insisted back then that she be accompanied when she went to draw water?

'I hoped that once I had gone through my purification and turned my back on the gods of Jericho, my days of recrimination would be over. But it seems that is not so.'

'How did . . . ?' I mumbled, pointing to the angry gash on Rahab's cheek.

'Rocks. This is not the only wound they inflicted on me,' she said, wincing as she touched her thigh. She pulled her robe tighter around her body. 'They said . . . they said I have brought disgrace upon you, that my being causes dishonour to you, to your family, and to your whole tribe. They accused me of trying to entice their husbands to sin. They called me . . . no,' she said, shaking her head. 'I will not tell you what they called me. I am sure you can imagine that for yourself.' She glared at me. 'You probably called me the same names when we first met. Perhaps you still do, when you talk of me to other men.'

'Rahab!' Her tone was so bitter. Toxic. So full of hatred. 'I speak of you only with honour, for your courage and your determination to learn of Yahweh and His ways. You must believe me!' I urged her, reaching out to grasp her arm.

154

She flinched, wrapping her arms around her torso. Alya put a gentle hand on my shoulder. I drew back.

'I was foolish to think that I could do this,' Rahab mumbled. 'I should have known I would never be accepted. They hate me. I can never be one of them.' The torrent of Rahab's rage was abating, replaced by a veneer of raw pain.

I knelt down in front of her and held her gaze.

'Rahab, these women, their words, their accusations, are false. They are wicked, untrue words, poison dripping from the mouths of stiff-necked women who are ignorant of the truth. Their hearts feed on violence. They have nothing better to do than to persecute those who they know nothing of. Their thoughts are *not* my thoughts, or the thoughts of my family – *your* family.'

Rahab stared at me, her green eyes pools of naked vulnerability. I knew she wanted to believe me, but her pain hindered her from letting down her guard. She shook her head.

'No. I was stupid to think that I could be one of your people. Me,' she scoffed, 'a Canaanite harlot.'

'Rahab,' Alya interrupted, 'you are a harlot no longer. That is in the past. You are a woman of Israel now, purified and sanctified. Yahweh Himself has welcomed you, deemed you worthy, and if the Lord God of Israel declares you to be one with us, then that is who you are.'

'Rahab,' I said, jumping on the back of Alya's speech. 'You will not leave.' Looking deep into her eyes, I said, 'You will stay here, with us, your Hebrew family. Stay in your tent until you are healed, if that is your wish. We will tend to you and protect you, and when you are ready to go back to the stream to draw water, Alya and I will accompany you. We will walk through the camp together on that day, and those malcontented women will see that Rahab the Israelite is beloved and accepted among the brethren. And from now on, one of our women will go with you when you draw water, or visit your family.'

Alya voiced her agreement, reaching out to draw her into an embrace.

I wasn't finished.

'I understand why you have no wish to tell me who these women are, and I will respect you in this. But I swear to you, if I find out who they are, I will deal with them. They will face my wrath and be brought to justice. They will pay for what they have done to you.'

A look of wonder crossed Rahab's face. She seemed stunned by my words, the anger on my face.

It was no idle threat.

On that note, I said farewell and left Rahab to rest. My sleep was fitful and, as soon as I rose, I sent for Attai and asked him to convene a meeting with the elders in my tent. I asked Alya to stay close by, outside for propriety's sake, but close enough to hear my words. I wanted her to be a witness, so she could relay to Rahab what happened.

The elders gathered, possibly expecting an update on our latest strategy or conquest. The shocked confusion on their faces when I started talking about what had happened to Rahab would have been comical, had I not still been seething with anger. After sharing with them the details of what took place the previous day, and the extent of Rahab's wounds, I asked if any of them had heard about the incident, or knew of any malcontent towards Rahab. A few of them looked at their feet, with sheepish expressions.

'Jerodim? Speak!' I said to one of them.

'Ah, well, I have heard of . . . some . . . discontent,' he said, choosing his words carefully, 'among a few of our women regarding the harlot.'

I twitched at his use of the word 'harlot'. 'Do you know who these women are who attacked Rahab?'

'No, no. What I heard was merely . . . idle gossip, harmless talk, as women are prone to do, *nu*?' he said with a nervous titter.

I glared at him. 'What happened to Rahab was not just idle gossip, nor was it harmless. Her wounds bear testimony to that.' Looking around the group of men, I knew I could question quite a few of them and find out more details, but I held back. Some inner sense told me not to. I wanted to respect Rahab's wishes and, although I longed to interrogate these men and find out more, I knew she wouldn't have wanted that.

So, I took a deep breath in, steeled myself, and stood up.

'Most of you know that Rahab saved the lives of Beerah and Salmah, through her own quick thinking and courage, and at great risk to herself. What you may not know, however, is that she also shared information with us regarding the cities and kingdoms surrounding Jericho – cities which we are currently engaging in warfare. What she shared with us has been invaluable in our battle planning, and has doubtless saved the lives of hundreds of our warriors.'

Shock was on the faces of every elder in the tent, bar those like Joel and Caleb, who had been privy to this information.

'Jerodim,' I said, swinging round to face him. 'Rahab is no longer a harlot, and she is not to be named as such. She has been purified and sanctified before Yahweh, who has deemed her worthy to be called a woman of Israel. She is to be held in high esteem for her deeds of bravery. Is that understood?'

Jerodim nodded and mumbled his agreement, obviously embarrassed at being singled out. I turned to look at each one of the elders in turn as I continued my rhetoric.

'Many foreigners live among us. Some have been with us since we left Egypt, and have been allowed to live in peace with our people. But of all of them, not *one* has turned from their own traditions and cleaved to our God like Rahab has. She is the only foreigner I know of who has forsaken her home, her friends, her gods, and even her family, to become a woman of Israel. For this she deserves to be treated with respect, not maligned and attacked.'

Mutters filled the tent, accompanied by some nodding of heads.

'Husbands are to instruct their wives and daughters in this matter and, from this day forth, if any woman is found maligning Rahab, her husband or father will be held accountable.'

Gasps of shock echoed around the tent.

I had their attention. Now for the final word.

'I do not know who Rahab's attackers are, because she will not tell me. She has no desire to bring retribution on her accusers.' Some of the elders were clearly surprised by this. I didn't give them time to comment or respond. 'But hear me now. If anything like this should happen again, I will root them out and deal with them. Rahab is under my personal protection and, as such, anyone who wishes to bring a reproach against her will do so first to me, and anyone who raises a hand against her will have me to answer to. *Is that understood?*' I thundered, my chest heaving.

Normally, when my meetings with the elders concluded, I would stay in my tent as they left, to deal with any queries raised by those who stayed behind. Today, however, as soon as I had finished my speech, I swept out of my tent.

Nodding first at Attai, who stood as watchman at the tent entrance, I walked towards Alya, who stood nearby, as instructed. We shared a look of mutual gratification, then she smiled at me and walked towards Rahab's tent to tell her the news.

29

Deception

'They have deceived us!' Caleb shouted, bursting into my tent.

'Who has deceived us?' I asked, looking around to see if any of the elders who sat with me understood his meaning. They looked just as confused.

'The travellers!' Caleb panted; his face reddened with anger. 'The ones who told us they came from a far-off land.' He looked around the room, pointing at the men gathered round. 'The ones *you* made a peace treaty with!'

'Caleb, be still.' I held up my palm and spoke with a firm voice. 'Come. Sit with us and explain your meaning.' He didn't want to sit down. Indeed, it looked like he was angling for a fight, such was his passion. However, after a moment's hesitation he joined our circle, still glowering at the confused, somewhat offended group of men.

'What do you speak of?' I asked him.

My heart sank as Caleb explained the meaning of his outburst. His anger was related to an incident that had happened just a few days before, when a dishevelled, motley group of men arrived at our camp at Gilgal, requesting an audience with me. Their clothes were worn and dirty and their wineskins patched (indeed, one of their skins seemed to have a slow leak, as it dripped throughout the duration of our meeting).

In the course of our conversation, they revealed that they were envoys from a distant city who had travelled a long time to meet with us. They had heard of the God of Israel, what He had done in Egypt, and they knew of the defeat of King Og, the giant. They had come to ask us to covenant with them.

In truth, their arrival threw us into a state of disarray. The tattered state of their personage and belongings gave credence to their claim of having travelled a long way, and their bread was so mouldy, it was inedible. We erected tents for them outside the camp, gave them food and water, and left them to rest while we met to discuss their request.

'The Law of Moses is clear on this subject,' Yaron, one of the elders, expounded. 'We are to totally destroy the people of the cities which Yahweh has given us as an inheritance, lest they teach us all their abominations, and we sin against the Lord God.'[21]

Mutters of 'Amen, amen' sounded around the enclosure.

'*But* to the cities that are far off,' he continued, 'the law says we are to make an offer of peace.'[22]

We discussed the interpretation of the law and its exact meaning in the context of the situation we found ourselves in. By the time evening came, the elders were of the opinion that we should follow the Mosaic laws, and covenant with the travellers.

'These people display great regard for Yahweh and the mighty works He has done,' one of the elders muttered to me at the end of the meeting, impressed by the devotion they had shown in travelling so far to covenant with Yahweh's people.

'After all, they can pose no threat to our great nation, can they?' commented another with a scornful laugh.

So, it was done. The terms of the covenant were agreed, sealed by a covenant meal, and a day or so later the travellers left, supplied with fresh food, water and clothing for their long journey home.

Or so we thought.

Our network of spies had just returned, reporting that they had encountered the travellers along the way, and that they had not journeyed from far. They were, in fact, our neighbours: Canaanites from the cities of Gibeon, Chephirah, Beeroth and Kirjath Jearim. Caleb was right; we had been deceived.

Pandemonium broke out as the elders argued among themselves. Some defended their decision to covenant with the travellers, others chose that moment to make pompous declarations about the fact that they had been suspicions about the identity of the travellers all along, but had not wanted to voice their misgivings for fear of appearing obstreperous.

Our error was blindingly obvious to me: we had not enquired of the Lord about whether to covenant with the travellers. We felt

---

21. Deuteronomy 20:16-18, paraphrased.
22. Deuteronomy 20:10,15, paraphrased.

sure that our interpretation of His laws was sufficient to justify our decision. What foolishness! Again! Why did I insist on following my own ways, instead of turning to Yahweh for His direction?

I slumped forward and groaned, putting my head in my hands. Running through my mind was a brief conversation I had had with Rahab a few days before, after the travellers had been settled in their tents on the camp outskirts, near her family. She told me they looked familiar to her; she felt sure she had seen some of them before. However, she couldn't give me any clear details or reasons for her reservations. When I pressed her about it, she seemed somewhat embarrassed about the fact that she had brought the subject up at all, so I dismissed her reservations with a quick word of thanks.

'Why did I not listen to you, woman?' I mumbled.

Rahab must have seen these men, or men like them, in Jericho. I wondered if she had even entertained some of them, but brushed that thought aside as soon as it entered my head. I could not walk that path now.

The fact remained: we had been tricked.

These Hivites from Gibeon were now under the protection of the nation of Israel and there was nothing we could do about it. The covenant had been sealed and, despite their deception, we could not go back on our word. While many heated discussions took place, I sought Yahweh's face. He decreed that the Gibeonites' lives be spared, but that they should be made woodcutters and water carriers, servants to our people for the rest of their days.

Regardless of their sentence, the Gibeonite's deception was successful.

They would be the only people group to be spared from the cleansing that would storm through the land like wildfire.

30

Transformation

She sat, hunched over by the firepit, staring pensively at a cauldron, a stirring stick lying idle in her hands.

'*Shalom*, Rahab.' She jumped. 'Are you well?' I enquired.

'Yes, my lord Joshua, very well.' Seeing that I waited on her response, she explained. 'I was thinking on my lesson with the priest.' One of Rahab's great joys was her daily lesson with the priests, where she learned about the history of our people and received instruction in Yahweh's laws. One of our women always accompanied her, and they learned early on to expect a deluge of questions on the walk home about whatever topic had been covered in that day's lesson!

'He read to me the laws of Moses regarding the treatment of strangers who live among Yahweh's people.'

'Ah yes,' I replied, quoting a passage which I had pondered on myself, in recent weeks. '"You shall neither mistreat a stranger nor oppress him, for you were strangers in the land of Egypt."[23] Yahweh's laws regarding the stranger reveal His kindness, *nu*?'

'Assuredly.' Her brow furrowed. She hesitated, then squinted up at me as I towered over her, and asked, 'What was it like? In Egypt, when you were slaves.'

Wooah! I hadn't expected that. I thought back to our years of captivity. How could I explain to her what life had been like back then? I sat down and watched her as I talked, so I could tell if what I was sharing was becoming too much for her.

'It was brutal. Our Egyptian taskmasters were without mercy. We were put to work in the fields or quarries, some of us in the houses of wealthy Egyptians, from a young age. As soon as our children were strong enough, they were made to gather straw for

---

23.   Exodus 22:21.

the brickmakers, or harvest crops. Many of them died without seeing ten winters. Food was scarce; only the strong survived.'

Studying Rahab's face, I saw only compassion, so I continued. 'Whippings and beatings were a daily occurrence; death was our constant companion. We learned to live one day at a time, to relish each moment we had together. We never knew when it would be our last. The stories of our ancestors fed our souls – we clung to the promises Yahweh had given to them about our own homeland, our land of promise. For many of us, the hardships we endured made us stronger, more resilient. For others, it broke them almost beyond repair.' I glanced up at her. 'Joel was one such man.'

'Joel? Alya's Joel? Surely not?'

I went on to tell Rahab some of Joel's story, of the trauma he endured in Egypt, and the difficulty he had experienced, learning how to be free once we were delivered from Egypt.

'Joel was physically strong and able to work. He stayed out of trouble, did everything he could to avoid being beaten. His friend, Jacob, was not so blessed. He grew weak from sickness and toil. One day he fell behind with his quota. His taskmasters flayed him. Jacob died of his wounds, in Joel's arms. Joel was just a young man when it happened.'

Rahab gasped; her eyes filled with tears.

'Forgive me, I will say no more,' I muttered. 'I do not wish to cause you distress.'

'No!' she cried. 'Please, I must know what happened.' I searched her eyes and saw anguish, but it was coupled with resilience. Rahab was no stranger to hardship or death.

'Joel's pain was strangling him. Even when we escaped Egypt and found freedom, he could not fully live. He barely slept because of the demons that hunted him in his dreams every night. He was angry, sullen, locked up. But, one day, everything that had been locked away in his heart burst out.' I grimaced. 'It was ugly.'

I stared up at the sky, thinking back to that day.

'Yahweh used me to break Joel free from the pain that had shackled him his whole life. I have often wondered, why me? Perhaps because I also had a childhood friend who was murdered by the Egyptians, so I understood his pain. But whereas Joel retreated when his friend died, I hit out.' I glanced at Rahab with a wry smile. 'I walked a path of violence in my youth.'

'You? A man of wrath?'

'Yes. I was not a man of good character, but Yahweh redeemed me. In His compassion He brought me out of my dark place and, perhaps because of the pain I had endured, I was able to help Joel, years later.'

'Truly, Yahweh is kind and compassionate.' Rahab spoke with such sincerity. A lump came to my throat. How had such an astonishing transformation taken place in this woman in such a short space of time? I looked down, fiddling with the callouses on my hand, before continuing.

'Up until that time, I hadn't really known Joel – none of us really knew him, even his own parents. We had lived with him, but we couldn't reach him; he was held captive inside his own mind. But, after that day, he awakened, as if from slumber. I have witnessed many miracles over the years of our sojourning: water flowing from a rock, manna from heaven, bitter water made sweet, but Joel . . .'

I gazed at Rahab, 'he was the greatest miracle of all. To see a life made new, transformed before your very eyes . . .' I shook my head. 'Now, *that* is a miracle.'

Rahab sat, knees drawn up, her chin resting on her hands, immersed in my words. 'What I would have given to see that,' she whispered.

'You will see miracles,' I told her. 'Yahweh's arm is not short. You are one of His people now, and you will see Him perform many miracles before you go the way of all the earth.'

She smiled; her eyes sparkled in response. 'When I look at Joel, I cannot believe he endured such hardship. He is so wise and calm and loving and joyful. There is no sign of the pain and adversity he faced.'

'Assuredly. What you see now is but the overflow of a deep well which he dug over many years. He draws much of his strength from Alya – their love, too, had to endure much.'

Rahab sat up, excited. 'Oh? Tell me of . . .'

'No, no! Not now! That is a story for another day, *nu*?' I stood to my feet, laughing at the disappointment on her face and her pouting lips. 'I have a meeting to attend, but I will see you later, yes?'

'You will tell me later about Joel and Alya?'

'If there is time, yes,' I chuckled. '*Shalom*, Rahab.'

'*Shalom*, my lord Joshua.' She turned back to her cauldron, stirring it absent-mindedly.

'Now there is another miracle taking place before our very eyes,' I thought to myself as I glanced back at her.

31

Blood Money

The sky was clear and cloudless. Sunshine spilled down on us, wooing us, inviting us to partake of its delights, wrapping us in a warm blanket of contentment. The joyful trill of desert sparrows heralded an invitation; summer was upon us and the land was blooming and bearing.

The olive groves near the ruins of Jericho were ripe and ready for harvest, as were the endless rows of grapevines which had ripened into fat, juicy orbs of deliciousness. A hawk wheeled lazily in the sky, its cry piercing the hustle and bustle that was part of the daily life of a sojourner, and a dry wind fanned the land, whipping at my cloak as I strode through the camp.

'The Lord has brought strong winds out of his treasuries to blow upon us today, *nu?*' I said to Attai, who murmured his agreement, clinging onto his headscarf. Because he was a lot shorter than me, he sometimes struggled to keep pace, especially when I failed to measure my stride to his. It resulted in him having to do a sort of skip every now and then to keep up with me. Although I would never have told him so, I found it quite amusing.

The morning was nearly spent and the sun was reaching its peak. It was time to seek refuge and rest under the awnings of our tents. Our midday breaks tended to be longer in the summer months, a circumstance which I welcomed. It meant more time to fellowship with my family ... and with Rahab. The sense of contentment in my heart over the last while was like a comfortable, warming sheepskin rug on a cold winter's night. I had become so used to the sense of equanimity that had pervaded our family gatherings of late, and especially Rahab's new peaceful persona, that it surprised me on my return home to find her sitting alone outside her tent, staring disconsolate at the ground.

'Rahab? You are downcast. What ails you?'

She started at my voice and then flushed like a child caught in wrongdoing. 'Nothing,' she said. There was anger in her tone.

'If it causes your brow to furrow like that, then it cannot be nothing,' I said, sitting down on a log near her. 'I would like to think we are able to talk about issues that trouble us – yes?'

She nodded. Frowning in concentration, she said, 'I met with Yacov this morning for my instruction in the Law of Moses.'

'Ah, I see. There is something on which you are unclear. Tell me,' I urged her. 'I may be able to help bring understanding to your heart.'

She hesitated, studying me for a while. 'Yacov said Yahweh does not speak to women.'

'Ah. Mmm. I see.' I had expected a conversation about the laws regarding strangers, or perhaps the burned offerings for various sins. Not this. Questions about women were not my forte. 'And this troubles you?'

'Certainly! Should it *not* trouble me?' A fiery flash in her eyes reminded me of the old Rahab. I liked it. Although I welcomed the softer, more playful side of her nature which had emerged since her purification, I appreciated the chance to spar once more with the woman who had shown such spirit when I first met her.

'Why does it trouble you?'

'Because it is wrong!' she blurted. 'I thought Yahweh was different from the gods of Canaan.' Her eyes grew wide with passion as she accused me. 'You told me that He is kind and good, and I believed you. Now I am told that He talks with men, but will not speak to women. He is no better than the ignorant gods of my people!'

'Rahab! Give heed to what you say,' I cautioned her. 'Guard your mouth and find wisdom.' The fire in her eyes did not diminish, but she did remain silent, although I noticed her jaw clenching in response. 'The question of whether Yahweh talks to women is . . . a matter that cannot be spoken of lightly.' I scratched my beard, frowning. 'I used to be of the same mind as Yacov, but . . .'

'But . . . ?' She peered at me like an inquisitor.

'Now I am not so sure.'

'Why?'

I smiled. 'It is difficult to disbelieve something that you have witnessed with your own eyes.' Rahab's face lost its hard edge.

A look of longing graced her countenance as I told her about Yahweh's desire to speak with His people, to know them and to be known by them in return. She soaked up my words, savouring them like tasty morsels.

'You hear His voice, don't you? How does He speak to you?'

I stared at the ground. 'The first time I heard His voice was at Mount Sinai.'

She nodded in anticipation. 'And . . . ? What was it like?'

I drew in a long breath and exhaled through pursed lips. 'It was like the sound of a fast-flowing river, but melodious and rich, like dripping honey, but deep in tone . . .' I screwed up my face, sighing in frustration. 'There are no words that can truly describe it, but when He speaks, you are changed. His voice – His presence – changes you.'

'Yes?' Rahab leaned forward as if to pull the words out of me.

I closed my eyes, battling with the impossible task of describing the indescribable. 'I felt Yahweh's presence in the cloud which He sent to guide us through the wilderness.'

'That was true? I heard the stories, but I thought they couldn't be true!' Rahab exclaimed.

I smiled. 'They are. I only had to gaze upon it to be filled with warmth and peace. Sometimes, it was like a heat that spread through my body with such power, I could not help but tremble in response. It . . . it was like an unseen weight that enfolds you in its grip – not a grip that constrains,' I clarified, 'but a grip that enables and empowers. It is the hand of strength and power.' I flushed. 'My words must sound like foolishness to you,' I said, glancing at . Her eyes were wide with wonder and she shook her head.

'No. Please, tell me more.'

I gazed into the distance, remembering my inauguration. 'When He speaks, power floods your body, like sparks of life, a quickening deep within you. When I am in His presence, everything else falls away, ceases to exist. He is all in all.'

I glanced at Rahab. Tears had filled her eyes.

I told her about Yahweh's messengers, His shining men, sharing with her some of my experiences, including the story of how the shining men caused the earthquake that destroyed Jericho. I also told her about the shining men who stood guard around her home. My mind accused me for sharing such a precious story with a woman such as Rahab. My heart told me she would treasure it as I did.

My heart was right.

Her tears overflowed as she pondered my words. Yahweh had seen her, a pagan prostitute. He had sent His shining men to redeem her life. She was found worthy in His sight.

We sat in silence for a while.

'The more I learn about Him, the more I long to know Him. My heart yearns to hear Him speak. If Yahweh desires to speak to me and it is my desire to hear His voice, why then can it not be so?'

'I believe Alya would be best able to answer your question in more detail.'

'Alya?' Rahab's eyes were wide with expectation. She sat up, ready to bolt. 'I should talk to her?'

'Yes, but Rahab,' I held up a warning hand, 'do not talk to others about this matter, *nu*? Some of the mysteries of God are best pondered in our hearts, not talked about with people.'

Rahab nodded. 'There is something I would ask you,' she said, wiping her tears away.

'Hmm?'

She focused on the ground. 'When . . . when Ayna was . . . taken from us, my father was given a reward.' She shook her head; a flash of anger covered her face. 'Every chosen family was given a reward – as if any amount of coin could replace a child. It was called the "honour bounty". My father never spent it. He kept it in its cloth purse, hidden behind a loose stone in the wall of our house. He could not bring himself to spend it, even when our need was great. It was blood money.'

She stared into the distance at the remains of Jericho.

'He still has it.' Rahab shook herself out of her daze and looked at me. 'We would like to give it into the treasures of Yahweh's Tabernacle.'

'Truly?'

'Yes.' There was no hesitation in Rahab's tone. In fact, the familiar tone of defiance rang out in an unspoken challenge. 'I heard how the plunder from Ai was given into the treasury of the Lord. We would like to do the same. We are agreed. Will you accept it?'

I thought for a moment before responding. 'Yes. If you are sure. What form does the "honour bounty" take?'

'Pieces of silver.'

'How many?' I asked, wondering what price the men of Jericho would place upon the life of a child.

'Thirty.'

32

Cry for Help

'I knew they would bring trouble to our people. Did I not say it?' Caleb shouted. 'Their lips drip with the poison of deception. They enticed us with their flattering speech and yet, now they are ensnared, they call for us to come and save them!'

I let him rant for a while longer.

I had learned long ago that it was much easier, and more fruitful in the long run, to reason with Caleb only after he had released the force of his pent-up emotions. When the flow of his anger had lessened, I sat him down and we discussed the issue at hand.

It had only been a matter of months since the Gibeonites had deceived us into making a covenant with them and yet, that morning, a messenger had arrived asking us to rescue them from their adversaries. Apparently, word had reached the other Amorite kings of the covenant which the Gibeonites had made with the nation of Israel, and they were much displeased.

I sent for the elders and Eleazar and, once they had assembled, we gave the Gibeonite messenger an audience. He looked almost as dirty and dishevelled as the envoys had when they came to deceive us into forming a treaty, and wasted no time in telling us that the kings of the surrounding Amorite nations had banded together to attack Gibeon because of our alliance.

'Which kings are they, who have united to make war on your people?' I asked him.

'The five Amorite kings, my lord,' he replied. 'The kings of Jerusalem, Hebron, Jarmuth, Lachish and Eglon.' Our spies had furnished us with much information over the previous months so I knew that not only were these not small, insignificant nations, but that their armies too were sizeable.

'What was taking place when you left Gibeon?'

'Their armies had assembled and were preparing to launch an attack on our city.' I could tell by the volley of mutters which echoed around the tent that Caleb was not alone in his reluctance to rush to the aid of the Gibeonites. The messenger glanced around the room, then lifted his head and focused his attention back on me.

'My lord, Gibeon is a great city, and our men of war are mighty,' he said, wisely ignoring Caleb, who snorted in derision. 'But against five other nations with great armies, we will not prevail. Our request is simple: do not forsake your servants. We call upon you to honour the terms of our covenant and help us make war on these kings who have joined forces against us.'

Another smattering of scornful jibes filled the room.

'Why should we come to the aid of a people who deceived us?'

'Your troubles are of no concern to us.'

'Fraudsters, all of you!'

'Go back to your people and fight your own battles!'

The messenger kept his eyes locked on mine and seemed undeterred by the barrage of insults and threats. 'They were wise to have chosen you as their messenger,' I thought. I couldn't help but admire the man's courage and fortitude in the face of such hostility. He did not grovel or beg, but stood straight, spoke clearly, and displayed an air of honour and respect.

I liked it.

I liked him.

'What is your name?'

For a moment he looked bemused, probably wondering why his name was significant. 'Yaksu, my lord.'

'And are you a leader among your people, Yaksu?'

'I am not yet of an age to be a leader, my lord,' he replied, before adding, 'but I am a trusted messenger.'

'Mmm.' I stared at him. He didn't break eye contact. 'Yaksu, go with Attai,' I said, motioning to Attai, who had been standing by the entrance to the tent, listening to the discussion. 'He will give you food and water. Rest while we discuss this matter. I will call for you when we have come to a decision.'

'My lord,' Yaksu said, inclining his head. He followed Attai, but before they had even left the tent, a barrage of protestations erupted. I silenced them with a wave of my hand, told the elders that we would come before Yahweh to seek His face regarding the matter, and left for the Tabernacle to do just that.

I would not make the same mistake again.

Sometime later, we reconvened in my tent. 'It is of no consequence what our individual opinions are in this matter,' I said to the elders. 'Yahweh has spoken. We will come to the aid of the Gibeonites.' Looks of outrage filled the tent, along with muttered comments and mumbled objections.

I stood up, once again silencing them with my raised hand. 'Yahweh has spoken. That is enough. However, should you need more certainty in your hearts about this decision, then know this: this warfare is not merely in defence of the Gibeonites, or in response to our covenant with them. In taking us to war against the Amorites, the Lord God has delivered them into our hands; *not one man* of them shall stand before us. This warfare will be part of the cleansing of this land. We will rid this territory of the plague of idolatry that has cursed this land for generations – and we will do it in the name of the God of Israel.'

To say the elders cheered would have been an overstatement. There was no applause in response to my rousing speech. However, a sense of purpose and zeal filled that place; many a head nodded in agreement and most of the elders bowed in acknowledgement of the Lord's voice through His chosen servant.

Me.

I felt no fear as I stood before the elders. No doubt. I knew Yahweh's will. I knew His voice and, finally, it seemed as though I knew the mantle He had placed on me. I stood tall.

Assured.

It felt good.

I sent Attai to call Yaksu and, while we waited for him to arrive, Eleazar drew near. He peered at me through bushy grey eyebrows, and murmured, 'You sounded just like Moses.'

I could not speak. My heart was full.

There was no greater endorsement that he could have spoken over me. I moved to stand behind my chair with my back to the room, away from peering eyes and questioning voices, until Attai returned with Yaksu. I stood in front of him so as to look him in the eye. He had to raise his head to meet my gaze, but did so with a calm dignity.

'We will come to the rescue of your people. You will travel with us, staying by my side throughout the duration of the journey and, Yaksu, if we discover that your people have deceived us again, you will be the first to die by my hand. But if your words are true, we will fight side by side and conquer the enemies of your people.'

A look of relief crossed Yaksu's face, followed swiftly by a smile of acknowledgement and a nod of his head. 'My lord.'

Turning to Caleb, I said, 'Call the men to arms. We leave at first light tomorrow.' We would leave a fair size contingent to guard the camp, but the majority of our warriors would march with us to Gibeon. We would need all our forces to defeat such a mighty foe. The word of the Lord would stand.

That night, after breaking bread, I wandered away from the firepit and stood staring into the darkness in the direction of Jericho and Ai. A smattering of stars winked against the black canopy of night and the buzzing of cicadas filled the air. A hush lay over the camp; the hush of families whose men are about to go off to war, where words are superfluous, and eyes speak of the issues of the heart with greater clarity than words ever could.

A quiet voice disturbed my contemplation.

'Your thoughts dwell on Yoram?'

I turned to see Rahab watching me. Yes. I was thinking of Yoram. He was always at my side when we went to make war, but not this time. How did she know that?

I nodded.

She shivered, drew her cloak tighter around her shoulders, and came to stand beside me, a silent companion, sharing the agonies that beset me, knowing full well that nothing she could say would assuage them.

33

Stand Still

He stood before me, muscles rippling, sword in hand, his other arm outstretched to stop me from going any further. His face was stern. He meant business.

I held up a clenched fist; the troops behind me came to an abrupt halt, probably wondering why we had stopped. They couldn't see the magnificent shining man who stood before me, blocking the way. I frowned, staring past him at our enemies, who were making good their escape. We had them on the run; why was he preventing us from pursuing them?

'Joshua, why have we stopped? They are getting away!' Caleb shouted, struggling to hold back the hordes of warriors that surged behind us, eager to continue the battle.

The need to explain myself was superseded by loud thuds and screams of terror. Numerous giant hailstones hurtled down from the heavens, slamming into the fleeing Canaanites, felling them with devastating accuracy. The shining man, seeing that I now understood the need to halt, sheathed his sword and stood like an ethereal statue, watching the gruesome display of power.

I had witnessed the stoning of a man many times; I knew well the cracking sound that a rock made when it collided with a man's skull, and the blood that spurted from his broken frame. I also knew what hailstones ricocheting off the skins of our tents in the winter months sounded like, as well as the tearing and ripping that often resulted. But I had never heard or seen the two together – until now.

It was horrifying, and yet I found I couldn't look away. A macabre fascination held me fixated on the mass execution.

Even Caleb, who was never short of words, stood next to me, stunned into silence.

Those who were not felled straight away scattered in every direction, colliding with each other, and attacking one another in their confusion. Within a short space of time, the hillsides sloping down from Beth Horon were strewn with the battered bodies of Canaanite warriors.

The rays of the afternoon sun made short work of melting the hailstones and soon, the crisp smell of melting ice mixed with the metallic odour of blood.

Our usual practice at the end of a battle was to finish off those who were mortally wounded, to give them as quick and merciful a death as possible. But as I looked out over the vast carpet of white and red, I realised there would be no need to end the lives of the wounded. This was Yahweh's battle and His alone; the outcome was irrefutable. He needed no help from men. He would finish this Himself.

Caleb turned to me. 'Shall I tell the men to rest?'

We had marched all night and taken the Canaanites by surprise that morning. My men had been fighting all day and were tired; it made sense to let them rest before facing the next battle, but something within me refused to stop. Yahweh's words had lit an unquenchable fire within my belly: 'I have delivered them into your hands; not a man of them shall stand before you.'[24]

'No.' Caleb's eyebrows lifted in surprise. I continued, 'We must continue to strike until our enemy is utterly destroyed from this land.'

He acknowledged my order and issued the command. We regrouped and marched back to Gibeon to confront the rest of the Canaanite armies. Our men fought courageously, spurred on by the knowledge that Yahweh Himself was fighting for us.

'With them is the arm of the flesh, but with us is the Lord God of the armies of Israel!' I roared, as we surged forward to meet them. 'Gird yourselves with strength, and let our enemies perish by our hands!'

Yaksu fought at my side, as agreed, along with Attai, who was also my shield bearer. I was impressed with Yaksu's swordsmanship as well as his fearlessness in battle. My admiration for this young Gibeonite messenger was growing.

Our tribal armies pursued our enemies as far as Azekah and Makkedah. The Lord God was true to His word: the Canaanites fell

---

24. Joshua 10:8.

before us in their thousands. Yet, as I looked across the landscape, the enemy's forces still swarmed over the land like a vast colony of ants. I had no doubt that we could defeat them, but it would take quite some time, and time was something we didn't have much more of. I shielded my eyes and squinted up at the sun. It was well on its downward journey; I estimated we had one, possibly two more hours of daylight.

That would not be enough.

My frustration grew. I slashed with my sword, cutting down all who stood in my path, all the while knowing that our valiant efforts would not be sufficient.

'We need more time,' I shouted to Caleb, wiping some blood from my cheek. Squinting up at the sun, I mumbled, 'Lord God, help us! We need more time to end this.'

A familiar tingling rose up my arms and down my back. I glanced to my right and saw the same shining man who had held us back from the hailstones. He stood, calm and majestic, in the midst of the blood-spattered chaos that raged all around him. Looking up at the heavens, he pointed to the sun, then stared back at me, a fiery challenge in his eyes.

I knew in an instant what I had to do.

My heart started thumping even faster. What madness was this?

I had to do it.

I had to obey.

Yaksu and Attai, noticing my demeanour, stopped fighting and came towards me, panting and dripping with sweat. 'Commander?' Attai said. 'What do you have need of?'

I didn't look at him or even acknowledge him, such was my focus. My chest heaved with passion. Staring upwards, I took a huge breath and roared with all my might, '*Suuuuuun!*'

The warriors within the sound of my voice froze; Canaanite and Israelite alike stared at me in shock.

'*Halt! Stand still!*' I roared, raising my sword high. '*Stand still!*'

They looked to the heavens, but seeing nothing out of the ordinary, continued fighting. The sound of metal clanging on metal resumed as if nothing had happened.

Had something happened, or had I just made an absolute fool of myself?

Time would tell.

Literally.

I turned to the shining man. He was gone. Fighting continued with renewed energy and it was only sometime later that I paused to look upwards and realised that the sun was still positioned where it had been when I commanded it to be still.

'It stands still, Commander,' Attai said, looking at me with something akin to fear. 'It has not moved since you commanded it thus.'

'Yahweh has heard my prayer,' I responded with great conviction, all the while thinking to myself, 'How is this possible? How can it be that the sun would obey a mere man such as I? How can Yahweh put such store in the words of a man?'

News spread and, within a short space of time, I could tell by the stunned expressions on their faces that most of the warriors under my command had heard what had happened. No one said anything to me directly, although I overheard Yaksu say to Attai, 'If the sun itself obeys your commander's order to halt, I'll not be stopping anytime soon.'

To my relief, none of them questioned me about it. How could I explain to them what was happening when I could hardly understand it myself?

A messenger brought word to me of the five Ammorite kings, who had apparently fled the battle and hidden themselves in a cave at Makkedah. I didn't have to think long before deciding what to do. They could wait. There was one thing my men and I needed now, and it was not a confrontation with five conquered kings. I gave the command to stop up the mouth of the cave with large stones and post guards by its entrance.

The battle continued, one relentless duel after another. Every time I turned around another Canaanite warrior met me, then another and another.

Time itself lost all meaning.

The sun stood still and my sword took on a life of its own until my hand cleaved to its hilt and my thoughts became a mindless fog. Eventually, the time came when I could see no aggressors challenging me, waiting to strike swords with mine.

We had done it!

We had obeyed the word of the Lord. The sun started to move again of its own accord and, before long, the evening drew nigh.

Not a single man of the Canaanites was left standing. Partnering with a debilitating exhaustion was a sense of elated jubilation: this territory had been cleansed! No longer would the depraved practices of these heathen nations hold the land to ransom. It was free! We had triumphed.

Two things stood out to me when that interminable battle against the Canaanites came to an end: the looks of awe and even fear on the faces of our warriors when they regarded me, and the complete and utter exhaustion that threatened to overcome me.

Eleazar caught up with me by the gates of Gibeon. He took me by the shoulders and said, 'There has never been a day like this, when the Lord heeded the voice of a man; for the Lord fought for Israel today.'

I didn't reply. I didn't have the words or the energy to do so. As darkness enveloped the camp and the time for sleep had at last arrived, I thanked Yahweh for His faithfulness. The last thing that flashed through my mind when my head touched my bedroll was the image of a beautiful woman wearing a pale-green robe, with flowing dark hair and mysterious green eyes.

34

Five Kings

They were not what I had expected.

The tales I had heard about these five kings told of their grandeur and magnificence, of the glory of their renowned cities and their much-heralded accomplishments. The men who stumbled out of the cave, shielding their eyes and blinking in the sunlight, looked nothing like that. They were dirty and bleary-eyed, and the rancid smell of urine and sweat hung about them.

They had been shut up in the cave for days while we finished the job of plundering their cities, laying waste to their seats of power. At first, when we rolled the stones away from the mouth of their cave, they looked relieved. However, when their eyes adjusted to the light and they realised that it was not their own people but a solid wall of Israelite warriors who stood facing them, their expressions turned from hope to fear. I stepped forward and looked each one of them in the eye in turn.

'I am Joshua, commander of the armies of Israel, and worshipper of the One True God. Name yourselves.' They shuffled their feet and exchanged uncertain looks, then one of them spoke.

'I am Adoni-Zedek, king of Jerusalem.' I inclined my head to him. He frowned and looked as though he was about to insult me. Probably thinking better of it, he glowered at me and dipped his head in response. The others followed suit.

'Hoham, king of Hebron.'

'Piram, king of Jarmuth.'

'Japhia, king of Lachish.'

'Debir, king of Eglon.'

Up until then they had stood, unshackled, in a dirty huddle, but on my command, five of my men stepped forward and bound their hands behind their backs, thrusting them down onto the ground.

Three out of the five kings tried to fight back, but my warriors were more than a match for each of them. They were clearly dehydrated; their saggy waterskins were empty, and their bodies tottered unsteadily. My natural instinct was to give them water, but I knew that would only delay the inevitable: these five kings were marked for death. Before they went to join their ancestors, however, there was something that needed to be done.

I called five of my captains of a thousand forward. Pushing to the back of my mind the thought that Yoram would have been among them, had he lived, I instructed them to place their feet on the necks of the kings. The kings protested on hearing my words, hurling insults at me. I ignored them. The five chosen captains hesitated, then one spoke on their behalf.

'Commander, forgive me, but this is not our portion. This honour is yours, as our victorious leader.'

I held his gaze for a while, then turned to face the mass of warriors gathered on the rocky terrain surrounding the cave. 'Our victory over these kings and their people came not by the hand of one man alone, but by many. This honour belongs to all who unsheathed their sword in the name of the God of Israel.'

Turning to look first at the five captains standing at the ready, then at those gathered around, I said, 'Each of my captains will place their foot upon the neck of a Canaanite king, for each of them has earned his place in the chronicles of war for his courage and valour.'

A stunned silence ensued. As the first five captains moved forward to lay their feet on the downtrodden necks of the fallen kings of Canaan, I spoke. 'I declare over you today the words that the Lord God Himself spoke over me: "Do not be afraid, nor be dismayed; be strong and of good courage, for thus the Lord will do to *all* your enemies against whom you fight."'[25]

A sense of awe swept through the place where we stood, as each captain in turn received an infilling of power, a sign of approval from the Lord God of Israel. All the captains of a thousand took their turn, placing their foot on the neck of one of the Canaanite kings, until only Caleb and I were left. Caleb gave me his trademark grin, and raised one eyebrow.

'Shall we?' he asked.

---

25. Joshua 10:25, my italics.

When it was done, the kings were dragged to their feet. They knew their time was up; not one of their faces bore even the slightest glimmer of hope. I drew my sword and walked up and down in front of them.

'You ran from the battlefield, believing your lives to be of more value than those of your people, fleeing into this cave like dogs rather than fighting and dying with honour alongside your warriors. This cave, which you thought would be your refuge, will become your tomb.'

Without hesitation, I plunged my sword through the heart of the king nearest me, Adoni-Zedek, followed swiftly by the others, until all five kings lay crumpled on the ground in a pool of their own blood.

It was done. The Battle of the Five Kings was finished.

The warriors lifted a mighty shout which echoed through the hills, spurred on by Caleb, who waved his sword high above his head. The bodies of the five kings would hang on trees until the daylight hours faded, when they would be sealed forever inside the mountainous tomb of their cowardice.

We would leave the next morning to return to Gilgal.

Gilgal. Home!

I couldn't wait!

The longing in my heart was great to see my family again ... and Rahab. I sat around the fire that night watching my men celebrate the great victory that had been wrought by their hands. They spoke of their conquests on the battlefield, of the conflicts they had faced and the wounds they had incurred. They revelled in the mighty hand of their God, who had showered hailstones on their enemies, and boasted in the vanquishing of the five mighty kings who had been slain.

I watched them with a sense of detached exhaustion, thinking only about how much Rahab's hair might have grown back during the time that I had been away.

35

Friendship with a Harlot

The days that followed the Battle of the Five Kings were restorative, steeped in rest and contemplation. Attai relayed a message to the elders that, following a short debrief, no more meetings about strategies or battles would take place for at least seven days; my men and I had earned that much. The only thing on our agenda now was time with our families and sleep – and I relished both!

I slept through most of our first day back, only surfacing to eat or drink before returning to my bedroll. The family understood my exhaustion and waited patiently until I was ready and able to talk about the battles we had faced, as well as the miracles we had seen Yahweh perform. On the second evening when we broke bread, the warriors among us shared some of what had happened, being careful not to include any graphic details while the children were still among us. Those would be discussed later when the men sat around the firepit.

The family were astounded when we shared about the hailstones, but when it came to the account of the sun standing still, I fell quiet. I found it difficult to talk about my own accomplishments, or moments when Yahweh moved through me in power. Joash and Naim shared the story from their perspectives, although neither of them were in my squadron, so they had not been present when I commanded the sun to stand still. A sense of awe rippled through the family when Davi shared the account of what had happened – or at least, what he had been told had happened.

'So . . . what did you do?' Joel stared at me, asking the question which was probably on the tip of everyone's tongue.

I glanced around the circle of expectant faces, hating being thrust into the spotlight. 'I said, "Sun, stand still."'

'Did you say it quietly, like that?'

I frowned. 'No. I shouted. It was ... an unction that rose up from my belly.' I cringed. That sounded so foolish. Why must he press me for details?

'And what happened?' Joel persisted.

'Nothing.'

'Nothing?' His eyebrows lifted.

'Yes.'

'So ... how did you know that Yahweh had heard your cry?'

'I didn't.'

Joel narrowed his eyes and stared at me, bemused. The rest of the family followed suit. Realising that they weren't going to move on until I had given them sufficient details, I quashed my awkwardness, stared into the firepit, and explained what had happened as succinctly as possible. It was only after I had finished, and conversation had moved on, that I glanced in Rahab's direction.

My heart stopped.

The look of fascination and – dare I say it – admiration on her face confounded me. Her eyes shone as she gazed at me, a baffled smile on her face. I looked away, focusing my attention on peeling a large orange, popping the segments into my mouth one by one. The following day, however, Rahab came to speak to me. It was our first private conversation since my return from battle.

It was Shabbat.

Rahab loved Shabbat; it was her favourite day of the week. She revelled in the opportunity to rest, talk to the family, ask questions and hear more stories, without the ever-present need to attend to chores.

'It is astonishing,' she told me as we sat under the shade of my tent awning in the heat of the day, snacking on nuts and grapes, 'that Yahweh would *command* His people to rest every seventh day! That He would deem it so important for us to rest and spend time together without labouring that He would make it law! I have heard many laws in my time, but never one like this. Never one that would give without requiring anything in return.'

Her face glowed with contentment. It warmed my heart to see her this way.

'Truly, Yahweh desires only good for His people,' I said with a smile.

'My lord Joshua,' she asked, staring at her sandalled feet, brushing the residue of dust off them. 'Why is it that a God like Yahweh, who is kind and compassionate even to one such as I, would require the killing of so many people in this land?'

I blanched. That was not a question with a straightforward answer and, even if I could answer it, I wasn't sure Rahab would understand. I wasn't sure I truly understood.

'That is not an easy question to answer, but I will try,' I responded, silently asking Yahweh to help me explain His inexplicable ways to this woman. I stared up at the sky and exhaled. 'Yahweh is the One True God, the Creator of all things. Besides Him, there is no other. He is a just God, a good God whose desire is to walk with His own special people – all who know Him and worship Him.'

Rahab nodded in agreement, tucking a strand of dark hair under her headscarf. Her hair had grown a lot more than I had expected during the time I was away. The glossy tendrils that I saw peeping out from Rahab's headscarf filled my heart with a bizarre sense of joy. I looked away before she noticed me staring at her.

'The people of this land worship the moon, the trees, fire, their own bodies, even making their own gods to worship, as you know. They worship the created when they should worship the Creator. Yahweh *made* the moon, the trees, fire, water . . . He made everything our eyes see, all that we touch.'

A gentle breeze swept through the camp, causing a small ringlet dangling on Rahab's forehead to dance in response. 'Even the wind that blows our hair, the stones and wood which they use to craft their idolatrous images, were created by Yahweh. He made them all, and yet they turn from Him and worship what He has made, instead of He who made them.'

Her brow furrowed in concentration.

'You have seen what the gods of man, such as Chemosh, require – their cruelty and depravity, their lust for mammon and even their demands for the life of a man, a child.'

Rahab flinched and wrapped her arms around her body. Much healing had taken place in her heart, but still, the memory of her little sister's death continued to haunt her.

'Rahab,' I said, turning to face her. 'This land is diseased. It . . . it travails because of the evil of the idol worshippers who dwell here, the innocent blood that is spilt without cause.' I couldn't think of a way to describe Alya's dream about the beast to Rahab in a manner which she would understand, so I decided not to tell her.

'Help me, Yahweh,' I prayed. 'How can I explain this to her?' I desperately wanted Rahab to understand Yahweh's goodness, to know the purity of His laws, and love His presence like I did.

'The worship of idols is like a canker. A plague of festering boils that spreads from person to person, unseen, often only recognised when it is too late to do anything about it. Like a boil, it must be cut out, or it will poison the whole body. I have seen it, Rahab. I have seen the darkness manifest in the eyes of my own people, good men who turned from walking the path of righteousness to embracing the evils of idolatry.'

'When did you see this?' she asked, biting her lip. 'What happened?'

I told Rahab of the rebellious uprising that occurred when some of our people turned to the gods of Egypt shortly after we had escaped slavery, how the dark evil could be seen in their eyes, and how it spread like an epidemic throughout our ranks. I also told her of the terrible price the idolators paid for their refusal to set aside their evil ways. So many had died, many by my own hand. It had happened more than forty years ago, but the pain of that day still lived on in my memory.

'I think I know of what you speak,' Rahab responded, realisation covering her face. She stared into the distance. 'I had a childhood friend called Cheness. We played together and, after Ayna was taken, Cheness knit her heart with mine. She understood my pain. We were bound in love throughout the years of our maidenhood, but when she was chosen to be a priestess, she changed. She went to live in the temple quarters with the other priestesses. My heart longed for her; I couldn't wait to see her again, but when I did see her some weeks later, I hardly recognised her. It was as if a darkness had overtaken her soul – like the darkness you spoke of. Her beauty was . . . tainted, the love between us lost. She talked only of the gods, of their favour, of the riches lavished upon her, and the men who sought her out.'

Rahab paused, leaning her chin in her hands. I saw in her eyes the same vulnerability that I had witnessed the day she told us about her sister's murder.

'Cheness was taken over by that darkness. I didn't know her any more. She was lost to me.' She gave a wry laugh. 'After Salmah and

Beerah gave me their pledge, I sought Cheness out. I begged her to turn away from the path of a priestess, to come and stay with me, and escape Jericho with me.' Rahab's eyes glistened with sadness. 'She laughed at me. I realised then that if you give just a little to the gods, in time they will take your very soul.'

I waited while she recovered her composure. Yahweh's words rang in my heart and mind, 'Neither will I be with you anymore, unless you destroy the accursed from among you.'

'Rahab, you speak the truth. Yahweh cannot dwell with sin – He is sinless, pure, perfect. There is no evil in Him, and that is His desire for His people: that we would walk a path of righteousness, living a life filled with joy and peace – like we do during Shabbat,' I said, smiling at her.

Rahab didn't smile back.

In fact, she shied away from me. Pulling her scarf further down over her face, she whispered, 'Why then was I spared? My people died. I was no less evil than they, so why was I spared? Why did this poisonous evil not infect me?'

'In truth, that is a question only Yahweh can answer.' I thought for a while. 'For my part, perhaps you were spared because you never allowed the poison to take root in your heart. We are all tempted with evil. Every day, each one of us is faced with a choice: what path will we walk? The path of righteousness – a path that is not without challenge, but which yields a harvest of peace and joy – or the downward path of unrighteousness, following our own ways, deciding for ourselves what we think is good and right and just. Rahab,' I said, waiting until she met my gaze. 'You had a choice. You could easily have given in to fear and betrayed my men. You would probably have been rewarded handsomely for your part in their capture. But you didn't betray them. You chose not to join with those who took your little sister from you. You chose a path that would take you away from that iniquitous cruelty. You chose redemption – and Yahweh honoured you for that.'

Tears spilled over. 'Why then does my heart accuse me?' she sobbed. 'Why do I feel so unworthy, so guilty for being here, among you and your people, when I should have died with the rest of mine?'

Memories flooded back to me; fleeting images and feelings from two score years ago, of a time when I felt the same burden of guilt that Rahab now felt.

'Because the path of righteousness is not an easy path to walk. We think that because we made a righteous decision, our steps will not falter, and we will not stumble on our way, but that is not so.'

Tenderness rose up in my heart. I had to tell her. I had to try to ease her suffering. I wanted her to know that I was well acquainted with the guilt that derided her day after day for being alive, taunting her for surviving when other had not, accusing her of being unworthy of that great honour.

So, I told her.

I told her about the first time I had come to Canaan, as a spy. I told her about the perils that our company of spies had experienced, of the giants we had seen, and the fear that had beset the hearts of all but two of us. I spoke of the darkness that consumed the other ten spies, of our people's refusal to enter our promised land, and the terrible consequences that had resulted.

I said, 'I know what it is to feel unworthy.'

Rahab's eyes were pools; deep, bottomless pools of water, drenched with a longing to be understood, to be accepted, to be known.

I told her about the agony I experienced each time one of my family died in the lead-up to our crossing of the Jordan River, of the guilt that ripped into my heart over and over again, of my relationship with my adopted brother, Mesha, and his death just weeks before we entered Canaan.

I didn't stop there. It was as though the floodgates of my heart had been flung open. All of a sudden, I wanted her to know me – not just the great leader some thought me to be, or the feats I had accomplished, but the man I really was. The man who had walked a path littered with pain and uncertainty, love and faith.

I told her about my fathers – all three of them. I told her about the faithful man who fathered me when my mother died, and of the gut-wrenching disappointment I felt when Nun passed away before we escaped from Egypt. I told her about my adopted father, Jesher, of his immense capacity for love and grace, and how he taught me some of life's greatest lessons. I told her of my spiritual father, Moses. I wept unashamedly when I spoke of his passing, of the sense of grief and abandonment that I had felt at that time, and my reluctance to take on the mantle of leading this great nation.

I shared with Rahab my fears about Canaan, about the beast that stalked the land, and the ever-present threat of idolatry that poisoned all in its path.

I shared with her my anxiety about not being a good enough leader.

I told her about my encounters with Yahweh, my passionate longing for His presence and His righteousness, and my desire to be worthy of His great calling.

I spoke about my hopes for the future, of all that was in my heart for our people, and my vow to serve the Lord fully for the rest of my days.

I also told her about the struggles I endured when I found out about the Canaanite harlot who had saved my spies. I looked into her gentle, warm eyes and confessed my pride and arrogance, my anger that Yahweh would choose a pagan harlot to bring about His plan for our people – and I asked her forgiveness for judging her so harshly before I even knew her.

I told her how astounded I was at the way she had embraced her new life, following Yahweh and learning of His ways with such passion and tenacity. I told her how much I admired her strength and resilience and I exhorted her to walk the path He had laid out for her.

I spoke to her as a friend; a friend who I now knew I could trust. A friend who would hold what I shared with her close to her heart, and not cast it to the ground or give it, like tasty morsels of gossip, to others less trustworthy.

We sat in the gentle warmth of the sun, hour after hour on that Shabbat, until shadows dappled the hills. The afternoon sun lingered in tranquil grace, finally giving way to the soft touch of twilight. Beneath the sunset's fading glow, the pearly clouds, laced with pink, whispered to us of peace, and murmured goodnight.

36

Taking the Land

It was over.

Our week of rest following the defeat of the five Amorite kings was a joy which I savoured with the same intensity I employed when sucking every last vestige of meat off the bones of our roasted animals on feast days.

But now it was over.

I knew that if we rested for too long, we would lose our momentum and struggle to regain our focus on taking this land for Yahweh. I held many meeting with my leaders, but the more we discussed the possibilities, the more daunting the process of resettling a whole nation became.

Discussions around the mat during our evening meals, more often than not, focused on these themes. I gained useful insight from hearing my family's differing perspectives on the issues at hand.

'The promise of a new land is a wonderful gift,' I said, wiping away the juices that dribbled down my chin, 'but my heart is anxious for our people. We are not skilled in farming, or tending vines, or harvesting crops. We are herdsmen. Sojourners. We know nothing of settling, of building houses, planting fields. The skills we learned in the wilderness will not be of much use to us here in Canaan. Our people have lived the life of a nomad for so long, they know little of the perils that await them in this land. We must prepare them for what lies ahead, lest they become discouraged or turn from the paths of righteousness.' I paused to look around the mat. Heads nodded in agreement.

'There will not be much call for tentmakers when we settle, *nu*?' Arad said, resting his chin on his hands with a frown. When Yoram died, his younger brother had taken over leadership of the family's thriving tentmaking business. He and his sons had made a good trade in the desert, but their future now seemed less promising. 'We will need stonemasons and builders to erect houses for our people to dwell in, not tentmakers, hmm?' he said, his brow furrowed with concern.

'Mmm.'

Joel grunted and turned to me with a wry smile. 'This is when all those years of labouring in the quarries of Egypt might have been of some use, *nu*? But there are only a few of us left who learned how to build with stone, and we will need many masons.'

Joel had always loathed working with stone, because of the trauma he experienced in the quarries of Egypt at the hands of the taskmasters. Carpentry was his great love – in fact, his love of wood was as great as his hatred of working with stone.

'Is that something you would be willing to do?' I asked with an air of nonchalance, not looking at him. 'Could you pass on your knowledge of stone craft to some of our younger men?'

Silence fell.

All eyes were on Joel.

Our eyes met.

Silence.

Joel tore off a piece of bread, dipped it in the bowl of relish, and put it in his mouth before replying. 'If it would help our people to settle in this land, yes. I will do it. Not that I have much skill to pass on, but,' he shrugged, 'even a little is better than none, hmm?'

I grasped Joel's shoulder. 'Thank you, Joel. *Thank you!* I will send out word tomorrow. We will find the other men who worked in the quarries and start apprenticing some young men to learn those skills.'

My heart constricted at the smile which Alya gave Joel, a smile of such love, such respect. Alya knew more than any of us how much of a sacrifice this would be for her husband, and she loved him for being willing to make it. To have a woman gaze at you in that way must be a wondrous thing. I sneaked a quick glance at Rahab. She was deep in conversation with the other women.

Talk moved on to our people's lack of skill in agriculture, vine tending and seed sowing, and we discussed how to go about training them in the required skills. Arad's sons were loud, fearless, strapping young men. All three of them were much like their father had been in his youth, quick to jump into any situation which they perceived as favourable, without first counting the cost or thinking it through. It seemed they had now decided that tentmaking would not be a viable source of income once we were settled, so they would learn the trade of stonemasonry.

'No, no! Do not be too hasty, my sons,' Arad said, holding his arms out to quieten their impassioned debating. 'Stone masonry is one pathway you could take, yes, but take thought first to what it would require of you, and what Yahweh would have you do, yes?'

'Your *abba* is right,' Joel said with a twinkle in his eye, in response to their spirited protestations. 'Do you remember what Yahweh told Joshua about the taking of this land?' He paused for a moment and, seeing only blank expressions on their faces, continued. 'The Lord God said He would not drive out the inhabitants of this land in just one year. Why not?'

Without pausing for breath, Joel continued his rhetoric.

'Because if He did, the land would lie fallow for too long, and the beasts of the field would become too numerous. No, no,' Joel said, wagging his finger in the air. 'We are not to rush in and take this land in our own strength, or in our own time. Yahweh said we must take it little by little, yes? *Little by little.*' Joel peered at the young men, one eyebrow raised, to make sure they understood his meaning.

Turning to me, he said, 'Is that not so?'

I grinned at him. 'It is. There is wisdom in your words, my friend.'

'Little by little, then, it shall be so. But in whatever manner the Lord decrees, we *will take this land*, nevertheless?' Caleb exhorted, lifting his fist high. 'We will rid the land of every giant that treads upon it, yes?' Caleb and his family often joined us to break bread in the evenings. When he was present, talk inevitably turned to giant slaying, or the quest of warfare. Tonight was no different. Gone were all thoughts of farming land, stone masonry or taking territory little by little, replaced in an instant with tales of past encounters with giants and other formidable foes.

'Have you encountered many giants in your time?' Rahab asked Caleb, blushing when everyone turned to stare at her. It was unusual for the women to speak up when talk turned to warfare.

'Many giants?' I could see a familiar glint in Caleb's eyes as he responded. 'Oh yes, we have faced many giants, and we have slain *every one of them* who dared oppose us. But the first, and the greatest of all, was the slaughter of Og, king of Bashan. That took place at the hand of but one man, our honoured commander.'

He turned and lifted his cup to me, inclining his head, one eyebrow raised. I knew what was coming. Caleb loved telling the story of the slaying of King Og, and would seize any and every opportunity to share the details of that particular encounter. Keeping my head low, I gave him a quick smile to acknowledge his tribute, returning my gaze to the ground for the duration of his discourse. He was in fine fettle tonight, embellishing the story with gestures and vocal enhancements, even leaping to his feet to demonstrate the final toppling of the titan. The family roared their approval when Caleb's story came to an end, clapping and whooping with great enthusiasm. He bowed with a flourish and sat back down, shooting me a mischievous grin.

He knew how much I hated being in the limelight.

Shortly afterwards, the women and children left the mat and we men moved closer to the firepit to discuss the things that men were prone to talk about. The subject of giants persisted. We had killed all the giants in the line of Anakin, but our spies had reported that some had been seen in Hebron, Debir and Anab. They would be our next target.

Later that night, after the children had been bedded and the communal area cleared, I stood near my tent looking out across the landscape. The night was cold and clear; the moon left a silvery trace across the vast star-strewn canopy overhead. Every now and then, a hoof stamped, a lamb bleated, or a child cried out. The camp was shrouded in sleep. I had always loved the peace and solitude of early morning and late evening. That was when I sensed Yahweh's presence most keenly.

I stood for a while soaking it all in, before turning towards the entrance of my tent. Seeing a figure standing in the shadows, I started, then realised who it was.

'Rahab?' I whispered. 'You are still awake? Why do you not take to your bed?'

She shuffled nearer. 'I could not sleep, my lord Joshua. I was thinking about giants.'

'Be at peace. There is no need to fear them.'

'I don't.'

'Oh. Then what ... ?'

'I was pondering what Caleb said about King Og and how you . . .'
She sighed and glanced at me with a look of curiosity. 'You are not
like the kings I have encountered before.'

I grunted and gave her a lopsided grin. 'That is probably because
I am not a king.'

'No?'

'No. Yahweh is our King. I am simply His chosen leader.'

'Nevertheless, you are ruler of this great people, and commander
of a vast army. The rulers I have encountered were proud and
aggressive, lording it over their people, treating us like . . . like refuse
to be trampled underfoot. You are not like that. You are a great
warrior and a much-respected leader, and yet you are humble, not
greedy for plunder – and you care for your people more than your
own soul. How is this so?'

I turned to face her and instantly wished I hadn't. Her
mesmerising eyes probed my soul, desiring truth, demanding
authenticity. I turned away.

'Rahab, I am just a man.'

'My lord Joshua, I have known many men,' she said, still staring
at me. 'You are not just a man.'

I remained silent. Would that she was right. Could she be right?
I wasn't comfortable with her thinking so highly of me. I also
wasn't comfortable with her calling me 'my lord'. I never had been.

'Rahab,' I drew a breath in. 'I would ask something of you.'

'Anything.'

'I would ask you not to call me "my lord Joshua".'

Her brow furrowed. 'Not call . . . ? Why? What would you have
me call you?'

'My warriors call me Commander, but my friends and family call
me Joshua.' I turned to face her. 'I would have you call me Joshua.'

37

A Wife for Joshua

My heart pounded erratically, despite my efforts to breathe calmly.

'Did she ask you to enquire of me?'

Alya's clear, calm eyes bore into me. 'No.'

'Then why do you speak thus?'

Many months had passed since the Battle of the Five Kings. More Canaanite cities had been conquered and the process of resettling of our people was underway. It was a laborious process, and we were learning as we went, for the most part, but I kept in the forefront of my mind Yahweh's words about taking the land 'little by little'. It kept me on track, stopped me from being swept up in the hasty pursuit of too much, too soon.

I had just returned that morning from the city of Gibeon, where a group of elders and I had engaged in days of discussions with the Gibeonites regarding the resettlement of their people. Following Yahweh's decision to spare them, but have them become servants to our people, we decided to divide them into groups and send them out to the new territories we had conquered. The Gibeonites knew how to farm this land and would be useful in teaching us the necessary agricultural skills. They were also experienced horsemen who would be able to help us train and ride the many horses of which we were now the proud, but somewhat clueless, owners. Camels we knew from our time in the wilderness, but horses were new to us and their temperaments were quite different from the stubborn but docile beasts we had been used to riding.

There was no small amount of dissent when we revealed our plans to the Gibeonite elders, but they knew their options were limited, especially when we reminded them that they were fortunate to have escaped with their lives. Our plan was to be executed with as much compassion as possible; family groups were not to be separated or sent to different areas, and the Gibeonites were not to be abused in any way, as we had been in Egypt.

Once again, Yaksu proved himself useful to me; I came to rely on him during the discussions that took place. After discovering that he had not yet taken a wife, I decided Yaksu would not be sent away to a resettlement area, but would remain with me as part of my household. His response when I told him of my decision was gratifying; not only did he find the plan agreeable, but he seemed honoured by being chosen to serve me.

The journey home that morning was arduous. The sweltering sun beat down on us and, as soon as we arrived back at Gilgal, I went to bathe in the cool waters of a nearby stream. I had just arrived back home when Alya accosted me. Handing me a cup of water, she asked, 'Yoshi, if there was a man of our people who desired to take Rahab as his wife, would she be free to marry him?'

What?

What kind of a question was that to ask me, and at such a time! My mind was a sudden blur of jumbled thoughts. Rahab, marry? Why? Who? Who wanted to marry her?

'Why do you ask this? Speak your mind,' I snapped.

Alya paused, obviously intrigued by my reaction. I could see the hazel brown tinges in her green eyes. I hated it when she looked at me in that fashion, as if seeing right through me to the uneven beating of my palpitating heart.

'Rahab has no knowledge of this,' she replied. 'I ask only out of concern for her.'

I frowned. Concern? 'Concern about what?' I thought to myself. 'Rahab has everything she has need of: a new family who have embraced her, food and shelter, protection . . . what more could she want?'

'What are your concerns?'

'Although Rahab is not young, she is still a woman of child-bearing age. She shared with me of her longing to be married, her desire to bear children. Her greatest desire is to be a wife, and a mother in Israel.'

I stared at Alya. My lips moved but no words came forth. The thought of Rahab being given in marriage had never occurred to me. She was part of our family and fast becoming one of my dearest friends, but the possibility of her wanting more than that had never entered my mind. My heart seized at the sudden possibility of her being betrothed, of her leaving us.

Leaving me.

'Has a man come forward to ask for her?' My voice rasped and cracked.

'No, not that I am aware of.'

'Mmm.'

'So . . . ?' Alya's head tilted.

'So?'

'So, would she be free to marry, if a man asked for her?'

My mind was frozen, eyes fixed on hers. I cleared my throat.

'She would.' I muttered '*Shalom*' and darted inside my tent, leaving Alya standing where I had left her. Closing my tent flap, I stood in the middle of the enclosure with my hands on my hips, my heart still racing, thoughts scattering like tumbleweed in a desert storm.

Marry?

Rahab, marry?

Why would she . . . ? Who would . . . ? Surely, she . . . ?

My internal babblings were interrupted by Attai who, having heard that I had returned from the stream, had come to speak to me about my schedule for the rest of the day. All thoughts of Rahab were abandoned as I turned my attention to matters that had long awaited my return, and the ever-growing list of people wishing to speak with me.

My sleep that night was troubled, filled with bewildering dreams of loss and abandonment. I awoke groggy and not in the best of moods. My head throbbed. The first thoughts to fill my mind were not those of resettlement or conquest, but of the beautiful woman who could be ripped away from our family.

'*Shalom*, Yoshi,' Alya called out when I poked my head out of my tent. 'Are you coming to break fast? We are waiting for you.'

I glanced over at the family mat. True enough, the whole family was gathered, including Rahab, and a lively stream of chatter could be heard.

'*Shalom*, Alya,' I responded, rubbing my forehead. 'Forgive me, but I will not join you today. Please have some food brought to my tent; I will eat alone.'

'As you wish,' she responded, but as she turned away, I saw a familiar expression on her face. Alya was notoriously hard to deceive. She had an uncanny ability of seeing through the flimsy veneer of words and platitudes. She knew I was not myself, and she was right.

The truth was, I didn't want to see Rahab. I didn't want to look upon her – or rather, I didn't want her to look upon me. I didn't want her to see the fear that I knew would burn in my eyes at the thought of her leaving us.

Leaving me.

I broke my fast alone in my tent and kept busy for the rest of the day. Feigning an urgent need to discuss the battle plan for our next conquest, I went to break bread with Caleb and his family that night, returning much later to find Joel waiting for me.

'Joel? *Shalom*. Is all well with you?'

'*Shalom*, Yoshi. Yes, yes, all is well,' he replied, 'but there is something I must discuss with you, if you have time?' It was late and another deep discussion was not what my heart longed for, but Joel was family and I always made time for family.

'Assuredly, come in.' I ushered him into my tent and we sat down. 'Drink?' I said, offering him some water, which he declined with a smile. 'What do you wish to speak about?'

Joel studied his fingers for a while before looking up. 'Yoshi, have you thought about taking a wife?'

I could feel the blood draining from my face as a flood of emotions washed over me. Anger. Frustration. Shock. Embarrassment. Pain. Rage. How dare he? How dare he speak to me in this manner?

I stood to my feet and challenged him. 'Have you been speaking with Alya?'

Joel stayed seated and spoke calmly. 'Yoshi, Alya is my wife. We talk about many things, you know that.'

He *had* talked with her. I knew it was so! She must have told him what she suspected. They had been talking about me, and now here he was, as brazen as a pup, asking me about taking a wife. How dare he speak to me thus? I glared at him.

'Joel, the hour is late and I have another busy day tomorrow. This matter must wait unt . . .'

'Yoshi, forgive me, but no.'

I blanched at his forthrightness. Joel was a gracious man, not given to strong shows of defiance or resistance.

'No?' I said, my fists clenching and unclenching.

'Please,' he continued. 'I will not take much of your time. You would honour me greatly by hearing me.' There was no arrogance in his tone, no insolence or falsehood. Quite the opposite; I saw in his eyes an appeal from the heart which I knew I could not deny.

Plonking myself down again, I crossed my arms and muttered, 'Speak your mind, and make haste.'

He gave a brief nod. 'Yoshi, Alya and I have noticed that you and Rahab seem to have . . . developed an understanding.' I glowered at Joel, but he looked away and continued talking. 'She is a remarkable woman, a woman of courage and beauty. She has proven herself to be hardworking and wise, and the children love her, as do our aged – as do we all,' he said, smiling to himself, probably picturing the way Rahab told stories to the little ones when they crowded onto her lap, or danced with them when they were bored.

He looked back at me and held my gaze with a look of authentic openness. 'Joshua, she is no longer the pagan harlot who came to live with our people. She is a woman of Israel, a woman of virtue who follows the ways of Yahweh. Her desire is to marry and bear children. Alya and I believe she would make you a good wife.'

I guffawed and uncrossed my arms. 'Rahab would not marry me.'

'Why not?'

'Because she is a beautiful young woman. I am too old to take her as my wife. I have . . . benefited much from her friendship, but her being given in marriage was not something that had entered my thoughts.'

'Yes, Alya thought as much.' He studied me long and hard before saying, 'So, your reluctance to ask for her hand in marriage is not because you don't desire her for your wife, but because you think she would not want you as her husband?'

Heat crept up my neck and into my face. The silence was painful; I couldn't look at Joel. He grasped my arm and spoke with fervour.

'Yoshi, Rahab is not a naïve young girl whose head is turned by every young buck who struts past her. She is a woman who has . . . seen much and experienced much, and who now desires to marry and bear her own children.'

'Children?' I laughed. 'Well, then, I am definitely not the right man to wed her. I am too old to have children.'

'Why? Abraham was nearly one hundred years old when he fathered Isaac. You have only seen . . . about seventy winters, *nu*? Yes, you are of mature years, but you are strong of body and mind, and able to father children . . .' Joel leaned forward and lowered his voice. 'You *are* still able to father children, yes?'

I scowled at him and nodded. The audacity of this man to even pose such a question!

'Yes. Good.' He leaned back. 'So, there is no reason for you not to take her as your wife.' I frowned at him and shook my head. 'You marvel that I speak of this,' he pressed me. 'Why? Do you see yourself as unworthy?' Noting the look on my face, he exclaimed, 'You do! You see yourself as unworthy of taking her as your wife. How is this possible?'

Joel sat back, utterly flummoxed by this revelation. After a while, when I still had not spoken, he said. 'Joshua, you are commander of the armies of Israel, leader of this mighty nation, our first giant slayer, a man of honour and integrity who loves his family and serves his people with faithfulness and humility. Yoshi, no man is ever too old for love. Love does not concern itself with how many winters we have seen; it has to do with the issues of the heart.' He leaned forward again.

'Marry Rahab, Yoshi! Take her for your wife. Have children. Find joy in this! Any woman would be blessed indeed to be betrothed to a man such as you.'

'Has she told you this?' I asked. 'Are these her words?'

'Uh . . . no. Alya has not asked Rahab concerning you, but she knows of her desire to be a wife and mother. She would make a good wife, Yoshi.'

Of course she would make a good wife – the best of wives – but for another man, a younger man, not for me.

Not for me.

38

A Husband for Rahab

Marry Rahab? Me, take Rahab as my wife?

Could I?

Should I?

What would my people think?

Would she even want to marry me?

The thought was ludicrous, outrageous. Marry Rahab? Father her children? Could this truly be my path?

No!

I could not countenance such a thing. I would not give myself false hope. I had felt the sting of disappointment before; I would not put myself through that again. I determined to block the notion of marriage, and of Rahab, from my thoughts, banishing these rebellious imaginings to the recesses of my mind, as I had done many times before.

It didn't work. Not this time.

The thought of marrying Rahab buzzed around like a tenacious bee hovering around spilt honey, refusing to be shooed away. I hardly slept that night, and awoke the following morning, restless and unable to sit still.

I couldn't eat.

I couldn't concentrate.

I couldn't stop pacing.

I knew I wouldn't be able to harness my thoughts into an orderly pattern until I had fully grappled with them. I needed to move, to walk, to think. I needed wide-open spaces. Pulling on my outer robe, sandals and headscarf, I pushed open my tent flap and peered outside. The dawn would still be some time coming. No one was stirring; the camp was swathed in slumber.

I made good my escape, taking the quickest path to the outskirts of the camp and into the nearby hills, greeting the night watchman on my way. Breathing in the chilly pre-dawn air, I paused to watch ethereal mists drifting down from the hills, blurring groves and vineyards in the dim moonlight.

Marry Rahab? Me? Surely not.

'Why not? Why should I not take a bride?' my heart protested. Joel was right. If Abraham fathered a son when he was one hundred, I could father children now. I could take a wife. I could be a father.

'But you have seen more than seventy winters,' the voice of my silent accuser taunted me.

'Yes, but I am still strong and full of vigour,' I argued back. My father had always spoken of my handsome face and manly appearance, as had others in my family from time to time, but they were my family. Perhaps they were just being kind. I thought on what Joel said about Abraham's introduction to fatherhood late in life. Possibilities filled the air around me like the stars that filled this dark cloak of night.

'Besides,' I thought to myself, 'Rahab is not an old woman like Abraham's wife, Sarah, was. She is half my age and well able to bear children.'

The fierce debate continued long and hard until the breaking of dawn, heralded by the chirping of desert sparrows, joined by the sleepy cooing of doves in the nearby meadows. Bright rays of sunlight revealed silken webs strung between long blades of grass, and tiny dew drops sparkling on damp leaves. The timeless orb rose higher and higher, bathing everything in its wake in a rosy glow.

So it was with me.

Daybreak banished the confusing wrestlings of the night watches and invited new dreams, bright and fresh. As I watched the sunlight swathe the pearly clouds in hues of pastel pink edged with gold, a surge of certainty rushed through me.

Why should I not take a wife? I *would* do it. I would speak to her father today, then meet with her straight afterwards. Although I knew that in our culture women had no say in who they were given to in marriage, I had to speak to Rahab. I needed to know if the thought of being betrothed to me was pleasing, or not. I could not marry her if she were unwilling.

'She might despise you,' the accuser sneered.

'Yes. She might,' I whispered to a spider that was edging its way to the centre of an intricate web. 'But I will ask her, nevertheless.'

The certainty of that decision was like a rush of power through me. I *would* marry Rahab! Her father would not refuse me. An unseen yoke broke off me. I wanted to jump and leap and shout and whoop! My heart was so full, I thought it would burst out of my chest. A deluge of yearnings and desires, long held back by walls of fear and disappointment, now burst out, free of restraint.

'I am to be a husband!' my soul sang out. 'I am to be a father!'

I remembered the day when my brother-in-law Hareph found out that he was going to be a father after believing for so long that his wife, Eglah, was barren. I always had a great love for Hareph, but never more so than on that day. I could still see him clearly in my mind's eye, rushing around, embracing everyone in sight, tears pouring down his cheeks, shouting, 'She is with child! I am to be a father!' That was a remarkable day, one that I would always treasure – and now I was to be like Hareph – a father! Even in my latter years, I was to be married!

Thankfulness burst out of me. 'Thank you, Yahweh! Thank you, thank you, *thank* you!' I had to tell someone; I could keep this to myself no longer. Wheeling about, I started striding towards the camp, breaking into a jog when I neared it.

'I am to be married!' I told the turtledoves that nestled in the branches of an acacia tree.

That thought resonated in my heart, over and over again, with uncontainable joy. I put my head back, saw the white puffy clouds overhead, and laughed to myself. 'It is as though I'm walking on a cloud,' I whispered, stifling another laugh.

I am to be married!

To Rahab!

As I neared the camp, I came upon a small enclosure where some sheep watched over their newly born lambs. The lambs gambolled around their pen, nuzzling each other, and playing a delightful game of chase. I felt just like them! The thought of skipping and frolicking with these little creatures was so appealing.

'I am to be a father,' I whispered, hugging that revelation to myself like a priceless treasure. 'I will be a husband, and a father.' A chuckle burst out of my mouth. This time I didn't try to suppress it. I didn't care. I wanted everyone to know. I wanted to shout out, '*I am to be married!*' but instead I just giggled like a young pup in love.

'But you are not a young pup,' my stern inner voice told me.

'No,' I silenced it. 'But I *am* to be married!'

The walk back to my tent took much longer than it usually did. I reached out to hold some of the babies that new mothers presented to me, played with some children on my way, and called out greetings to nearly everyone I passed. I couldn't help but notice the inquisitive expressions on their faces. I could see them wondering what could have happened to bring about such a change in their usually quiet, serious leader.

What indeed!

Hope! Hope had happened.

Dreams that I had tried my whole life to bury, but which I now realised had never truly died, rose to the surface, gloriously resurrected, as if they have been standing in the shadows for decades, just waiting to be summoned. Now that I had realised the condition of my heart, there was no holding back. I loved her. I loved Rahab. That realisation was liberating.

'I am to be a husband! I am to take a wife!' my soul sang out. 'A wife! Rahab! My love. My wife! And we shall have children! *Lots* of children!'

By the time I arrived back home, my family had long since broken their fast and gone about their daily chores. The thought of missing the morning meal did not perturb me – I had no appetite for food anyway – but I did want to find Joel and Alya and tell them of my decision. Attai, who was standing outside my tent, came striding towards me when he saw me, concern masking his face. 'Commander, I could not find you. Is all well?' he asked. I knew he got frustrated when I disappeared without telling him where I was going but today, I just didn't care.

'All is well, Attai, all is well! *Shalom,*' I said, slapping him on the back. 'This is a beautiful day, yes? A day for rejoicing and giving thanks.'

'Uh . . . yes, Commander,' Attai stuttered. 'What are we giving thanks for?' he asked, bemused.

'Oh, there is much to be thankful for,' I said, giving him a wink before heading towards my tent.

'Commander?' Attai scurried after me. 'Caleb is waiting for you in your tent. He wishes to speak with you.'

'Yes, yes, thank you Attai,' I said. 'I will attend him now.'

'Caleb,' I said, entering my tent to find Caleb in conversation with Salmah.

'Caleb! Salmah! *Shalom, shalom!*' I greeted them, kissing them on both cheeks. Salmah had recently returned from a mission; Caleb must have brought him to me to hear his report. 'Ah well,' I thought to myself, 'I will listen to his report as quickly as possible, then go and find Rahab's father.'

'*Shalom*, Commander,' Caleb responded, always careful to address me properly when others were around.

'Salmah,' I said, turning to him. 'You have much to report about your recent mission, yes?'

'Uh . . . well, yes, Commander,' Salmah said, looking flustered. He turned to Caleb, seeming unsure of what to say.

Caleb grinned at him and turned to me. 'He has much to tell us, yes, but that is not why we have come to see you, Commander. Salmah has come to ask your permission to take a wife for himself.'

'Sit, sit!' I gestured to the benches, then turned to Salmah. 'This is wonderful news! It is good for a man to take a wife. That is a noble endeavour, yes?' I knew I was blabbering and chattering – the bemused expression on Caleb's face confirmed as much – but I couldn't stop. The joy was pouring out of me and would not be contained.

I turned to Salmah. 'You have waited longer than most to take a wife, but you do not need my permission. If it is in your heart to do so, and you have spoken to the woman's *abba*, there is no reason why you should need my permission. Go! Take a wife, and may the Lord increase you and bless you all the days of your life! Who is it you plan to marry?'

'Rahab, Commander. I would take Rahab as my wife.'

39

Frozen

Frozen.

Everything was frozen: the look of nervous pride on Salmah's face, the oblivious smile on Caleb's, the painful beating of my heart ... frozen. I had taught my men countless times about the danger of hesitating in battle. The man who hesitates is lost. Strike first, strike sure.

I had hesitated. I had waited too long, and I had lost.

'I have spoken to Rahab's *abba*,' Salmah continued. 'He has given me his blessing and we have agreed the bride price.'

My heart jolted and started hammering erratically, beating faster and faster.

'And is Rahab agreeable?'

Salmah smiled, a nervous, awkward smile. 'I believe so, Commander, but since she is under your protection, I felt it only right to ask for your permission.'

'My permission ... yes.' *Nooooo!* my heart screamed. No, no, no, no, *nooooo*! You cannot have her! She is mine!

Another awkward silence.

'And ... uh ... you are aware of her past ... indiscretions?' I kicked myself for asking such a stupid question. Salmah had been there, in Jericho, in her house. Of course he knew of Rahab's past; he knew her before I even met her. All of a sudden, images of Salmah with Rahab flashed through my mind; the times I had seen him talking with her, helping her settle into the camp, explaining our ways and laws to her, helping her pack her tent to move into the camp near us. Near me.

What a fool I was! Why had I never realised, never thought anything of it? But then, why would I? I had never even considered the possibility that she might want to marry.

Until now.

'I am, Commander, but I have observed her for some time and I believe with all my heart that she has put her old life away, and has fully embraced her new life as a worshipper of Yahweh.'

'Yes.' I stared at him. Salmah had been watching Rahab? For how long? 'Assuredly.'

Caleb stepped forward. 'So . . . ?'

'So?' A numbness was sweeping over me. I felt dizzy. My head had turned to wood, my tongue was swollen and thick.

'So does he have your permission to marry Rahab?' Caleb asked, looking at me with an expression of bewildered curiosity.

'My permission to . . .' I turned back to Salmah. I was not to be Rahab's husband. This man was to take her as his wife. This man was to embrace her, love her, protect her, father children with her. 'Yes,' I croaked. I cleared my throat. 'Yes, you have my permission.'

'There, you see! I told you he would bless your union, *nu*?' Caleb embraced Salmah with much back-slapping, then Salmah put his hand on his heart and turned to me.

'Thank you, Commander, with all my heart, thank you!'

I nodded. I think I smiled. In truth, the numbness had taken over. I could feel nothing. 'Caleb,' I called, as Salmah left my tent.

'Yes?'

'Salmah – is he a good man?' I asked. 'Does he have sufficient means to provide for Rahab and her family?'

Caleb stared at me. 'You know him as I do. You know he is a good man. He is one of our most trusted spies.'

'Yes, yes, of course,' I mumbled, regretting this line of questioning I had started, but unable to stop the words from tumbling out of my mouth. 'Will he be . . . gentle with her?' I flushed and forced a stern look on my face. 'I would not have her used by a man, as she was in Jericho.'

'Uh . . . there is much kindness in Salmah; he is not a man taken to much wrath.' Caleb was clearly perplexed. 'This *is* a blessing, is it not? For Rahab to be married, and to a good man like Salmah? This *is* what you wanted for her, *nu*?'

'Yes. Yes, assuredly.' I coughed. 'This is a great blessing.'

My heart ripped open.

Caleb went on his way. I stood in the middle of my tent, motionless, unseeing, staring at nothing. Gone. It was all gone.

The dreams, hopes, plans. The joy. Gone. The fragile veneer of my resurfaced dreams had been shattered in one lethal blow.

A quiet cough drew my attention. Attai stood by the entrance. 'Commander, can I be of service?'

Can you be of service? His question replayed in my mind, like a dragonfly hovering over a stream, unable to land. Can you be of service? No. There is nothing you can do. There is nothing I can do. There is nothing anyone can do. It is done. Then, one stubborn thought poked through the fog of my numbness. I had to know. I had to ask.

'Yes,' I replied. 'Can you ask Rahab to come and see me.'

Attai left and, within minutes, Rahab stood before me, a beautiful, ethereal, unattainable vision of loveliness.

'You wanted to see me, my lo . . . Joshua?' she said, still trying to adjust to calling me by my first name. I had always loved the way she said my name but today, it sliced through me like a dagger.

'Yes.' I fiddled with some scrolls on the table, not wishing to look her in the eye. 'Salmah has asked for permission to take you as his wife.'

'Yes.'

'Is it your wish to be joined with him?'

'My father has already agreed the match.'

'Yes. But was this pleasing to you?'

She hesitated. 'Salmah is a good man, kind and gentle, and knowledgeable in the ways of Yahweh. We talk often about the law and commandments and I have learned much from him. He . . . he does not see me through a clouded veil of the woman I once was. He sees me only as the woman I have become.'

'Mmm.'

'It . . . it has always been my desire to marry, to belong to one man, to be known by him alone and to know him in return, to bear his children, but I never thought it would be possible, until now. I am grateful that he has asked for me.'

Silence fell. The numbness turned to dizziness.

'Say it,' I told myself sternly. '*Say it!*' I turned to face her. 'If this is your desire, I will not deny you. You are free to marry Salmah.'

'Thank you.' She gazed at me, clearly wanting to say more, but unable to find the words. After a few moments, she lowered her head and turned to leave.

'Rahab,' I called out.

She swung round.

'Was he . . .' I gulped. 'Is Salmah the husband of your heart?'

She stared at me, her limpid green eyes wide with vulnerability and tenderness, her lip quivering. She held my gaze for a while before whispering, 'No, my lord Joshua.'

She smiled at me, a smile of such sweetness, such longing.

It broke me.

40

The Ravings of a Madman

I took nothing with me.

Hunched and shuffling like a sleepwalker, my headscarf pulled way down over my face, I took the shortest route out of camp.

I could stay in my tent no longer, knowing that she was just a stone's throw away. I had to get out. How could this be? To lose the woman I loved, not once but *twice*. Merav, and now Rahab. How could this be? Was I such a fool? Why did I not speak out sooner? I cursed myself for my cowardice, or had it been ignorance? Possibly both. I knew not and cared not. Whatever the reason, it was too late to do anything now.

It was done.

I continued walking like a mindless wanderer, tripping over roots and stones, grimacing when I realised that my feet had led me to the same place I had visited just a couple of hours ago, in the hills surrounding the campsite. Was it really only this morning that I had felt such joy, such exhilaration? It felt like such a long time ago.

I felt old. So old.

And cold.

I shivered. Hope had evaporated, leaving behind it a heavy load of despair.

Seeing a grove of palm trees on a hillside, I made my way towards it and slumped down, leaning my back against the trunk of the large palm. My head lolled back and I looked out across the plains, staring first at the ruins of Jericho, then at the myriad of tents camped at Gilgal. She was there, in one of those tents, but she was not mine. She would never be mine. Not now.

A stubborn surge of aggression rose in me.

'This cannot be! I must stand against the betrothal,' I muttered. I could deny Salmah permission to take Rahab.

'No, you can't. It's too late. You can't change your mind now,' the voice of my accuser challenged me. 'What reason would you give?'

My mind whirled with different possibilities. What reason could I give for rescinding my permission? I could find Salmah unworthy, but of what? The image of his kind, intelligent face entered my consciousness. I had never found anything untrustworthy or dishonourable in the man, which was why he was one of our most respected spies.

'Curse you, Salmah,' I hissed. 'Why are you such a good man?'

What if . . . ? A loathsome thought crept into my mind, slinking in the shadows like a putrid ghoul.

What if Salmah were to die?

My mind clutched onto that thought, yanking it from its hiding place in the shadows and pulling it into the forefront of my mind. How? How could that be? How could I bring that about?

'It would have to be soon, before they are wed,' I mumbled to myself, scratching my beard. All newlyweds were given a year off active service. I would not have long to arrange it; their betrothal would probably not be a long one, owing to their ages. But how? I could promote Salmah to lead a troop, send him into a dangerous battle with little or no back-up.

Or perhaps Yaksu could help? He might be able to find some Gibeonites to assassinate Salmah. Yes! That would work. No one need know. Yaksu would ask no questions and, if he did, I could have him killed or sent away. Salmah would be in his grave long before their marriage was consummated, then Rahab would be free to marry again. I could take her as my wife. I would bed her, give her children. I would . . .

'Listen to yourself!' my conscience screamed at me. 'These are the ravings of a madman, not the thoughts of Joshua ben Nun. Who are you? Who have you become?'

I froze, stunned into reality, sickened by the thoughts I had entertained. Jealousy, treachery, murder? No, this was *not* who I was. I shook my head in disbelief, trying to shake the evil thoughts out of my mind, shocked that I had even contemplated ending a man's life so I could take his woman. How had this happened? How could I have sunk so low?

'Yahweh,' I groaned. Swivelling onto my knees, I crouched down, head in my hands. 'Forgive me, I beg of you. Forgive me.' Grabbing a large stone, I screamed, hurling it with all my might at a nearby palm. It whizzed through the air and smashed into the trunk. Slamming my fists into the ground over and over again, I roared my rage and pain to the hard, unforgiving soil until my knuckles were raw and bloodied.

Gasping and groaning, I sat back and closed my eyes.

'Yahweh, help me. Please. Help me.'

A pair of doves in a nearby tree cooed with a mournful cry, their call followed by the twittering of sparrows. The doves call I welcomed; the sparrows only vexed me. I opened my eyes and glared at them; how could they sing with such joy when my heart was shrivelling in pain?

Out of the corner of my eye I saw a figure walking across the plain, towards the hill where I sat. I frowned. Who could this be? I would send them away, whoever they were. I had no need of company right now. Scrunching up my eyes, I peered at them. It was Attai; I recognised the bag he had slung over his shoulder. He must have followed me from a distance. I waited until he neared the bottom of the hill and was just about to shout at him to return to camp when he stopped under the shade of a large sycamore tree. Placing his bag on the ground, he drew his knees up and sat with his back to me, looking out over the plains.

He reminded me of myself. Many a time I had followed Moses, staying just close enough to be summoned if needed, but not so close as to intrude. Although Moses had been a mighty prophet, he was not a practical man, so I made it my business to carry a good supply of food and water with me whenever we ventured away from camp. I grunted, wondering if that was what Attai carried in his bundle, simultaneously realising that I had brought nothing with me, and had no weapon with which to defend myself.

I had brought nothing but a broken heart and a large measure of self-loathing.

'Perhaps it is good that you have come, after all,' I muttered, staring at the still figure of my faithful manservant.

I don't know how long I sat there for, not moving, not speaking. My grief was too deep for tears. It was the grief of a lost hope, fragile and fragmented. The midday sun beat down mercilessly, draining the life out of me. For a fleeting moment, I wondered what it would be like to die out here. I considered wandering off, just leaving it all behind. Disappearing. Taking my headscarf off, I wiped the sweat from my face and the back of my neck, and was considering removing my outer robe when I saw Attai stand to his feet. He picked up his bag and made his way up the hill towards me.

When he reached me, he said nothing and didn't make eye contact. Glancing at my bloodied hands, he took the waterskin that was slung over his shoulder and poured water over each of my hands in turn, wiping away the flecks of dirt and blood which had started to harden. His touch was surprisingly gentle. Attai handed the waterskin to me, still not looking in my eyes. I drank with huge gulps as he unravelled his bag and took out a small cloth bundle which he unwrapped and laid on the ground in front of me. Seeing a selection of oranges, dates, barley cakes and cheese, I realised how hungry I had become. I hadn't eaten for nearly a day.

I also saw my dagger in his bag.

He didn't give it to me and I didn't ask him for it.

Attai didn't go back to his position at the hill's descent. Instead, he sat by a nearby palm, leaning up against it as I did, still not looking at me.

He said nothing, but knew everything.

From his post outside my tent, he would have heard it all. He was a silent sentinel, just like I had been for Moses for nearly forty years. Just as I had shared much of the pain that Moses bore, I believe Attai shared mine.

We sat for hours not speaking, just looking out over the plains, watching the stream of humankind trickling in and out of the camp. Twilight reached out with her mysterious silken fingers. I would have done anything to have been able to gaze upon Yahweh's magnificent pillar of fire at that moment.

Only when the sun had fully disappeared and the canopy above us was strewn with stars did we make our way back to camp in the moonlight, walking side by side, still in silence.

41

Absconding

I spent the night in the Tabernacle praying and meditating, unable to sleep. By the time the dawn broke, I knew what I had to do. There was no doubt in my mind.

The day was spent holed up in my tent in discussion with Caleb and Eleazar. Neither of them knew the details of what had happened but, of the two, I knew Eleazar would have discerned some of my heart's agony. Caleb would doubtless find out sometime after I had left.

Alya brought me my meals, watching over me like a mother hen with a wounded chick, even though she was younger than me. Compassion welled up, spilling out of her soft green eyes. The gentle touch of her hand on my shoulder told me that she knew what had happened, but I was grateful she did not speak of it. Her silent ministrations were a balm to my soul. Words would have broken me.

'Yoshi, let me come with you,' Joel pleaded with me when I told him my plan.

'No.' I looked into his wise grey eyes, noting how his wrinkles didn't make him look old, but regal. 'Thank you, my friend, but I need you to stay here. Caleb and Eleazar will have command of the camp, and they will continue to liaise with the elders concerning the resettlement, but I must know that my family is safe and well cared for. Please, do this for me.'

Joel also spoke nothing of the reason for my sudden departure. He didn't mention Rahab, but he knew. In the months afterwards, as I stared up at the night sky, I often wondered if perhaps he felt responsible for the pain I endured during that time. If he had not spoken to me that night of marrying Rahab, I might never have thought of taking her as my wife. The hopes and dreams that had been dashed against the rocks and cruelly destroyed would still have been locked away, safe behind their high walls of fear and denial.

Tears welled up in Joel's eyes. He gulped and drew me into a tight embrace. Even though I was at least half a foot taller than him, it felt as though he was encompassing me. He held me for a long time; I didn't resist, choosing instead to draw strength from the tightness of his arms around me, and the love that overshadowed me. When we finally drew apart, both of us wiped away tears, but both were able to smile.

Attai's response to my plan, however, was not as congenial.

'Why can I not come with you?' he asked. 'I am your manservant. Where you go, I go.'

'Not this time, Attai. I will be gone for a long time and I have no wish to separate you from your family. I will not be alone. Yaksu will accompany me.' The sullen expression on Attai's face showed his obvious displeasure, but another expression flickered in his eyes; a glint of what I only came to realise the following morning to be rebellion.

Yaksu and I were up and ready to leave in the early hours of the morning, long before the dawn broke. We would go on ahead and the troops that had been chosen for the first few missions would follow on later that morning, under the command of their captains. Yaksu came to my tent, leading two camels. He had suggested taking horses, but I refused.

'I will leave those beasts for the younger men to conquer, *nu*? A camel will do well for me,' I said, forcing a smile.

I could not have faced any more goodbyes, so Joel agreed to tell the family of my departure and convey my love to them later that day. Only he and Alya were present to see us off in the chilly darkness of early morning.

'Please, give this to Salmah and Rahab at the betrothal feast,' I mumbled, pushing a roughly wrapped bundle into Joel's hands.

He nodded, and asked, 'May I?'

I nodded. He pulled back the layers to reveal two brand-new sets of clothing: the first, a man's robe of spun linen in pale brown, along with an outer robe in blue with vibrant threads of red and gold running through it. The second, a soft, flowing women's robe in palest green, with a jewelled headdress bedecked with emeralds and gold coins.

Joel gazed at the outfits, smoothing the folds of linen with a reverent touch before covered them again. As he and Alya embraced me, I saw out of the corner of my eye a movement to my right. Attai strode out of the darkness, leading two more camels loaded with baggage. I frowned and started to protest, but he cut me short.

'Commander, I am your manservant and I will accompany you on your travels.'

'Attai, I have . . .'

'Mara and I have spoken,' he said in a loud voice; then, realising the need for quiet, he whispered, 'I must be with you. Do not fear, I will not be separated from my family; they are coming with us. Mara will cook, clean and look after us, and the children will help. They are older now; they will not be burdensome. Indeed, I believe they could be a blessing to us on our travels.'

I frowned and made ready to complain, but Attai lifted his chin, stared up at me with an air of loving defiance, and said, 'Commander, it is decided. We are coming with you.' His defiant frown morphed into a smile. 'You will thank me,' he said with a twinkle in his eye. 'My wife is a good cook, and you have not yet tasted Yaksu's food, have you?' He pulled a face and turned to Yaksu, who grimaced in response.

'There is some truth in what he says, Commander,' he said, wrinkling up his nose. 'I am not known for my skills in cooking.'

I stared from one to the other, knowing that I was beaten, but feeling relieved at having been forced to surrender. I had come to appreciate Yaksu in the past few months, but he was not Attai. Attai knew my routine, my habits, my likes and dislikes. Attai knew my heart.

'Do my words hold no power in this matter?' I asked, my face breaking into a smile.

'No,' Attai said, gesturing to the darkness, whereupon Mara and the two little ones emerged from the shadows, dressed for travelling.

Attai helped Mara and their little girl, Leah, up onto one camel, then mounted the second camel with his son, Eshton. Yaksu and I did the same; then, holding our arms up in farewell to Joel and

Alya, we glided through the camp, dodging the glowing remains of countless firepits, heading in the direction of Jericho.

The plains around Jericho were still black and blistered. The ash-covered ruins lay gloomy and sullen in the light of the moon, like a dismal beacon, a warning to those who would dare to defy the living God of Israel. The heavy rains we had experienced of late had succeeded in enticing new growth. Fresh grassy shoots poked their heads out of the scorched ground, a tenacious green carpet of hope pushing its way through the confines of ashy death.

I grunted.

'Yes, there will be new life,' I thought as I stared, mesmerised by the brave green stems. 'One day my heart will heal. One day it will bear new life, new hope.'

One day, but not now.

Not yet.

42

The Distance Between Us

It was like a well-greased pedal on a potter's wheel; the slow, steady pressing and releasing of the pedal. Down, up, down, up . . . press, release, press, release. The hypnotic rhythm of the treadle wheel draws you in, compels you to move in harmony with it. Speed is the enemy; haste leads only to destruction. The wheel is your instrument, creating music which rises and falls with each pressing of your foot.

Such was the life of a sojourner.

I slipped back into the familiar, dependable rhythm of packing, moving on, making camp, breaking camp, packing, moving on . . . as if I'd never left it.

Attai was right to have insisted on accompanying me; he was proving invaluable, not only as a manservant, but as a friend. He had walked with me through some extremely hard times, from the death of Moses and then Yoram, to my tenuous grasp on leading an entire nation and now, losing Rahab. Although he was not a man given to many words, Attai had a discerning heart and, when he did speak, his words were filled with wisdom.

He was also a good listener.

He had been right about bringing Mara; she was an accomplished cook and a good homemaker. Although at first I struggled to feel at ease around her, once I got to know her I found her presence enriching, and loved watching her bustling around our campsite, rebuking my men when they brought dirt into my tent. While Attai was a man of few words, Mara had words enough for both of them! She was a force of nature, and refused point blank to call me Joshua, insisting instead on addressing me in the same way her husband did.

'*Shalom*, Commander,' she would say each morning, giving me one of her cheerful smiles. 'Did you sleep well?'

Invariably I would reply, '*Shalom*, Mara. I did, thank you,' even when my sleep had been troubled, although I was sure Mara knew when my response was baseless. Nothing much slipped past her. Although she and Attai were only half my age, she took on the role of 'camp mother', and soon became known as '*Ima* Mara'. Initially, she had been suspicious of Yaksu – I think she saw him as a threat to Attai's position. However, it didn't take long before she grew to know and trust him, and what followed was inevitable: Yaksu became part of her little family, and both she and Attai embraced him as a brother.

Mara's presence, and that of her children, prevented me from cutting myself off entirely from the lifestyle of family. I was grateful for it. Leah and Eshton were delightful children, well-mannered and helpful; Esthon reminded me of Yoram as a little boy. He watched me constantly and, whenever he saw that I was not busy, he would come and sit in front of me, asking me questions about our people's history, my experiences as a warrior, or my knowledge of Yahweh. I had never been the storyteller in our family – my *abba* Jesher was a superb storyteller and, when Joel took over that role, he had proven to be just as entertaining and knowledgeable – but I found myself being pulled into the world of storytelling, whether willingly or not.

Strangely enough, I didn't mind.

Leah would clamber onto my lap while Esthon sat by my feet and both would listen, enthralled, when I told them the stories of Abraham, Isaac, Noah and especially Moses. They were amazed that I had known the great prophet Moses who they had heard so much about, and even more astounded when they found out that I had been his manservant.

'Just like my *abba* is your manservant?' Leah asked, her big brown eyes wide with amazement.

'Yes, just like your *abba*,' I replied, throwing a quick wink in Attai's direction.

The night-times were the hardest. When everyone went to their tents, I was left alone, staring into the night sky, listening to their laughter and murmured conversations. That was usually when a shroud of hopelessness would settle on me. I missed my family desperately, but could not be with them right now. They were too vivid a reminder of what had been, of my life as it was before I lost Rahab, and I could not be reminded of that now. It was time to put that all behind me and move on.

If only I could.

You would think that with all the battles I was fighting, the strategising that was taking place, the constant travelling from place to place, my mind would be too full to dwell on one woman. Not so. My thoughts in both day and night were filled with her and, try as I might, I could not banish her from my mind. I wondered how she was faring, what their betrothal feast had been like, and whether she and Salmah were married yet. I pictured her in the pale-green gown I had given her for her betrothal, seeing in my mind's eye her beautiful green eyes framed by the emerald and gold headdress. I tormented myself with thoughts of Salmah bedding her, and would often wake in the night, drenched with sweat from wrestling in my sleep.

Month after month it continued until, nearly two years after leaving Gilgal, I gave up trying to rid her from my thoughts. Instead, I let myself sink back into the memories of what had been, and my concerns about what could take place in the future. I gave myself over to thinking through the details of my conversations with Rahab, trying to unravel and understand the emotions that had beset me, and were still doing so.

I think that was when things started to change.

I couldn't say with any certainty when it was that my heart decided to heal, or my mind turned from dwelling on what was past to looking with hope to the future. I only know that one day I felt lighter. Sometimes you only know the true weight of the burden you have been carrying once you are released from it.

It was so with me.

We had just returned from conquering the hilly territory of Tappuah. Their warriors had fought back valiantly but once again, our forces were victorious. Yahweh had been true to His word. Little by little, city by city, town by town and village by village, the banner of the God of Israel was spreading over Canaan, and the land that had been plagued with evil was being redeemed.

The warriors who fought the Battle of Tappuah had finished their term of service and would be returning to Gilgal the following day.

New troops would be arriving, led by none other than my trusted general, Caleb. I hadn't seen him for so long, my heart raced at the thought of spending time with him again. I stood on the crest of a hill near Tappuah, looking out over the surrounding territory. A cool breeze fanned my sweaty body. I closed my eyes, took a deep breath in and sighed. I felt contented.

Contented?

I opened my eyes and realised with a start that it was true! I *did* feel contented. Peaceful. The nagging pain in my heart wasn't there anymore. I could breathe without tension or effort. I couldn't remember the last time I had felt like that.

'Yahweh,' I murmured. 'I sense Your peace.'

It felt good. So good. Everything I had done over the last two years had been out of pure obedience to Yahweh. I knew what I was commissioned to do and I did it, but there had been little joy or peace, or contentment in it. Only the satisfaction of knowing that I was being obedient to His call. That had been enough.

Now, however, I felt a lightness in my heart.

I didn't feel the heaviness leave – I don't know when it left. I just realised that it wasn't there anymore.

My reunion with Caleb was just as I had expected: lots of back-slapping, laughing and eating! Mara provided a veritable feast; we ate and drank and talked and laughed until we were full to bursting with food and with joy. Later that night, after the others had gone to their beds, Caleb and I sat round the fire. Talk turned to family.

'How are they?' I asked. 'Joel and Alya? Tell me what has taken place. What have I missed? Who has given birth to children? Are Arad's sons still set on becoming stonemasons?'

'They are,' he replied, telling me of their latest escapades while trying to learn the art of stone masonry. 'The family are all well, but they yearn for you, my friend,' he said, his characteristic grin turning into a concerned glance. 'Have you given thought to when you might return?'

I looked away, not because I didn't want to answer him, but because I didn't know the answer to that question. In truth, from the day I left until now, I hadn't let myself think about returning, only of continuing to do what I knew I had to do. My entire focus had been on taking the land, little by little, little by little . . . but now . . .

Go home?

Home.

One question lurked in the back of my mind. I needed to face it. Before any more talk could take place about going home, I had to know.

Looking directly at Caleb, I asked, 'How does Rahab fare?' I asked, 'And Salmah?'

His eyes flickered and he hesitated.

'What is it? Speak your mind,' I urged. 'I must know.'

'They are well. Both of them. She . . .' He stared at me. 'Rahab is with child.'

43

Timnath Heres

'Rahab is with child . . . Rahab is with child . . . Rahab is with child.'
It echoed in the cavities of my mind. I waited for the dagger to rip
into me.

It didn't.

Yes, I felt a sadness, a kind of subconscious ache, knowing that
it was not my child she was carrying, but that knowledge was
combined with a warm sense of pleasure.

'So, she is to be a mother in Israel,' I said, smiling to myself.
'Rahab, a mother.' I glanced at Caleb. 'That has been her heart's
desire for many moons. This is good news.'

Caleb voiced his agreement, obviously relieved at my reaction,
and talk turned to his family, of Iru and Serah's children and their
children, of his wife's health and the grandchildren they had been
blessed with.

The following morning, I arose later than usual, feeling restless.
I felt the need to get out of camp, not for battle or conquest, but just
to explore, to look, to try to see with new eyes.

Attai and I mounted our camels and rode to the nearby settlement
of Timnath Heres. We had taken the town a week or so ago, and
left a troop of men to clear the site and burn the bodies on a funeral
pyre, but I had not been back since. We rode half way up the hill
that Timnath Serah was built on and rapped our camels on their
necks until they bent their legs, allowing us to dismount. Tying
their reins around the broad trunk of a widespread tamarisk tree,
we left the growling beasts there while we looked around.

It was a glorious, balmy day. Rays of sun sparkled down on us,
nourishing and warming my skin, while the breeze whispered
to me of promises, of blessings to come. This was not a day for

rushing or busyness. This was a day for leisurely pastimes and contemplation . . . and exploring.

We strolled up the hill, noting the olive groves that covered the east slopes of the settlement, the forests on the south, the fenced enclosures that must have been built to house animals, and the pastureland that stretched for miles around. Offset from the main pathway, we came across a well surrounded by shady acacia trees and some well-placed rocks. Judging from the worn path leading down to the well and its surrounding area, this must have been a bustling meeting place for the women of the town. An image of Alya, Samina and the other women in our family gathering around the well, chattering and laughing, brought a smile to my lips.

Attai pulled up the rope that dangled in the well, and found a small wooden container tied to its end. Scooping some of the water out of it with his hand, he first sniffed it, then took a sip. Lifting his eyebrows, he nodded and pursed his lips.

'The water is good, Commander. Fresh and sweet.' He handed the bucket to me. I drank some water, then went back for more. He was right. It was good.

We walked a little further into the centre of the town, noting the skilled masonry of some of the houses. Although many of them were the usual mud-brick constructions common to Canaanite settlements, some had been made of hewn stone, with wooden doors and shuttered windows. Their design and construction showed mastery and great skill.

I pushed open the door of one such home and peered inside. The musty smell of stale air filled my nostrils, followed by the rich, earthy fragrance of herbs. Attai followed me inside, looking around the little home with great interest. Bunches of herbs hung from the beams in a corner of the room near a pile of cooking pots and utensils, some in wicker baskets, others tied and hung upside down to dry. The rushes that had been laid on the floor that must have been fresh and smooth when picked were now dry and crinkled, crumbling when we trod on them. A small alcove had been carved into the wall of the family room. In my experience, that was where the family idols would have been housed. The alcove was empty. Any idols would have been destroyed, and items of value confiscated by the troops who cleared the village in the days following the battle. Despite the desolation of the rooms, I could tell this must once have been a cosy little home for a small family.

My heart filled with sadness at the thought of the family who might have lived here before. Ousting any thoughts of grief or regret, I turned my mind instead to thinking about the new family who might fill this home with laughter and joy. Putting my hand on the wall near the doorway, I murmured, 'Yahweh, bless this home. Fill it with Your presence, Your life. Your peace.' Taking one last look around this little house that seemed to have captured a special place in my heart, I stepped outside and stood, arms crossed, looking up and down the street.

'Attai, what are your thoughts about this town?' I asked.

He looked around the little home one more time before closing the door with great care. Coming to join me, he responded, 'Its position is pleasing, Commander – the view from here is magnificent. The olive groves and surrounding lands are fertile, and there is much pasture for flocks and herds. The homes here seem sturdy, well placed, and the water supply is plentiful.'

Attai did not often look me squarely in the face, possibly due to our difference in height, or in respect to my rank, but this time he did. Peering at me with intent, he said, 'This would be a good place to settle, *nu?*'

As usual, Attai had read my mind.

I gave him a quick smile, saying nothing. We continued walking over the crest of the hill and down the other side. Nearer the outskirts of the town, we came across another building which called to us, inviting us to enter. Much larger than the first one, it was built in the shape of a square, all its rooms surrounding a large, central, open-aired courtyard. We stood in the entrance hall looking at the courtyard with great satisfaction. It was decorated with shrubs and flowering plants in clay pots, their fragrant blossoms giving off a sweet, welcoming aroma. A fresh herb garden had been planted down one side of the courtyard. Although it was neglected and somewhat overgrown, it showed much promise. On the other side were two large palm trees, under which sat a wooden bench.

In the centre of the courtyard was a large firepit, filled with ashes long since dead, and an upturned clay dish. Burned-out oil lamps hung from the timber beams around the outskirts of the courtyard.

I walked over to the bench and sat on it, leaning back, soaking in the warmth of the sun and the silence. Closing my eyes, I imagined the snap of fire, the sound of music and laughter floating in the air, and the delicious aroma of meat roasting over the fire. A cheerful trill caused me to open my eyes; sitting on a branch of one of the nearby shrubs was a plucky little bulbul. Its inquisitive eyes sparkled as it cocked its head and peered at me. Puffing out its creamy chest, it warbled a melodious burst of triumphant song before spreading its wings and taking off in flight through the opening above me.

The bulbul's song was as a proclamation, a heralding of things to come – a call to step onto a new pathway. A challenge to fly!

Yes! I said in answer to the bird's unspoken invitation. I will accept the challenge! I was ready for a new adventure.

I stood to my feet, stretched and continued my tour of the property, Attai by my side. All the bedrooms had wooden pallets in them, with dusty bedrolls still in place. In one room, we found a heavy, ornate chest of camphorwood, now emptied of its treasures but striking in form, nevertheless. There was a separate room for cooking and preparing food, and a large outside oven. This dwelling had everything you could want, and a lot that I wouldn't have thought of asking for.

'The man who lived here must have been a leader of his people,' Attai said, taking in the beauty of his surroundings. Turning to face me, he said in a matter-of-fact tone, 'This would be a good home for you to dwell in, Commander.'

'Me?' I frowned. 'I have no need of large rooms and extravagant furnishings.'

'Mmm. You said the same when you were offered Moses' tent, but it has served you well, especially when you had need of space to host visitors and meet with large groups of people.'

I grunted and looked away.

I hated to admit it, but he was right.

'And would it please you and Mara to live in a town like this?' I asked, looking at him sideways.

Attai stared at me for a moment, then his face broke into a grin and he laughed out loud. 'It would, Commander. Assuredly, it would.' Looking rather sheepish, he said, 'I must confess to feeling drawn to the first house we entered.' He sighed. 'To dwell in a home with walls, to settle and not have to keep moving – that seems good to me. Very good.'

'My heart rejoices to hear that,' I responded. 'That home deserves to be filled with the laughter of children and stories.'

Attai and I went outside and sat on a rocky outcrop near the entrance of the large house. Far off in the distance, I could see the faint silvery glint of the sun shining on the Jordan River. Before it lay the distant planes of Jericho, now covered with a vibrant, waving carpet of green. I recalled the green shoots I had seen two years ago when I left Gilgal; brave stems of grass pushing their way through the hard, scorched soil.

There was something about this place, something fresh and new, and yet oddly familiar at the same time. I felt as though I belonged here, like this town had been set apart specifically for me and my kin, as if it had been waiting for me to come and claim it. Here, the sting of the past two years faded away, dispersed by the tantalising lure of new beginnings. I saw it all around me. I smelled it in the air, fragranced with citrus fruit and blossoms.

I sensed it within me.

Hope reborn.

'Timnath Heres. Portion of the Sun,' Attai murmured. 'That is a good name for a town, yes?'

It was the perfect name for this town. Portion of the Sun. I squinted up at the beams of sun that shone down, embracing the freedom of the open spaces that surrounded us. No tents surrounded me here, no flapping ears listening to every word I said, or prying eyes watching my movements. This was a place I could settle down in. Here, I didn't feel hemmed in. Here I felt free, peaceful, invigorated. This was a place of life, of peace, of family, of . . . ? A word dangled on the tip of my tongue, evading capture.

That was it! Redemption! This was a place of redemption.

'Yahweh,' I prayed within myself. 'This is the place I desire to dwell in for the remainder of my days. I petition you now, let it be so. Grant me this land, for my family and I to settle in.'

I knew at that moment that my time of sojourning was coming to an end. The morning after our trip to Timnath Heres, I woke with a fierce longing to see my family and an equally strong desire to settle down and cast aside this life of journeying once and for all.

We left for Gilgal two days' later.

44

Return

We heard them long before we saw them. The sound of ululating filled the air, mingling with exuberant shouts that reverberated across the plains. A vast number of our people had gathered outside the western border of the camp to welcome us home. Many of them held palm branches in their hands, which they waved in the air and then flung on the ground before us as we drew near to the camp. The camels grunted and pulled at their reins, unsettled by the raucous noise and the strange green carpet that was forming beneath their hooves.

They were not the only ones.

I was horrified.

My plan to slip into camp in the dim light of evening had been well and truly thwarted. The noise increased as we drew nearer and, when we dismounted, the crowds erupted into a frenzy of dancing and celebration. Standing at the front of the multitudes were Caleb (who had returned the day before) and Eleazar, along with Joel and Alya, who had tears running down her cheeks.

'This was not of my doing, I swear to you,' Caleb said as he embraced me, looking singularly unrepentant at the ruckus that greeted me. 'I told only the elders of your coming, but it seems word has spread. Your people are welcoming you home, Commander!' he said with a flourish, gesturing to the masses surrounding us.

I glowered at him but, before I could respond, Eleazar drew me into a warm embrace and whispered to me, 'Smile, Joshua. Smile at your people. Acknowledge their welcome. They honour you – do not scorn them. They were not able to bid you farewell when you left, do not rob them of the opportunity of welcoming you home.' Drawing back, he raised his eyebrows in a challenge. 'You have been away a long time and your presence has been sorely missed, *nu?*'

'Yoshi,' Joel and Alya whispered as they embraced me. We would catch up later, there was time enough for that. Eleazar and Caleb took up their positions either side of me and we walked towards the camp together. Joel, Alya, Attai, Mara, the children and Yaksu walked behind us, leading the camels. I had hoped that the palm branch carpet would end once we dismounted, but that was a vain hope. Branch after branch was flung before us, as was the custom when welcoming a conquering hero home.

It was excruciating.

I fixed a smile upon my face and greeted those whose faces I recognised, but every time I lifted my hand to acknowledge the crowd, a fresh roar would arise and a new outburst of ululating erupted. In the end I stopped raising my arm, and just tried to smile and nod. Eleazar tried, albeit unsuccessfully, to stifle the laughter that threatened to break out, but Caleb didn't even bother. He roared at my discomfort. 'I'll deal with you later,' I thought, forcing myself to smile and greet those who thronged around us.

Attai, Mara and Yaksu didn't seem to mind the exuberance of our welcome – in fact, I was sure I saw a smirk on Attai's face as he glanced across at me. The crowds thronged the pathways through the camp, right up to the entrance to our family's circle of tents, whereupon Eleazar stepped forward and held up his arms, dismissing the people.

'Go home to your families,' he shouted. 'Celebrate and rejoice, for Yahweh has brought our commander safely home to us.' After a short tenure of murmurs and attempts at more ululating, the crowd dispersed and Eleazar turned to smile at me, his face full of compassion, his eyes twinkling with delight.

Never before had I felt such gratitude towards him.

I invited Eleazar and his family to break bread with us, but he refused with great grace. 'We will talk more in the days to come, my friend, but for now, it is time for you to be reunited with your family.'

He was right, as usual.

I greeted every single member of the family with a kiss on both cheeks, an embrace, some murmured words of acknowledgement. Never had it been made so clear to me how big our family had grown! Each child demanded a cuddle, each youngster wanted to tell me a story of what had happened during my absence, show me their missing tooth or increased height, or ask me a question. Joel stayed by my side, my guardian protector, and finally steered me towards the circle of mats, where a feast had been laid out.

I walked around the outside of the circle to find my place at the mat, when a pale-green apparition caught my attention.

She was there, standing in front of me, her hands folded over her swollen belly, a nervous smile on her face. Salmah stood next to her, his arm around her shoulders, smiling with great warmth. He was wearing the robes I had given him for their betrothal.

'Salmah, Rahab,' I said, walking towards them. Placing a hand on each of their shoulders, I said, '*Shalom, shalom.* It is good to see you both again. I see the Lord has blessed your union, yes? When will your child be born?' Conversation transitioned into a brief discussion around the likely time of their child's appearance, then Alya showed us to our places and the feast started.

'Blessed be You, Lord God of the heavens,' Joel prayed, lifting his hands to the skies, 'for bringing back to us our brother, our uncle, our friend, Joshua. May Your blessings be upon Him and abound towards him and may his strength increase day by day as he seeks to serve You.' Lowering his hands, he looked around the circle of faces. 'Amen?'

Cries of, 'Amen! Amen!' echoed around the mat, along with a smattering of applause, whoops and cheers.

I had always loved our family celebrations. We knew how to rejoice, how to feast, how to laugh and how to love. But today, I found it all too much.

Too much noise.

Too many questions.

Too much talking.

Too many people.

Everyone talking, laughing, singing, shouting, all at the same time.

I realised that I had become used to a much quieter existence. 'Or perhaps I am just getting old,' I wondered, staring around me at the faces of these beautiful people who I was blessed to call family.

I saw Alya watching me. She knew.

When the meal was done and the music-making began, I saw her lean across and whisper in Joel's ear. Shortly afterwards, he announced to the family that as wonderful as it was to have me back with them, I needed to rest, and would now retire. Silencing any protestations, he assured the family that there would be time enough in the next few days to share more stories and ask more questions, 'But for now, we bid Joshua a good night, yes?'

Blessings for good sleep filled the air as I clambered to my feet, suddenly finding myself overcome with weariness. I threw Alya a grateful glance, and Joel got up to walk with me to my tent.

'Thank you, my friend,' I whispered to him.

He smiled in acknowledgement and whispered back, 'I hope you were not grieved at our inviting Rahab and Salmah to join us tonight. They were both very anxious to see you again.'

'Not at all,' I reassured him. 'It was good to see them.' It was. It truly was good to see them. Both of them.

'Sleep well, my friend,' Joel muttered, embracing me, and sending me into my tent without further ado.

My dreams that night were not filled with images of a beautiful woman in a pale-green gown. I dreamed instead of a picturesque town nestled on the slopes of a hill, crowned with rays of sunshine, and bedecked with olive trees and blossoming shrubs. In the dream, I heard the gentle call of the wind, and the melodious trill of a bulbul.

45

Inheritance

'You cannot hide away in your tent for much longer, Commander. You will have to face your people soon. It might just as well be today, yes?' Attai said with a lopsided grin on his face.

'You suppose that I have been hiding?' I responded with a frown.

Attai said nothing, but raised one eyebrow in response. Our relationship had changed a lot over the last two years. Although we had not spoken about it in so many words, we both knew that an irreversible shift had occurred: Attai was no longer my servant, he was my friend. He was still respectful, and his service to me continued to be exemplary but, as my friend, he now had no problem calling me out on anything he felt I needed to deal with.

Like this.

I huffed, stalked over to the tent flap, and peered out. Two days had passed and, apart from taking meals with my family, Attai was right, I had been hiding in my tent. I had become used to living within a small family unit, alongside rotating squads of soldiers. My men did not demand anything of me other than to lead them with courage and clarity, and they certainly didn't expect me to pass the time of day with them or engage in idle chitchat. The thought of walking through the camp, being confronted with so many people wanting to talk to me, ask questions or tell me things, was overwhelming.

But I knew it had to be done.

Maybe Attai was right. Perhaps I should venture out. I knew myself well; the longer I thought about it, the less likely it was to happen. I must do it now. Hesitate and you lose. I knew that from bitter experience.

Swinging round to face Attai, I declared, 'I had thought of taking a walk today. I must go to the Tabernacle. There is much I must seek the Lord's face about. Come, walk with me.'

I was rewarded with a broad smile. 'Yes, Commander.' Attai inclined his head, as if to acknowledge that it had been my idea. Both of us knew it wasn't.

I strode from my tent, rounded the corner, and came face to face with Rahab.

'Oh! *Shalom*, Rahab.'

'*Shalom*, my l . . . Joshua.' We shared a smile at the thought that she still struggled to call me by my name after all this time.

'Are you well?' I asked her. 'And the child?'

She caressed her swollen belly and gazed up at me. 'We are both strong and well, thank you.' She flinched. 'The strength of his kick tells me he is nearly ready to meet us.'

'He? You believe it to be a boy child?'

'I do.' A flush crept up her face. 'I may be wrong, but my heart tells me that the child I carry is a boy.'

'I hope you are right,' I replied. 'Salmah's cup of happiness would overflow, *nu*?'

'Assuredly.' She gave a little giggle, then her face turned serious. 'Joshua, I wanted to apologise for not being among the throng that welcomed you home the other day. We wanted to be there, but Salmah did not want me to be jostled in a big crowd, since I am so near my time.'

'He is a wise man indeed. Please, do not concern yourself; I would have had it no other way. You must guard your child carefully until he is safely delivered.' Rahab smiled at the mention of 'he'. 'My soul delighted to see you both at the feast; you look so happy.'

'Thank you, we are. Yahweh has blessed us; I have much to be thankful for.' She hesitated before staring up at me with her soft green eyes. 'Joshua – is it well with you?'

I paused to consider her question before replying, 'It is, Rahab. I am contented. I am at peace.' The look of relief on her face warmed my heart. She gazed at me with such openness, it reminded me of the conversations we used to have, when we shared our hearts so freely. Before I knew what was happening, I started to tell her about my life and experiences over the last two years, especially my recent trip to Timnath Heres.

I helped her lower herself onto a blanket-strewn boulder and sat down next to her. Attai moved a discreet distance away, giving us space to talk in private.

'And this town, Timnath Heres, this is where you will dwell?' she asked, her eyes lighting up with anticipation.

'If the Lord is willing, yes.'

'Oh!' She clasped her hands to her mouth. 'It sounds wonderful! Joshua, my heart rejoices for you. When will you be able to settle there?'

'*Eiysh!*' I shook my head. 'Not for some time yet. There is still much to do. We are seeking the counsel of the Lord as to how to divide the land. Each tribe is to be allocated a portion of land, to be distributed by lot before the Lord. Some of our people have settled east of the Jordan River, as you know, but the allocations for the rest of the tribes are yet to be done – and even when the lots are drawn, there are still many adversaries to drive out before we can fully settle.'

'I see. So, Joel and Alya, and the family – will they dwell at Timnath Heres with you, or will they live among the tribe of Benjamin in their allotted land?'

Oh.

Over our time of desert wandering, I had become so used to dwelling with my adopted family, I tended to forget that they were not my blood family, and were from a different tribe. Whenever I thought of Timnath Heres, I pictured them with me. It never occurred to me that they might choose not to live in the land allocated to my tribe of Ephraim, but to join their kin in the Benjaminite lands. My heart sank.

'Uh . . . there is still much to be decided,' I muttered. 'Indeed, I am on my way to the Tabernacle now to seek the Lord for His counsel on the matter,' I said, rising to my feet. I helped Rahab up, embraced her, and we parted ways, promising to break bread together soon. With Attai by my side, I made it to the Tabernacle without too much disruption, where I spent much time petitioning the Lord.

Over the next few weeks, the elders and I met to enquire of the Lord regarding the future of our nation. Never again would I make the fatal mistake of following my own path instead of consulting Yahweh regarding the way forward.

The lots for tribal land allocation were drawn some days later. Although I tried not to show it, my thoughts were anxious during that process. I had set my heart on living on the hillside in my Portion of the Sun; how would I bear it, if it was given to someone else?

Yahweh heard my cry: the lot of the tribe of Ephraim fell on the hill country to the west of the Jordan River and, among the settlements that fell to the Ephraimites was the town of Timnath Heres. I laid my request before Yahweh in the presence of Eleazar and the elders, and His response to my petition was indisputable: the town was mine.

Timnath Heres was mine!

My land!

My inheritance!

My *home*.

I had never owned land before. I had never owned anything of consequence before. All my worldly possessions fitted into a few bundles, as befitted the life of a sojourner. But not anymore. I would be a sojourner no longer.

I had a home!

The thought of settling down in that spacious corner of the world filled me with such joy, such gratitude and excitement, I could hardly contain myself. Not usually given to dramatic outpourings of emotion, the elders gathered round were shocked when I fell to my knees, weeping, shouting and laughing all at the same time. Up until that moment, only a handful of people knew of my deep desire to settle at Timnath Heres but within a short space of time, the whole camp knew that the God of Israel had seen fit to give an inheritance, a Portion of the Sun, to His servant, Joshua, son of Nun.

Rahab's innocent question about whether my family would move to Timnath Heres with me, or live with their kin in the land allocated to the tribe of Benjamin, had buzzed in the back of my mind for weeks, like an irritating insect. I had not yet spoken to Joel about it. I didn't know how to broach the topic. I comforted myself with the knowledge that the land given to the Benjaminites bordered the land of Ephraim, so the journey to see my family would only take a day or so, but it was a meagre comfort.

I didn't want to have to travel to see them.

I wanted to wake up every morning and break our fast together.

I wanted to hear the little ones squeal and giggle when their *imas* washed their faces with cold water, to listen to their stories and cuddle them when they hurt themselves.

I wanted to hear Samina humming as she rocked her grandchildren in her arms, and see Yoram's sons grow up to be as handsome and trustworthy as he had been.

I wanted to watch our elderly nodding off in the warmth of the sun, to be able to help them when they faltered, and sit with them as they watched the world go by.

I wanted to hear Arad's sons argue and fight among themselves about the construction of their latest project, and laugh at Arad's impassioned responses to their wrangling.

I wanted to watch Joel wipe the sleep out of his eyes, smoothing down his thatch of thick hair each morning, and see the loving look that Alya gave him in response.

I wanted to break bread with my family each evening, to look around the circle of mats at the unique people gathered there, and wonder again how it was that I had been so privileged to be included as one of them.

I wanted my family with me, not a short distance from me.

I wanted them at Timnath Heres.

The thought of them not being with me was a torment. Would I be forced yet again to let go of those I loved, to mourn and grieve once more for what I had lost? I had to know. Either way, I had to know.

I decided to mention it to Joel in passing, instead of arranging a meeting specifically to discuss it, in the hope that that would eradicate any pressure on him to decide in my favour. Much though I wanted him and the family with me, as patriarch it had to be his decision, and I would not sway him either way. So, one evening as we sat around the firepit discussing the latest migration of thousands of our people who were leaving to settle in their new homelands, I focused on the flames and asked, 'So, have you given much thought to when you will be leaving Gilgal to join your kin?'

'My kin?'

'Your kin in the tribe of Benjamin,' I mumbled as casually as I could, squinting into the dancing flames while my heart beat a crazy, uneven rhythm.

'My kin in the ... ?' Joel said, swivelling round to face me, a look of confusion on his face. 'Yoshi, *you* are our kin. We believed we would come and dwell at Timnath Heres with you – unless that is not your wish,' he added, lifting his hands in surrender.

My heart lurched with hope and wonder as I stared into Joel's confused, devoted face. 'You would forsake your inheritance among your people to come and live with me in Ephraim?'

'Yoshi, we would journey to the ends of the earth with you, if that was what you desired.'

'Joel,' I whispered. 'I ... yes ... yes ...' My voice cracked. I couldn't speak. I nodded, and kept nodding, until Joel grasped my arms and pulled me into one of his all-encompassing embraces.

'Yoshi,' he whispered. 'Yoshi, my brother.'

46

Farewell

The magnificence of that word still caused a shiver to run down my spine.

Home.

It was time. Time to go home. Everything fell into place once I knew that Joel and the family would be coming with me. I could see the future laid out before me like a newly hewn pathway on a moonlit night, clear and bright. We had lived at Gilgal for years and yet, all of a sudden, it felt strange – wrong – to be there. It wasn't home anymore; my heart had moved on. Countless times during the day, my thoughts drifted off to the sun-blessed house on the side of a hill.

Home.

My home.

Timnath Heres.

Sometimes the longing in my heart grew so great, I felt an almost physical pain in my chest. At times like these, words were not my friends. They darted around inside my head and would not be brought to order, especially when my heart was full.

It was full now.

Full of joy and excitement, but also trepidation at the thought of the steady stream of goodbyes which I knew our departure from Gilgal would necessitate.

Eleazar had been my close companion since I first started serving Moses. As young men, we had often been sent on errands together and, over time, I watched him transition from a timid, clumsy youth into the wise, discerning high priest who now stood before me. He had walked with me through the peaks and valleys of life for so long; the thought of bidding him farewell and going our separate ways caused me many sleepless nights.

'I have become too used to keeping company with you every day,' I said, when the day I had been dreading finally arrived. 'Your tent has been a sanctuary for me, a place of safety and solace. How will I walk the path laid out for me without you by my side? Who will I take counsel with when you are not there?'

'My friend.' His warm eyes brimmed over with emotion as he clasped my shoulders. 'Yahweh is with you. He has always been with you, and He will not forsake you now. Besides, this is not farewell. We have walked together for many years, and we will walk together for many more, *nu*?'

As usual, he was right.

We spent a lot of time together over the coming years in Shiloh, where the Tabernacle had been set up, presiding over various gatherings and settling disputes. We grew old together as the years passed by, just as we had grown up together in our youth, and I was at Eleazar's side when he went to join his fathers. He had seen ninety-nine winters.

Caleb was another irreplaceable friend to whom I dreaded saying goodbye. Although the complete opposite to Eleazar in character, Caleb had been the fiercest advocate, the bravest of warriors and the most loyal of friends.

During the time of the land distribution, he received word of three giants, sons of Anak, who were believed to be living in the mountainous regions of the south, near Hebron. In typical boldness of spirit, he requested a meeting with the elders to petition them to give him the city of Hebron. After reminding them in no uncertain terms of the part he had played in spying out Canaan, slaying giants, training our warriors, and protecting our people, he concluded with a passionate declaration.

'Moses swore to me that the land where I had walked would be my inheritance, and my descendants', because I *wholly followed the Lord my God.*' He pivoted, making eye contact with each and every elder. 'I am eighty-five years old, yet I am as strong today as I was when I spied out this land.' Staring at them with fiery eyes, Caleb flexed his arms in front of his chest. ' As strong as I was then, so I am now.' Raising his voice, he shouted with a mighty cry, 'Now therefore, *give me this mountain and watch me drive out the giants who dwell there!*'

No discussion took place regarding Caleb's request. No discussion was needed; the decision was unanimous. From that day forward, the mountainous region of Hebron belonged to Caleb, son of Jephunneh.

Unlike Eleazar, I wasn't sure when I would next see Caleb. I didn't want to say goodbye to him. I didn't know *how* to say goodbye to him. We met one last time in the privacy of my tent while Attai kept watch outside. Words were elusive when it came to conveying the depths of emotion in a man's soul; they continued to evade my tenuous grasp.

I waited for Caleb to speak; he was never short of words. He stared into my eyes; I saw a flash of uncertainty. Doubt. Vulnerability.

He had no words.

His stare pleaded with me to break the silence, to say what he couldn't.

I had no words.

His expression morphed into realisation. Acceptance. Gratitude. Love.

Caleb's eyes started watering. He grabbed me, drawing me into a bear hug. We clung to each other like our lives depended upon it. I could feel his heart beating through the thin veneer of his robe. I held him to me until his heartbeat started slowing.

'When will we meet again?' I asked when we released our hold.

He thought for a moment. 'Listen for talk of a mighty giant slayer. That's where you will find me!' With a final grin, he wiped the tears from his cheeks, swung round and swaggered out of my tent.

I did see him again many times over the years, although most of them were unexpected and unplanned, in typical Caleb fashion. Usually, the first I would hear of his intention to visit would be the jingle of harnesses and growling of disgruntled camels as they climbed the hill to Timnath Heres, or the stomping of feet as he entered my home, uninvited, flinging his bags onto the floor in my entrance hall.

I was unable to be with Caleb at his passing, due to my own frailty and old age at the time, but I sent word, and he knew I was with him in spirit. I would always be with him in spirit, just as he had always been with me.

There was one more parting that I dreaded with all of my heart.

How to say farewell to the woman who had consumed my thoughts for so many years; the woman whom I had despised like no other, then grew to love like no other? She had captured my heart, taught me so much about redemption and forgiveness. I thought back to when I had first heard of her. The horror that filled my heart at the thought of a pagan harlot coming to live among us had been all-consuming, as was my loathing of everything that she stood for.

I huffed, mumbling to myself, 'And yet now, I cannot find it in my heart to bid you farewell.'

The day of Rahab's birthing came shortly after my return to Gilgal. Alya was with her when she gave birth to a strong, healthy boy child who they named Boaz, 'In Strength'. It was a fitting name for the child. It spoke to me of the legacy of his mother, whose strength of heart had carried her from the perversion of whoredom in Jericho to a life of purity and joy as a mother in Israel.

Salmah and Rahab were staying in Gilgal for a while longer, until Rahab was fully rested and able to make the trip to the Judean tribal lands, so we would be leaving before them. I spent hours rehearsing what I would say to her and Salmah, and asked Joel and Alya to accompany me to Rahab and Salmah's tent to bid them farewell. Many tears were shed when Rahab said goodbye to Alya, who she now called her 'Hebrew *ima*'. While they embraced, I took Salmah by the shoulders.

'Salmah. Brother.' A deep love welled up within me for this brave, steadfast man. At first, I had been unsure of Salmah's ability to love and cherish Rahab as I felt she deserved – as I would have done. Now, however, there was no doubt in my mind that he was the right man to nurture and protect this extraordinary woman. Kissing Salmah on each cheek, I spoke over him a blessing.

'May the Lord bless you and keep you. May He increase the work of your hands and keep evil from your dwelling place, and may the memory of your name be blessed.' Salmah responded in like mind, we embraced, then I turned to face Rahab.

'My sister,' I said, staring once more into the impossible depths of her beautiful green eyes. I opened my mouth to declare a blessing over her. Glancing down at the babe in her arms, a strange, unforeseen unction rose up within me. The words I had planned to say evaporated and instead, I heard myself speak words that were not mine and that, if I were honest, I didn't fully understand.

'The head of this child will be crowned with the blessing of the Lord God of Israel. For from your lineage will arise One whose name will be exalted above all others.'

All conversation ceased.

All eyes were on me.

Little Boaz gazed at me, wide-eyed, his eyes shining with wisdom far beyond his tender age.

'The Lord will establish Him and raise Him up, and He will walk in the favour of God, flourishing like an olive tree in the courts of the Lord.'

No one spoke after that.

We held each other tightly before taking our leave, the words of the prophecy still ringing in our ears.

47

A Little Touch of Paradise

It was even better than I had remembered.

A little touch of paradise.

A secret treasure nestled in the heart of the dappled hills . . . and it was mine!

My first few days at Timnath Heres were like a dream. I walked around in a haze with a gawky smile on my face, hardly able to believe what was happening. The family camped out in my home the first night after we arrived and, early the following morning, I took them on a tour of the town so they could choose where they would like to live. They were very taken with Timnath Heres and, over the course of the day, each family chose their dwelling place and moved their belongings into their new homes – all except for Joel and Alya. They came to live with me in what became known as Bayit Gadol, 'The Big House'.

It was a time of jubilation, thanksgiving, and much weeping. Homes! We had homes! We would not be packing everything up and moving on, repairing the rips in our tents yet again, or battling the forces of nature in all kinds of weather. We would be staying here, in our sunny little piece of paradise on the hillside! I surprised Yoram's widow, Samina, one day shortly after we arrived. She was standing in the middle of her family room, her apron held up to her face to mop the tears that were flowing.

'Samina!' I popped my head through her open door. 'What ails you? Is it the children? Are you unwell?'

She swung round and burst into a fresh volley of tears when she saw me, gabbling a string of unintelligible phrases. I held her to my chest, stroking her hair, until she had calmed down enough to talk.

'We are home, Yoshi,' she spluttered. 'We are home. Yoram would be so happy to see us here, together, in Timnath Heres. He spoke so often of the home he would make for us and now . . . here we are. Home. In our promised land, and it is so beautiful, but he is not here to see it.' She started sobbing again.

Now I understood.

Happy tears, mixed with the overflow of long-borne grief. I knew well the conflict of joy and sorrow when they were bound together.

Joel and his sons worked from morning till night each day crafting furnishings for one member of the family or another to put in their new homes. Joel set up his workshop outside Bayit Gadol, on the east-facing wall. The front of his workshop opened up onto the street, and he used the tough waterproof material from our tents to cover the wooden beams and create a roof. I had always loved the sound of sawing and tools scraping on wood, and never ceased to be amazed at Joel's skill at carving ornate patterns into furniture. We never had much use for furniture in the wilderness. Sojourning was a simple nomadic life and we could carry only the bare essentials. But now . . . !

Our women, all of a sudden aware of the endless possibilities for their new homes, were in a frenzy of homemaking, cleaning and creating, while the men set to work at their potters' wheels or carpenters' benches, trying to provide what was suddenly deemed by their wives to be 'essential'.

'A weaving loom! I must have a loom,' Jana told her startled husband. 'Just think of all the clothing I could make if I had my own loom!'

Joash's brow furrowed. 'But you have always used *ima's* loom.' He turned to face Alya. 'You don't mind if Jana continues to use your loom, do you, *ima*?'

'Of course not. My loom is yours, Jana, whenever you have need of it,' Alya responded, giving me a knowing smile as she turned her attention back to her washing.

She knew as well as I did that the days of borrowing looms were now over, and that each wife would want her own weaving loom, her own table and benches, flat rocks arranged around a deep firepit and, of course, a full selection of pots and dishes.

The days were full and flavoursome, packed with a sense of anticipation, and bursting with possibilities. Each day, we found new ways of doing things. One tradition, however, didn't change. Each evening, the whole family would gather at Bayit Gadol to break bread together. Every afternoon, some of the women would come together to cook and prepare the evening meal and, for a short time, my home was filled with the cheerful sound of women chattering and children playing.

Yaksu had come to Timnath Heres, along with his family and a few other Gibeonite families who now lived among us, working in the fields, shepherding, or serving in our households. Each Gibeonite family had been given a place to live, and although they were simple dwellings, they seemed content with their lot. During his first year at Timnath Heres, Yaksu took a wife, and within a few short years, they brought forth a little brood of children to join our growing community.

One day, I arrived home from a trip to the northern lands to find Joel and his sons gathered in the courtyard of my home. They presented me with a gift they had been working on in secret: a huge rectangular cedarwood table, with matching benches. It was an object of great beauty with impressive proportions, inlaid with silver, and carved with Joel's trademark design of fruit and leaves.

'Joel, this is . . . this is wonderful!' I ran my fingers across the intricate designs, stroking the smoothness of the table's surface, feeling the grooves of the carvings. 'I have not seen anything like it before!'

It was superb.

Huge.

Solid.

Ornate.

Impressive.

Totally unnecessary.

I had long since come to terms with being hailed as the conquering commander and leader of the children of Israel, realising that I would never be able to escape the acclaim that came with that title. But, despite my learning to tolerate it, one thing still had not changed after all this time.

In my heart of hearts, I was still a simple man with simple needs.

I made sure that we used the table and benches over the next few days, showed them to everyone who visited during that time, and sang the praises of Joel and his sons. However, it wasn't long before Joel walked into the courtyard to find me sitting on the floor on the familiar, well-worn, colourful woven mats which we had used in the wilderness, sharing a snack with some friends. Warmth flushed my face as I scrambled to my feet.

Joel had the measure of me straight away.

'No, no, please,' he said, gesturing to me to stay seated. He sat with us on the ground and joined in the conversation. A little while later when conversation was in full swing, he turned to me and whispered, 'It is good to sit on these mats again, *nu*? Why change something that has worked so well for so long?'

'Joel,' I whispered in return. 'The table is magnificent. Truly. I beg of you, do not think that . . .'

He held up his hand to stop me. 'Yoshi, be at peace. These mats hold precious memories for our family. Some ancient ways should not be changed, no matter how grand or impressive the new ways might seem, yes?'

I stared into his eyes to check whether his words were true, or if he was just being placatory. There was no guile in his response and his eyes were full of warmth and humour. We used Joel's table and benches whenever we had visitors, all of whom were suitably impressed by its size and design. However, as soon as the visitors left Timnath Heres, our family went back to congregating on mats around the firepit, as we had done in years past.

Although my new life at Timnath Heres was pleasing to the soul, my time was not all leisure and feasting. For the first few years, I was kept busy with what seemed like a never-ending series of meetings regarding the resettling of our people, as well as ongoing land disputes. Attai still served me, spending his days by my side at Timnath Heres, as well as travelling with me to Shiloh or other regions for conquest and matters of state.

I no longer fought actively in the battles over territory. For the most part, the twelve tribal armies now fought their own battles. That strategy proved successful, and the desire to claim the land allotted to them was the motivation needed for the warriors to engage the enemy in battle. Little by little, just as Yahweh had instructed, we were taking the land, cleansing and redeeming it in the name of the God of Israel.

A few years after I had settled at Timnath Heres, the day finally came when I no longer needed to oversee territorial conquests or strategise about which town to subdue next.

Yahweh had given His people rest.

48

Home

'Where are you in such a hurry to get to?' I asked a chubby little black beetle who scurried across the pathway in front of our feet. 'Shall we follow him?' I said, turning to Leah, who giggled and nodded in response.

We looked around to see if anyone was watching, then followed the little creature, staying a discreet distance behind so as not to frighten him. His movements delighted me; the intermittent tapping of his hind quarters on the ground, his clumsy yet persistent attempts to climb over twigs that blocked his way. We followed him for quite some time, until he came to a sandbank where we saw a small hole. Crouching down on our haunches to get a better look, the last thing we saw were his spindly little legs pushing his rotund body through the hole.

'I wonder who waits for him there?' I mused.

'His family, of course,' Leah said, wrinkled her cute little button nose.

'His family. Of course,' I chuckled. 'Speaking of family, we'd better get you home, yes? Your *ima* will be wondering where you are.'

Leah slipped her soft little hand inside mine and we meandered up the pathway to her home.

Life at Timnath Heres was everything I had hoped it would be, and more. I found a contentment in my heart that had never before lodged there as I learned how to celebrate the smaller, seemingly unimportant things in life. The memory of battles, giants and hardships had dimmed somewhat since I had come home. I could still recall them, but whereas before they had been clear and distinct, they were now becoming blurred, slowly but surely being relegated to the back of my mind.

In my years of wandering and warfare, the simple things had often been swallowed up by the vastness of battles to be fought, giants to be defeated, or territory to be conquered. Now, however, I found myself noticing things that in bygone days would have passed me by.

The twittering of the birds. Had their song always been so pure, so joyful? How was it that I had been surrounded by them, but hardly noticed?

The tiny little wildflowers that grew among the tufts of grass lining the pathways. Delicate pink or white cyclamen, each petal pale and creamy, its tip dipped in a pink blush. Exquisite artistry, each petal uniquely shaped and coloured. I had looked at them so many times, but never really seen them.

The way Attai's son, Eshton, favoured his left leg when playing the hopping game, or how little Leah watched him, trying to copy his movements.

More often than not, I would find myself sitting in the shade outside Bayit Gadol, just watching the world go by. One of Joel's benches had been placed there, and each morning, Alya would bring out some plump cushions for us to sit on. When I sat on the bench, nothing was expected of me. Nothing waited for me to pay it heed. I wasn't expected to hold compelling conversations or make any decisions. It was just me and my thoughts. I chuckled to myself as I remembered how my adoptive father, Jesher, had done the very same thing. I wondered back then what he found so appealing about just sitting, watching, when there was so much to be done.

Now I knew.

'So this is what peace feels like,' I murmured, issuing a big sigh before snuggling into the cushion behind me. 'You knew that, didn't you, *Abba*? You knew about peace, and rest. Contentment. That was your secret, *nu*?'

Just that morning we had received word from Salmah and Rahab of the birth of their second child, a little girl. They named her Ayna, after Rahab's little sister. The news of another child being born to them didn't shake my peace or cause my thoughts to become disquieted. My newfound peace held, solid and immovable, as I prayed a blessing on the little girl who I knew would bring so much joy to the woman who had endured so much pain.

One morning soon afterwards, I sat near the edge of the hill under my favourite tree: a large sycamore with thick, knotted trunk and sturdy branches. Its heart-shaped leaves were large and leathery, providing a dense, shady bower in the heat of the day. The spread of this particular sycamore was significant; it must have stood there for many, many moons. Our women used the leaves of sycamores for their healing properties, and for wrapping food in for baking on the coals. The sap of the sycamore tree was sweetness itself, notwithstanding the fruit, which appeared regularly on our platters around the mat, and its wood, which was highly prized by carpenters.

No one touched my tree. It was an unspoken rule. They could use the leaves, sap, fruit and wood of any other sycamore tree in the town, but not this one.

This tree was special.

It was my 'thinking tree'.

The family soon came to realise that whenever I went missing, more often than not they would find me sitting under my sycamore, gazing at the surrounding landscape, as I was today. I leaned back against the trunk of the tree and looked up into the dense, vibrant green canopy above me. Laying my hand on the trunk, I whispered, 'You must have seen much within your lifetime, old friend, *nu*? The stories you could tell, if we could but hear you, mmm?'

I drew my knees up and rested my forearms on them, staring into the distance, when a voice called out.

'Yoshi?' Alya walked towards me, an empty water pitcher in hand. 'What are you thinking about?'

'The stillness.'

She tilted her head, waiting for me to explain.

'I have been surrounded by people and noise for so long, I forgot what stillness sounded like – felt like – until I came here. Come!' I urged, patting the ground next to me. 'Sit with me. Listen!'

She put her pitcher on the ground and sat down next to me. We sat in silence, feasting on the luxurious splendour of stillness, until the faint whistling of the wind provided a soft backdrop to the cooing of nearby turtledoves. Squeezing my forearm, Alya gave me a warm smile and kissed my cheek, before slipping away.

I walked the fields and groves around Timnath Heres, pausing every now and then just to look and listen, to let the stillness permeate my soul. It felt so good, so cleansing. Then, looking out over the landscape to the west, a trembling came over me.

I looked around. A shining man? Where?

I could see nothing but a solitary, sleepy lizard watching me with wary eyes from the branch of a nearby tree.

The trembling persisted.

Crouching down, I closed my eyes and prayed. 'Yahweh, speak to me. What do you wish me to hear?' I heard no words. The beauty of silence continued to caress me, like gentle waves on a beach.

Opening my eyes, I saw the rich, red soil. I took a handful and watched it run through my fingers. A burst of conviction filled me; a knowing, a sense of completion. That was it! That's what Yahweh wanted to tell me. This land was clean! The land that my feet had trodden on – this place that I now called home, and all the land surrounding it – was now rid of the foul beast that had tormented it for so long. The demonic high places that had littered these hills were gone. Idols and altars of death were destroyed, temples to bloodthirsty deities demolished.

This land was free!

Sanctified.

Redeemed.

And the wind sang a new song ... a pure song ... a joyous song.

It whistled through the trees, joining the cry of my heart, vowing to serve none but the One True God, the Creator Himself, Yahweh.

At last, this land was cleansed and free ... as was my soul.

49

Me and My House

'Choose this day, therefore, whom you will serve,' I shouted, raising my voice as much as my weakened body would allow. 'Choose!' I repeated. 'Choose now, this day. *Who will you serve?*'[26]

I looked around, locking eyes with the elders and leaders of Israel who had gathered at Shechem to hear the last dying words of Joshua, son of Nun. For more than two score years I had lived a life of rest and peace at Timnath Heres, but over the last few weeks, an urgency had gripped my spirit, confirming what my body had already told me: my appointed time had come.

'Are these Yahweh's words to you?' Joel asked, when I told him a few days earlier.

I gave a weak chuckle. 'I do not need Yahweh to tell me I am dying, Joel. I am old, advanced in years. I know in my bones that my time has come, and I am ready to go the way of my fathers.'

Messengers were dispatched to the elders of all twelve tribes of Israel, summoning them to an assembly: the last assembly of Joshua, son of Nun with the leaders of Israel, to be held at Shechem.

'Shechem?' Joel queried. 'Not Shiloh, at the Tabernacle of Meeting?'

'No. Shechem. We will meet at the great terebinth tree, for it was there that our ancestor Abraham built an altar to the Lord when he arrived in the land of Canaan.'

Joel said no more. He and Attai made the arrangements and a few days later, those of our family who were able to, travelled with me to Shechem for the holy assembly. I was grateful that it was not too far. Even settled in the back of a cart, nestled among cushions and lying on thick sheepskin rugs, the journey was arduous. The jolting of the oxen pulling the cart jarred my body. It felt like endless slashes from a blunt blade.

---

26. Joshua 24:15, paraphrased.

Alya travelled in the back of the cart with me, meeting my needs as best she could, but by the end of the day, I was biting my lip to stop myself from crying out in pain. Nevertheless, after a full night's sleep and Alya's healing ministrations, I was dressed and ready by mid-morning the following day. I knew the words I must speak to them, but one phrase circled my mind over and over again, one challenge which I knew I must lay before them: *Who will you serve?*

Not being strong enough to stand for the duration of my oration, I perched on a wide-armed chair covered with thick sheepskins. Joel and Attai stood either side of me and Phinehas, who had succeeded Eleazar as high priest, stood nearby.

'Behold, I am going the way of all the earth,' I started out, 'but there is much that the Lord God would have me say to you before I go to meet my fathers.' I reminded them of the story of Abraham, how God brought him from Ur of the Chaldeans to this land of Canaan. The elders listened as I spoke. They knew the story as well as I did; in fact, many of them probably could have told it better than I. *'But wait!'* I urged them in my heart. *'Listen!* Hear the word of the Lord!'

'The Lord God spoke a promise to Abraham. You know it well, yes? Say it with me then, let us declare it aloud together!' I exhorted them. The whole congregation lifted up their voices.

'I will make you a great nation;
I will bless you
And make your name great;
And you shall be a blessing.
I will bless those who bless you,
And I will curse him who curses you;
And in you all the families of the earth shall be blessed.'[27]

A spasm of coughing assailed me. Attai was by my side within seconds, a waterskin in his hands. I drank, cleared my throat and continued.

'The Lord told Abraham, "To your descendants I will give this land."[28] *We are Abraham's descendants!* We are the fulfilment of that great promise. You, and you, yes, and you, and you also!' I pointed out individuals. 'Each one of you has been brought here

---

27. Genesis 12:2-3.
28. Genesis 12:7.

by the outstretched hand of the Lord God of Israel. And today, the Lord your God says, "I have given you a land for which you did not labour, you dwell in cities which you did not build and eat of vineyards and olive groves which you did not plant."'[29]

Murmurs of agreement and thanksgiving broke out among the crowd.

'Amen! Amen!'

'Now therefore,' I stared with steely eyes, daring them to contradict me, 'Fear the Lord!'

An image of the horned beast in Alya's dream flashed into my mind, its scorpion tail plunging down again and again into the backs of our people.

'*Hold fast* to the Lord your God!'

The stone altar in Jericho's temple . . . the lifeless body of a beautiful young child laid on it, hair matted with blood, eyes frozen in terror.

'Serve Him in sincerity and truth . . .'

The nubile bodies of young priestesses, clad in erotic garments, slumped over the steps of the temple . . .

'. . . and *put away* the gods which your fathers served on the other side of the River.'[30]

Frenzied crowds, drunk on blood and lust, the incessant pounding of drums . . . the swish of a blade plunging downwards.

'Fear the Lord, and *serve Him only!*'

A roar erupted from the crowd. I waited until the noise subsided before continuing with my final challenge. My voice may have been diminished by age, but my passion was just as it always had been.

'And if it seems evil to you to serve the Lord, then choose for yourselves this day whom you will serve . . . *Choose!* Choose now, this very day. *Who will you serve?* The gods of the Amorites, or the One True God, Yahweh?'[31]

Another roar sounded out. Hands raised in solidarity, faces fierce with intent.

Leaving my walking stick, I leaned against the chair and reached out with both arms. Joel and Attai stepped forward and helped me to my feet, supporting me as I stood before the elders

---

29. Joshua 24:13, paraphrased.
30. Joshua 24:14, my italics.
31. Joshua 24:15, paraphrased

and leaders. I looked around, inclining my head to the members of my family who were present – both my adopted kin and those like Attai who were kin of my heart. Acknowledging them before the congregation, I took a deep breath and shouted with as much strength as I could muster.

'*But as for me and my house, we will serve the* LORD.'[32]

My voice, although thin and frail with age, echoed around the enclosure with implausible strength. 'Serve the Lord . . . the Lord . . . Lord.'

The assembly burst into spontaneous cheers and shouts of praise to Yahweh.

'The Lord our God we will serve!'

'His voice we will obey!'

'We will serve the Lord!'

An accusing voice taunted me. 'How long do you think they will continue in the ways of Yahweh after you have gone from this earth?'

Frowning with concentration, I raised my arm to silence their cries, then pointed to the great terebinth tree towering over us. 'Look at this tree! The same tree that Abraham sat under when he arrived in Canaan. He sacrificed to the Lord at this very place.' Pointing to a huge stone engraved with the words of the Law, I peered at them one more time.

'Behold, this stone shall be a witness to us, for it has heard all the words of the LORD which He spoke to us. It shall therefore be a witness to you, lest you deny your God.'[33]

The anointing that had fallen upon me while I spoke, now lifted off me with the weightlessness of a cloud.

I could do no more.

'It is finished,' I whispered, sinking back into my chair.

Later that day, Joel was approached by some of the elders present at the assembly, asking him to speak to me on their behalf about the place of my burial. They were of the opinion that I should be laid to rest there, at Shechem, where our patriarch Joseph's bones had been laid to rest.

'Ah, yes,' I mumbled, more to myself than to Joel. 'To be buried here at Shechem, alongside Joseph ben Jacob, would be a great honour. A great honour indeed.' I mused for a moment before

---

32. Joshua 24:15, my italics.
33. Joshua 24:27.

focusing my attention back on Joel. 'Please thank the elders,' I said, grasping Joel's arm to stop him from standing to his feet, 'but tell them I have no wish to be buried here at Shechem.'

Joel froze, his brow furrowed.

'No wish to...?' he stammered. 'Yoshi, forgive me, but do you not understand what a great honour this is that they bestow on you?'

'I do, my friend, I do, and I am thankful for it. But you see, I have no wish to lie here with great men who have been revered and honoured throughout the ages. I would like to be buried near my family in the place where my heart found its rest.'

I gazed into Joel's soft sea-grey eyes, noting the thinness of his facial skin and the abundance of wrinkles. It would not be too long now before he joined me, and we would be reunited again.

'I would like to be laid to rest at Timnath Heres, under my sycamore tree near the top of the hill, overlooking this land of Canaan. From there, I will be able to hear the children playing, the sound of metal on wood as your sons ply their trade, and the chattering of our women on their way to the well. I will be serenaded by the turtle doves that nest in my tree – you know the ones I speak of, *nu*?'

Joel nodded. His eyes filled with tears.

I patted his arm and sighed. 'Aah, the cooing of those doves has brought me much comfort over the years. They are old friends; I know them well.'

Joel grasped my hand, stroking it tenderly as he gazed at me, tears trickling down his cheeks.

Yes,' I gazed into mid-air, smiling as I pictured the view from my sycamore. 'From there, I will be able to see the mighty Jordan River in the early morning light, and the vast plains of Jericho. And I will remember the mighty arm of our God, how He brought us into this land of our inheritance. There, I will be at rest, knowing that I have obeyed Yahweh's call. I have done all that He commanded me to. I have brought His people into the land of their inheritance, and it is now redeemed and at peace.'

My land.

My home.

50

Cloud

I was surrounded. Surrounded by love. Enclosed by my family, who were packed inside my bedchamber like animals on market day. I chuckled to myself at the thought. Hearing the rumble of voices, I realised that many of them were in the courtyard outside. Large though my bedchamber was, it was nowhere near large enough to house all of us.

Joel and Alya sat near my head, either side of my bedroll, Alya wetting my dry lips with a damp cloth every minute or so. Attai knelt next to Joel, his eyes fixed on me; my faithful sentinel, with me to the very end, just as I was with Moses. I looked around the room, trying to catch the eyes of as many as I could, to acknowledge their presence, until an overwhelming tiredness came over me and my eyes drifted shut.

My breathing was shallow but steady. A comforting sense of warmth surrounded my aching bones; a warm sheepskin of the softest wool was being placed around me. I snuggled into its embrace, stroking the smooth, velvety fibres with my cheek, and opened my eyes to thank whoever had put it there.

There was no sheepskin around me.

Everyone was in their place, just as they had been, but my eyes were drawn to the warm glow of a form standing at the end of my bed.

'You're here!' I rasped. 'You have come!'

I could hear Joel and Alya asking me who I was speaking to, but their voices faded into insignificance as I gazed upon the One who stood before me. He was just as magnificent as he had been on the day He appeared to me before the Battle of Jericho, although today He held no weapon, was clothed in a simple cream robe and bare-footed.

He glowed with an ethereal light which cascaded from his person, not blinding in essence, but soft and warm and welcoming. I was struck by the contours of His face, His high cheekbones and glowing hair, but most of all, his eyes. Kind eyes. Liquid love poured out of them, flowing into the deepest parts of my soul. I gasped as I felt the force of its impact. Love radiated out of him, wrapping me in a sublime sense of contentment mixed with anticipation.

The Man stretched His hand out towards me.

'Come.'

My whole being responded to his call; spirit, soul and body combined in one glorious awakening. I reached for his hand and was instantly aware of being pulled away from my body. Pain ceased to exist. The aching joints and bruised limbs that had held me prisoner as I lay on my bedroll vanished in an instant. I was floating, gliding towards him.

As weightless as a feather.

He grasped hold of my hand; his grip was firm but gentle, and so warm. I was astonished to see that the skin on my hand was no longer stretched taut or peppered with sun spots. The leathery wrinkles and gnarly veins had disappeared, leaving a membrane that was soft, plump and glowing with good health.

As the Man drew me towards Him, the area behind Him opened up. It was then that I saw them: the shining men! Hundreds of them – or were there thousands? I couldn't tell. They were bathed in light, but within that light, every colour imaginable seemed to coexist. The light was not static or limited to one dimension but alive, dancing through the air in a glorious, golden, rosy celebration.

The shining men were of every size and appearance imaginable, but two stood out to me. Raising their arms in salute, their faces aglow with welcome, were the two shining men who had shown me how to defeat giants, protecting and guiding me over the years. The first was dark-skinned with handsome, sharp features; his companion had blond hair and eyes of burnished bronze. It was the first time I had seen them without weaponry or armour; their only clothing was a robe that sparkled with life and light.

It suited them well!

As I turned back to the Man, all thoughts of the shining men flew from my mind. The glory and purity that radiated out of Him surpassed all else. I felt exposed, completely naked before Him, but without shame. The absence of sin was so tangible, it was all-encompassing. I was free of fear, doubt, worry, pain . . . it simply didn't exist there. Although I knew my family would mourn my passing, I could feel no sadness. In that place, there was simply nothing to be sad about.

The Man, knowing my thoughts, gave me a smile; beams of sunlight illuminated the atmosphere. Still holding my hand, He gestured ahead with his other arm. I was reluctant to tear my eyes away from Him but when I did, my heart leaped and I gasped in ecstasy.

It was there!

My cloud!

My beautiful obsession.

Pulsating with energy, the same glimmering flurries of light that had adorned the sky over our wilderness camp year after year, now filled the atmosphere before me as far as the eye could see. Infinite rippling clouds shimmered among the glistening hues of rainbow colours, like ruffles of satiny swirls.

The shadowy beings which, at times, I thought must have been mere figments of my imagination, were there, right in front of me! They were *not* imagined; they were gloriously real! I could see their exquisite features, clear and defined. The individual feathers on their wings fluttered as they swooped up and plummeted down, swirling and dancing with complete abandon, sparkling and swaying in praise of the One who stood by my side swathed in a shimmering sheath of light.

Innumerable pairs of wings billowed in time to an ancient, instinctive, unrehearsed rhythm, lifting their voices in a climax of worship. Strings, all manner of pipes, bells, horns and drums combined with the sounds of running water, whistling winds, the cracking of fire and the calls of bird and beast.

I let go of the Man's hand and reached out. Wisps of cloud wrapped themselves around my fingers, caressing them with profound affection.

So alien, yet so familiar.

It felt like home.

The peace and joy I had felt at Timnath Heres faded into a dull memory in comparison.

The Shining Men

The Man watched, gazing at me in tender welcome. I breathed in the fragrant air and shivered with anticipation. This was it! This was what I had been waiting for. My whole life – the glories and heartache, mountaintops and valleys – had led to this precise moment.

This magnificent new adventure.

This homecoming.

And I was ready – *so* ready for it!

I took one last glance at my beloved family, bidding them a fond farewell until such time as I would see them again.

Then, reaching out to grasp the Man's hand again, I took a deep breath, fixed my eyes on the exquisite tableau laid out before me, and stepped into the cloud.

The Shining Men is the third book in a trilogy.

The first book in the trilogy, *Into the Wilderness*, is a vivid reimagining of the Israelites' exodus from captivity in Egypt and the beginning of their new life as desert wanderers, told through the eyes of Joshua, manservant to the prophet leader, Moses. Journey with Joshua into the wilderness; witness signs, wonders and miracles . . . and have your courage tested to the limit as you join Joshua in battling the relentless forces of darkness.

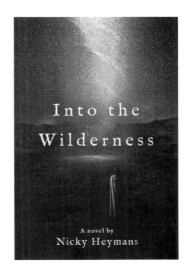

The second book in the trilogy, *Then There Were Giants*, centres around the years that Joshua and his fellow Israelites spent wandering in the desert. Join them as they learn how to survive in the desert, experience heart-warming moments as well as the brutality of warfare, and face their greatest adversaries yet – giants!

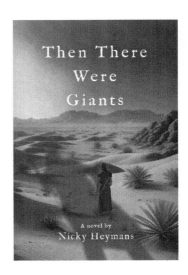

For more information, or to email the author, please go to

www.nickyheymansauthor.com